NEW WORLDS FOR OLD

NEW WORLDS FOR OLD

BY

H. G. WELLS

WILDSIDE PRESS

www.wildsidebooks.com

CONTENTS

CHAPTER   PAGE

I. THE GOOD WILL IN MAN   1

II. THE FUNDAMENTAL IDEA OF SOCIALISM   . . 21

III. THE FIRST MAIN GENERALIZATION OF SOCIALISM 27

IV. THE SECOND MAIN GENERALIZATION OF SOCIALISM 56

V. THE SPIRIT OF GAIN AND THE SPIRIT OF SERVICE 88

VI. WOULD SOCIALISM DESTROY THE HOME?   . . 114

VII. WOULD MODERN SOCIALISM ABOLISH ALL PROP-
ERTY?   137

VIII. THE MIDDLE-CLASS MAN AND SOCIALISM   . . 162

IX. SOME OBJECTIONS TO SOCIALISM   177

X. SOCIALISM A DEVELOPING DOCTRINE   .   .   . 205

XI. REVOLUTIONARY SOCIALISM   219

XII. ADMINISTRATIVE SOCIALISM   243

XIII. CONSTRUCTIVE SOCIALISM 261

XIV. SOME ARGUMENTS *AD HOMINEM*   .   .   . 291

XV. THE ADVANCEMENT OF SOCIALISM .   .   . 325

NEW WORLDS FOR OLD

CHAPTER I

THE GOOD WILL IN MAN

§ 1

THE present writer has long been interested in the Socialist movement in Great Britain and America and in all those complicated issues one lumps together as "social questions." In the last few years he has gone into it personally and studied the Socialist movement closely and intimately at first hand; he has made the acquaintance of many of its leaders upon both sides of the Atlantic, joined numerous organizations, attended and held meetings, experimented in Socialist politics. From these inquiries he has emerged with certain very definite conclusions as to the trend and needs of social development and these he is now rendering in this book. He calls himself a Socialist, but he is by no means a fanatical or uncritical adherent. To him Socialism presents itself as a very noble but a very human and fallible system of ideas. He does in all sincerity regard its spirit, its intimate substance, as the most hopeful thing in human affairs at the present time, but he does also find it shares with all mundane concerns the qualities of inadequacy and error. It suffers from the common penalty of noble propositions; it is hampered by the insufficiency of its supporters and advocates and by the superficial tarnish that necessarily falls in our atmosphere of greed and conflict darkest upon the brightest things. In spite of these admissions of failure and unworthiness in himself and those about him, he remains a Socialist.

In discussing Socialism with very various sorts of people he has necessarily had time after time to encounter and frame a reply to a very simple seeming and a really very difficult question: "What *is* Socialism?" It is almost like asking, "What is Christianity?" or demanding to be shown the atmosphere. It is not to be answered fully by a formula or an epigram. Again and again the writer has been asked for some book which would set out in untechnical language, frankly and straightforwardly, what Socialism is and what it is not, and always he has hesitated in his reply. Many good books there are upon this subject, clear and well written, but none that seem to tell the whole story as he knows it; no book that gives not only the outline but the spirit, answers the main objections, clears up the chief ambiguities, covers all the ground; no book that one can put in the hands of inquiring youth and say, "There! that will tell you precisely the broad facts you want to know." Some day, no doubt, such a book will come. In the meanwhile he has ventured to put forth this temporary substitute, his own account of the faith that is in him.

Socialism, then, as he understands it, is a great intellectual process, a development of desires and ideas that takes the form of a project, a project for the reshaping of human society upon new and better lines. That in the ampler proposition Socialism claims to be. This book seeks to expand and establish that proposition and to define the principles upon which a Socialist believes this reconstruction of society should go. The particulars and justification of this project and this claim, it will be the business of this book to discuss just as plainly as the writer can.

§ 2

Now, because the Socialist seeks the reshaping of human society, it does not follow that he denies it to be even now a very wonderful and admirable spectacle. Nor does he deny that for many people life is even now a very good thing. For his own part, though the writer is neither a very strong nor a very healthy nor a very successful person, though he finds much unattainable and much to regret, yet life presents itself to him, more and more with every year, as a spectacle of inexhaustible interest, of unfolding and intensifying beauty,

and as a splendid field for high attempts and
stimulating desires. Yet none the less is it a
spectacle shot strangely with pain, with mysterious
insufficiencies and cruelties, with pitfalls into anger and
regret, with aspects unaccountably sad. Its most exalted moments are most fraught for him with the appeal
for endeavour, with the urgency of unsatisfied wants.
These shadows and pains and instabilities do not, to
his sense at least, darken the whole prospect; it may be,
indeed, that they intensify its splendours to his per-
ceptions; yet all these evil and ugly aspects of life come
to him with an effect of challenge; as something not to
be ignored but passionately disputed, as an imperative
call for whatever effort and courage lurks in his composition. Life and the world are fine, but not as an
abiding place; as an arena — yes, an arena gorgeously
curtained with sea and sky, mountains and broad pros-
pects, decorated with all the delicate magnificence of
leaf tracery and flower petal and feather, soft fur and
the shining wonder of living skin, musical with thunder
and the singing of birds; but an arena, nevertheless,
an arena which offers no seats for idle spectators, in
which one must will and do, decide, strike and strike
back, — and presently pass away.

And it needs but a cursory view of history to realize —
though all knowledge of history confirms the generaliza-

tion — that this arena is not a confused and aimless conflict of individuals. Looked at too closely, it may seem to be that, a formless web of individual hates and loves; but detach one's self but a little, and the broader forms appear. One perceives something that goes on, that is constantly working to make order out of casualty, beauty out of confusion, justice, kindliness, mercy, out of cruelty and inconsiderate pressure. For our present purpose it will be sufficient to speak of this force that struggles and tends to make and do, as Good Will. More and more evident is it, as one reviews the ages, that there is this much more than lust, hunger, avarice, vanity, and more or less intelligent fear, among the motives of mankind. This Good Will of our race, however arising, however trivial, however subordinated to individual ends, however comically inadequate a thing it may be in this individual case or that, is in the aggregate an operating will. In spite of all the confusions and thwartings of life, the halts and resiliencies and the counter-strokes of fate, it is manifest that in the long run, human life becomes broader than it was, gentler than it was, finer and deeper. On the whole — and nowadays almost steadily — things *get better*. There is a secular amelioration of life, and it is brought about by Good Will working through the efforts of men.

Now this proposition lies quite open to dispute.

There are people who will dispute it and make a very passable case. One may deny the amelioration, or one may deny that it is the result of any Good Will or of anything but quite mechanical forces. The former is the commoner argument. The appeal is usually to what has been finest in the past, and to all that is bad and base in the present. At once the unsoundest and the most attractive argument is to be found in the deliberate idealization of particular ages, — the thirteenth century in England, for example, or the age of the Antonines. The former is presented with the brightness of a missal, the latter with all the dignity of a Roman inscription. One is asked to compare these ages, so delightfully conceived, with a patent medicine vendor's advertisement or a Lancashire factory town, quite ignoring the falsities of mediæval law or the slums and hunger and cruelty of Imperial Rome.

But quite apart from such unsound devices, it is, we may admit, possible to make a very excellent case against our general assertion of progress. One can instance a great number of things, big and little, that have been better in past times than they are now. For example, they dressed more sumptuously and delightfully in mediæval Venice and Florence than we do — all, that is, who could afford it; they made quite unapproachably beautiful marble figures in Athens in the time of Peri-

cles; there is no comparison between the brickwork of
Verona in the twelfth century and that of London when
Cannon Street station was erected; the art of cookery
declined after the splendid period of Roman history for
more than a thousand years; the Gothic architecture of
France and England exceeds in nobility and quality and
aggregated beauty every subsequent type of structure.
This much one agrees is true and beyond disputing. The
philosophical thought of Athens again, to come to greater
things, was to the very climax of its extinction bolder,
more free, more finely expressed than that of any epoch
since. And the English of Elizabeth's time was, we are
told by competent judges, a more gracious and powerful
instrument of speech than in the days of Queen Anne or
of Queen Victoria.

So one might go on in regard to a vast number of things,
petty things and large matters alike; the list would seem
overwhelming until the countervailing considerations
came into play. But, as a matter of fact, there is hardly
an age or a race that does not show us something better
done than ever it was before or since, because at no time
during the last thousand years has human effort ceased
and absolutely failed. Isolated eminence is no proof
of general elevation. Always in this field or that,
whether it was in the binding of books or the enamelling
of metal, the refinement of language or the assertion of

liberty, particular men have by a sort of necessity
grasped at occasion, — "found themselves" as the saying
goes, — and done the best that was in them. So always
while man endures, whatever else betide, one may feel
assured at this or that special thing, some men will find
a way to do and get to the crown of endeavour. Such
considerations of decline in particular things from the
standard of the past do not really affect the general
assertion of a continuous accumulating betterment in
the lot of men, do not invalidate the hopes of those who
believe in the power of men to end forever many of the
evils that now darken the world, who look to the reser-
voirs of human possibility, as as yet a scarcely touched
supply, who make of all the splendour and superiorities of
the past no more than a bright promise and suggestion
for the unworn future our every act builds up, into which,
whether we care or no, all our achievements pour.

Many evils have been overcome, much order and
beauty and scope for living has been evolved since man
was a hairy savage holding scarcely more than a brute's
intercourse with his fellows; but even in the comparatively short perspective of history, one can scarcely deny
a steady process of overcoming evil. One may sneer
at contemporary things, it is a fashion with that un-
happily trained type of mind which cannot appreciate
without invidious comparison, so poor in praise that it

cannot admit worth without venting a compensatory
envy; but of one permanent result of progress surely
every one is assured. In the matter of thoughtless and
instinctive cruelty — and that is a very fundamental
matter — mankind mends steadily. I wonder and
doubt if in the whole world, at any time before this, an
aged, ill-clad woman or a palpable cripple could have
moved among a crowd of low-class children as free from
combined or even isolated insult as such a one would be
to-day caught in the rush from a London Board School.
Then, for all our sins, I am sure the sense of justice is
quicker and more nearly universal than ever before.
Certain grave social evils, too, that once seemed innate in
humanity, have gone, — gone so effectually that we cannot now imagine ourselves subjected to them; the cruelties and insecurities of private war, the duel, overt
slavery, for example, have altogether ceased; and in all
Western Europe and America chronic local famines and
pestilences come no more. No doubt it is still an unsatisfactory world that mars the roadside with tawdry
advertisements of drugs and food; but less than two
centuries ago, remember, the place of these boards was
taken by gibbets and crow-pecked, tattered corpses
swinging in the wind, and the heads of dead gentlemen
(drawn and quartered, and their bowels burnt before
their eyes) rotted in the rain on Temple Bar.

The world is now a better place for a common man than ever it was before, the spectacle wider and richer and deeper and more charged with hope and promise. Think of the universal things it is so easy to ignore; of the great and growing multitude, for example, of those who may travel freely about the world, who may read freely, think freely, speak freely! Think of the quite unprecedented numbers of well-ordered homes and cared-for, wholesome, questioning children! And it is not simply that we have this increasing sea of mediocre well-being in which the realities of the future are engendering, but in the matter of sheer achievement I believe in my own time. It has been the cry of the irresponsive man since criticism began, that his own generation produced nothing; it's a cry that I hate and deny. When the dross has been cleared away and comparison becomes possible, I am convinced it will be admitted that in the aggregate, in philosophy, and significant literature, in architecture, painting, and scientific research, in engineering and industrial invention, in state-craft, humanity and valiant deeds, the last thirty years of man's endeavours will bear comparison with any other period of thirty years whatever in his history.

And this is the result of effort; things get better because men mean them to get better and try to bring betterment about; this progress goes on because man, in spite of evil temper, blundering, and vanity, in spite of indolence and base desire, does also respond to Good Will and display Good Will. You may declare that all the good things in life are the result of causes over which man has no control, that in pursuit of an "enlightened self-interest" he makes things better inadvertently. But think of any good thing you know! Was it thus it came?

§ 3

And yet, let us not disguise it from ourselves, for all the progress one can claim, life remains very evil; about the feet of all these glories of our time lurk darknesses.

Let me take but one group of facts that cry out to all of us — and will not cry in vain. I mean the lives of little children that are going on now — as the reader sits with this book in his hand. Think, for instance, of the little children who have been pursued and tormented and butchered in the Congo Free State during the last year or so: hands and feet chopped off, little bodies torn and thrown aside that rubber might be cheap, the tires of our cars run smoothly, and that detestable product of political expediency, the king of the Belgians, have his pleasures. Think, too, of the fear and violence, the dirt and stress, of the lives of the children who grow up amidst the lawless internal strife of the Russian political chaos. Think of the emigrant ships even now rolling upon the high seas, their dark, evil-smelling holds crammed with humanity and the huddled sick children in them — fleeing from certain to uncertain wretchedness. Think of the dreadful tale of childish misery and suffering that goes on wherever there are not sane factory laws; how even in so civilized a part of the world as the United States of America (as Spargo's *Bitter Cry of the Children* tells in detail) thousands of little white children of six and seven, ill-fed and often cruelly handled, toil without hope.

And in all agricultural lands too, where there is no sense of education, think of the children dragging weary feet from the filthy hovels that still house peasants the whole world over, to work in the mire and the pitiless winds, scaring birds, bending down to plant and weed. Even in London again, think just a little of the real significance of some facts I have happened upon in the Report of the Education Committee of the London County Council for the year 1905.

The headmaster of one casually selected school makes a special return upon the quality of the clothing of his 405 children. He tells of 7.4 per cent of his boys whose clothing was "the scantiest possible — *e.g.*, one ragged coat buttoned up and practically nothing found beneath it; and boots either absent or represented by a mass of rags tied upon the feet"; of 34.8 per cent whose "clothing was insufficient to retain animal heat and needed urgent remedy"; of 45.9 per cent whose clothing was "poor but passable, an old and perhaps ragged suit with some attempt at proper underclothing — usually of flannelette"; thus leaving only 12.8 per cent who could, in the broadest sense, be termed "well-clad."

Taking want of personal cleanliness as the next indication of neglect at home, 11 per cent of the boys are reported as "very dirty and verminous"; 34.7 per cent whose "clothes and body were dirty but not verminous"; 42.5 per cent were "passably clean, for boys," and only "12 per cent clean above the average."

Eleven per cent verminous; think what it means! Think what the homes must be like from which these poor little wretches come! Better perhaps than the country cottage where the cesspool drains into the water-supply and the henhouse, vermin invades the home, but surely intolerable beside our comforts! Give but a moment again to the significance of the figures I have italicized in the table that follows, a summarized return for the year 1906 of the "Ringworm" nurses who visit the London Elementary schools and inspect the children for various forms of dirt disease.

Departments	Number of Children Examined	Clean	Partially Cleansed	Verminous
Boys . . .	34,345	32,726	847	1,139
Girls . . .	36,445	22,476	4,426	12,003
Infants . .	42,140	6,675	2,661	*29,675*
Mixed . . .	5,855	4,886	298	897
Special . .	977	624	133	296
Total . .	119,762	67,387	8,365	44,010

Does not this speak of dirt and disorder we cannot suffer to continue, of women ill-trained for motherhood and worked beyond care for cleanliness, of a vast amount of preventible suffering? And these figures of filth and bad clothing are paralleled by others at least equally impressive, displaying emaciation, under-nutrition, anæmia, and every other painful and wretched consequence of neglect and insufficiency. These underfed, underclothed, undersized children are also the backward children; they grow up through a darkened, joyless childhood into a gray, perplexing, hopeless world that beats them down at last, after servility, after toil, after crime it may be and despair, to death.

And while you grasp the offence of these facts, do not be carried away into supposing that this age is therefore unprecedentedly evil. Such dirt, toil, cruelty have always been, — have been in larger measure. Don't idealize the primitive cave, the British hut, the peasant's cottage, damp and windowless, the filth-strewn, plague-stricken, mediæval town.   In spite of all these crushed, mangled, starved, neglected little ones about the feet of this fine time, in spite of a thousand other disorders and miseries almost as cruel, the fact remains that this age has not only more but a larger percentage of healthy, happy, kindly-treated children than any age since the world began; that to look back into the domestic history of other times is to see greater squalor and more suffering. Why! read the tombstones and monuments in any old English Church, those, I mean, that date from earlier than 1800, and you will see the history of every family, of even the prosperous county families, *laced* with the deaths of infants and children.   Nearly half of them died. Think too how stern was the upbringing.   And always before these days it seemed natural to make all but the children of the very wealthy and very refined, fear and work from their earliest years.   There comes to us too, from these days, beautiful furniture, fine literature, paintings; but there comes, too, much evidence of harsh whippings, dark imprisonments, and never a children's book, hardly the broken vestige of a toy.   Bad as things are, they are better — rest assured — and yet they are still urgently bad.   The greater evil of the past is no reason for contentment with the present.   But it is an earnest for hoping that our efforts, and that Good Will of which

they are a part and outcome, may still go on bearing
fruit in perpetually dwindling misery.

§ 4

It seems to me that the whole spirit and quality of
both the evil and the good of our time, and of the attitude not simply of the Socialist but of every sane
reformer toward these questions, was summarized in a
walk I had a little while ago with a friend along the
Thames Embankment, from Blackfriars Bridge to Westminster. We had dined together and we went there
because we thought that with a fitful moon and clouds
adrift, on a night when the air was a crystal air that
gladdened and brightened, that crescent of great buildings and steely, soft-hurrying water must needs be
altogether beautiful. And indeed it was beautiful: the
mysteries and mounting masses of the buildings to the
right of us, the blurs of this coloured light or that,
blue-white, green-white, amber or warmer orange, the
rich black archings of Waterloo Bridge, the rippled
lights upon the silent flowing river, the lattice of girders,
and the shifting trains of Charing Cross Bridge — their
funnels pouring a sort of hot-edged moonlight by way
of smoke — and then the sweeping line of lamps, the
accelerated run and diminuendo of the Embankment
lamps as one came into sight of Westminster. The big

hotels were very fine, huge swelling shapes of dun dark-gray and brown, huge shapes seamed and bursting and fenestrated with illumination, tattered at a thousand windows with light and the indistinct glowing suggestions of feasting and pleasure. And dim and faint above it all and very remote was the moon's dead wan face veiled and then displayed.

But we were dashed by an unanticipated refrain to this succession of magnificent things, and we did not cry, as we had meant to cry, how good it was to be alive! We found something else, something we had forgotten.

Along the Embankment, you see, there are iron seats at regular intervals, seats you cannot lie upon because iron arm-rests prevent that, and each seat, one saw by the lamplight, was filled with crouching and drooping figures. Not a vacant place remained, not one vacant place. These were the homeless, and they had come to sleep here. Now one noted a poor old woman with a shameful battered straw hat awry over her drowsing face, now a young clerk staring before him at despair; now a filthy tramp, and now a bearded, frock-coated, collarless respectability; I remember particularly one ghastly long white neck and white face that lopped backward, choked in some nightmare, awakened, clutched with a bony hand at the bony throat, and sat up and stared angrily as we passed. The wind had a keen edge that night, even for

c

us who had dined and were well-clad. One crumpled figure coughed and went on coughing — damnably.

"It's fine," said I, trying to keep hold of the effects to which this line of poor wretches was but the selvage; "it's fine! But I can't stand *this*."

"It changes all that we expected," admitted my friend, after a silence.

"Must we go on — past them all?"

"Yes. I think we ought to do that. It's a lesson perhaps — for trying to get too much beauty out of life as it is, and forgetting. Don't shirk it!"

"Great God!" cried I. "But must life always be like this? I could die, indeed, I would willingly jump into this cold and muddy river now, if by so doing I could stick a stiff dead hand through all these things into the future,— a dead commanding hand insisting with a silent irresistible gesture that this waste and failure of life should cease, and cease forever."

"But it does cease! Each year in its proportions it is a little less."

I walked in silence, and my companion talked by my side.

"We go on. Here is a good thing done, and there is a good thing done. The Good Will in man —"

"Not fast enough. It goes so slowly — and in a little while we too must die."

"It can be done," said my companion.

"It could be avoided," said I.

"It shall be in the days to come. There is food enough for all, shelter for all, wealth enough for all. Men need only know it and will it. And yet we have this!"

"And so much like this!" said I.

So we talked and were tormented.

And I remember how later we found ourselves on Westminster Bridge, looking back upon the long sweep of wrinkled black water that reflected lights and palaces and the flitting glow of steamboats, and by that time we had talked ourselves past our despair. We perceived that what was splendid remained splendid, that what was mysterious remained insoluble for all our pain and impatience. But it was clear to us: the thing for us two to go upon was not the good of the present nor the evil, but the effort and the dream of the finer order, the fuller life, the banishment of suffering, to come.

"We want all the beauty that is here," said my friend, "and more also. And none of these distresses. We are here — we know not whence nor why — to want that and to struggle to get it, you and I and ten thousand others thinly hidden from us by these luminous darknesses. We work, we pass — whither I know not, but out of our knowing. But we work — we are spurred to work. That yonder — those people are the spur for us who cannot answer to any finer appeal. Each in our measure must do. And our reward? Our reward is our faith. Here is my creed to-night. I believe out of me and the Good Will in me and my kind there comes a regenerate world — cleansed of suffering and sorrow. That is our purpose here — to forward that. It gives us work for all our lives. Why should we ask to know more? Our errors — our sins — to-night they seem to matter very little. If we stumble and roll in the mud, if we blunder against each other and hurt one another."

"We have to go on," said my friend after a pause.

We stood for a time in silence.

One's own personal problems came and went like a ripple in the water. Even that whiskey dealer's advertisement upon the southern bank became through some fantastic transformation a promise, an enigmatical promise, flashed up the river reach in letters of fire. London was indeed very beautiful that night. Without hope she would have seemed not only as beautiful but as terrible as a black panther crouching on her prey. Our hope redeemed her. Beyond her dark and meretricious splendours, beyond her throned presence, jewelled with links and points and cressets of fire, crowned with stars, robed in the night, hiding cruelties, I caught a moment's vision of the coming City of Mankind, of a city more wonderful than all my dreaming, full of life, full of youth, full of the spirit of creation.

CHAPTER II

THE fundamental idea upon which Socialism rests is the same fundamental idea as that upon which all real scientific work is carried on. It is the denial that chance impulse and individual will and happening constitute the only possible methods by which things may be done in the world. It is an assertion that things are in their nature orderly; that things may be computed, may be calculated upon and foreseen. In the spirit of this belief, science aims at a systematic knowledge of material things. "Knowledge is power," knowledge that is frankly and truly exchanged, that is the primary assumption of the *New Atlantis* which created the Royal Society and the organization of research. The Socialist has just that same faith in the order, the knowableness of things and the power of men in coöperation to overcome chance; but to him, dealing as he does with the social affairs of men, it takes the form not of schemes for collective research but for collective action and the creation for all the social activities of man of a comprehensive design. While science gathers knowl-

21

edge, Socialism, in an entirely harmonious spirit, criticises and develops a general plan of social life. Each
seeks to replace disorder by order.

Each of these systems of ideas has of course its limits;
we know in matters of material science that no calculated quantity is ever exact, no outline without a fog-
ging at the edge, no angle without a curve at the apex,
and in social affairs also, there must needs always be
individuality and the unexpected and incalculable.
But these things do not vitiate the case for a general
order, any more than the different sizes and widths and
needs of the human beings who travel prevent our having
our railway carriages and seats and doors of a generally
convenient size nor our sending everybody over the
same gauge of rail.

Now science has not only this in common with Socialism that it has grown out of men's courageous confidence in the superiority of order to muddle, but these
two great processes of human thought are further in
sympathy in the demand they make upon men to become
less egotistical and isolated. The whole difference of
modern scientific research from that of the Middle Ages,
the secret of its immense successes, lies in its collective
character, in the fact that every fruitful experiment
is published, every new discovery of relationships explained. In a sense scientific research is a triumph

over natural instinct, over that mean instinct that makes men secretive, that makes a man keep knowledge to himself and use it slyly to his own advantage.   The training of a scientific man is a training in what an il-literate lout would despise as a weakness, it is a training in blabbing, in blurting things out, in telling just as plainly as possible and as soon as possible what it is he has found.   To "keep shut" and bright-eyed and to score advantages, that is the wisdom of the common stuff of humanity still.   To science it is a crime.   The noble practice of that noble profession, medicine, for example, is to condemn as a quack and a rascal every man who uses secret remedies.   And it is one of the most encouraging things for all who speculate upon human possibility to consider the multitude of men in the last three centuries who have been content to live laborious, unprofitable, and for the most part quite undistinguished lives in the service of knowledge that has transformed the world.   Some names indeed stand out by virtue of gigantic or significant achievement, such names as Bacon, Newton, Volta, Darwin, Faraday, Joule, but these are but the culminating peaks of a nearly limitless Oberland of devoted toiling men,—men one could list by the thousand.   The rest have had the smallest meed of fame, small reward, much toil, much abandonment of pleasure for their lot.   One thing ennobles them all in

common, — their conquest over the meanness of concealment, their systematic application of energy to other
than personal ends!

And that, too, Socialism preëminently demands. It
applies to social and economic relationships the same
high rule of frankness and veracity, the same subordination of purely personal considerations to a common end
that science demands in the field of thought and knowledge. Just as science aims at a common organized body
of knowledge to which all its servants contribute and in
which they share, so Socialism insists upon its ideal of
an organized social order which every man serves and by
which every man benefits. Their common enemy is
the secret-thinking, self-seeking man. Secrecy, sub-
terfuge and the private gain: these are the enemies
of Socialism and the adversaries of science. At times,
I will admit, both Socialist and scientific man forget this
essential sympathy. You will find specialized scientific investigators who do not realize they are, in effect,
Socialists, and Socialists so dull to the quality of their
own professions, that they gird against science, and are
secretive in policy. But such purblind servants of the
light cannot alter the essential correlations of the two
systems of ideas.

Now the Socialist, inspired by this conception of a
possible, frank and comprehensive social order to

which mean and narrow things must be sacrificed, attacks and criticises the existing order of things at a great number of points and in a great variety of phraseology. At all points, however, you will find upon analysis that his criticism amounts to a declaration that there is wanting a sufficiency of CONSTRUCTIVE DESIGN. That in the last resort is what he always comes to.

He wants a complete organization for all those human affairs that are of collective importance. He says, to take instances almost haphazard, that our ways of manufacturing a great multitude of necessary things, of getting and distributing food, of conducting all sorts of business, of begetting and rearing children, of permitting diseases to engender and spread, are chaotic and undisciplined; so badly done that here is enormous hardship and there enormous waste, here excess and degeneration, and there privation and death. He declares that for these collective purposes, in the satisfaction of these universal needs, mankind presents the appearance and follows the methods of a mob when it ought to follow the method of an army. In place of disorderly individual effort, each man doing what he pleases, the Socialist wants organized effort and a plan. And while the scientific man seeks to make an orderly map of the half-explored wilderness of fact, the Socialist seeks to make an orderly plan for the half-conceived wilderness of human effort.

That and no other is the essential Socialist idea.

But do not let this image mislead you. When the Socialist speaks of a plan, he knows clearly that it is impossible to make a plan as an architect makes a plan, because while the architect deals with dead stone and timber, the statesman and Socialist deal with living and striving things. But he seeks to make a plan as one designs and lays out a garden, so that sweet and seemly things may grow, wide and beautiful vistas open, and weeds and foulness disappear. Always a garden plan develops and renews itself and discovers new possibilities, but, for all that, what makes all its graciousness and beauty possible, is the scheme and the persistent intention, the watching and the waiting, the digging and burning, the weeder clips and the hoe. That is the sort of plan, a living plan for things that live and grow, that the Socialist seeks for social and national life.

To make all this distincter I will show the planlessness of certain contemporary things, of two main sets of human interests in fact, and explain what inferences a Socialist draws in these matters. You will then see exactly what is meant when we deny that this present state of affairs has any constructive plan, and you will appreciate in the most generalized form the nature of the constructive plan which Socialists are making and offering the world.

CHAPTER III

§ 1

THE first — the chief aspect of social life in relation to which the Socialist finds the world now planless and drifting, and for which he earnestly propounds the scheme of a better order — is that whole side of existence which is turned toward children, their begetting and up-bringing, their care and education. Perpetually the world begins anew, perpetually death wipes out failure, disease, unteachableness, and all that has served life and accomplished itself; and to many Socialists, if not to all, this is the supreme fact in the social scheme. The whole measure of progress in a generation is the measure in which the children improve in physical and mental quality, in moral coördination, in opportunity, upon their parents. Nothing else matters in the way of success if in that way the Good Will fails.

Let us now consider how such matters stand in our world at the present time, and let us examine them in the light of the Socialist spirit. I have already quoted certain facts from the London Education Committee's

27

Report by which you have seen that by taking a school haphazard — dipping a ladle, as it were, into the welter of the London population — we find more than eighty in the hundred of the London children insufficiently clad, more than half unwholesomely dirty, — eleven per cent verminous, — and more than half the infants infested with vermin ! The nutrition of these children is equally bad. The same report shows clearly that differences in clothing and cleanliness are paralleled with differences in nutrition that are equally striking.

"The 30 boys of the lowest class showed considerable failure to reach the average weight for their age of the school; the average shortage per boy for his age being as much as .7 kilogram. The effect upon weight was more striking than upon height, as the average failure in height was one centimetre. The 141 boys of the next class worked out at exactly the average. The 49 well-clad boys showed an average excess per age-weight of .54 kilogram and age-height of 1.8 centimetres."

And who can doubt the amount of mental and moral dwarfing that is going on side by side with this physical shortage ?

Now it may be argued that this is not a fair sample of our general population, that these facts have been culled from a special section of the population, that here we are dealing with the congestion of London slums and altogether exceptional conditions. This is not so. The school examined was not from a specially bad district.

And it happens that the entire working-class population of one typical English town, York, has been exhaustively studied by Mr. B. S. Rowntree, and here are some facts from his result that quite confirm the impression given by the London figures.

"It was quite impossible to make a thorough examination of the physical condition of all the children, but as they came up to be weighed and measured, they were classified under the four headings, 'Very Good,' 'Good,' 'Fair,' or 'Bad,' by an investigator whose training and previous experience in similar work enabled her to make a reliable, even if rough, classification. . . .

"'Bad' implies that the child bore physical traces of underfeeding and neglect.

"The numbers classified under the various heads were as follows : —

	Very Good per cent.	Good per cent.	Fair per cent.	Bad per cent.
BOYS				
Section 1. (poorest)	2.8	14.6	31.	51.6
Section 2. (middle)	7.4	20.1	53.7	18.8
Section 3. (highest)	27.4	33.8	27.4	11.4
GIRLS				
Section 1. (poorest)	2.1	14.6	31.	52.3
Section 2. (middle)	7.5	21.2	50.4	20.9
Section 3. (highest)	27.2	38.	23.1	11.7

"It will be seen that the proportion of children classed as 'very good' in Section 3 is about ten times as large as in the poorest section, and that *more than half of the children in the poorest section are classed as 'bad.'*

"These 'bad' children presented a pathetic spectacle; all bore some mark of the hard conditions against which they were struggling. Puny and feeble bodies, dirty and often sadly insufficient clothing, sore eyes, in many cases acutely inflamed through continued want of attention, filthy heads, cases of hip disease, swollen glands — all these and other signs told the same tale of privation and neglect. It will be noticed that the condition of the children in Section 2 (middle-class labour) comes about halfway between Sections 1 and 3. In considering the above table it must of course be remembered that there was no absolute standard by which each child could be judged, but the broad comparison between the different classes is unimpeachable. The table affords further evidence of serious physical deterioration amongst the poorest section of the community."

And if York and London will not satisfy, let the reader take Edinburgh, whose Charity Organization Society has produced an admirable but infinitely distressing report of the physical conditions of the school children there. It gives a summary account of the homes of 1400 children in one of the Edinburgh Elementary Schools, selected because it represented a fair mixture of prosperous and unprosperous people. I take the first 10 entries of this list just as they come, representing 38 children, and they are a fair sample of the whole list. No amount of writing could make these little thumb-nail sketches of the reality of domestic life among our population to-day more impressive than they are, thus barrenly given.

1. A bad home. Woman twice married; second husband deserted her six or seven years ago and she now keeps a bad house in which much drinking and rioting goes on. Daughter on stage sends 10/— a week, son is out of work. A son is in an institution. All as filthy as is the house. The food is irregular. Two children have had free dinners from school this and last winter, clothes were also given for one each time. The boy attends regularly. The woman is a hard drinker, and gets money in undesirable ways. The eldest child has glands, neck; hair not good but clean; fleabitten. The second child, adenoids and tonsils. Housing: five in one room. Evidence from Police, School Charity, Headmistress, School Officers, and Doctors.

2. The drinking capacity of this family cannot be too much emphasized. The parents can't agree, and live apart, the man allowing 7/6 a week when girl is with mother, and 5/—when she comes to him. She is verminous and very badly kept, Mother can't get charring, as she lives in so bad a neighbourhood, so means to move; at present she keeps other women's babies at 6d. a day each. Elder boy out of work, a tidy lad, reads in Free Library. One child has died. Housing: three in one room. House not so very untidy. Evidence from Police, Church, and Officer.

3. A miserable family and in very wretched circumstances. Father deserts home at intervals, but last time seemed "sent back by Providence," as the works in the town he was in were burnt down. Children starving in his absence; one had pneumonia, and died since of the effects. The eldest child has adenoids; the second, uticaria; lice, bad; clothes full of pediculi.

Housing: six in two rooms.   Mother hardworking, does her best, but has chronic bronchitis; does not keep house overtidy.   The two elder boys are very idle, tiresome fellows, and worry the father a great deal.   They improved and found work during the year following the visit, in which time the father got into decent work in the city.   The S.P.C.C. branch had to interfere on behalf of small children.   Three dead since marriage, when parents were at ages 23 and 20.   Food good when there is any. School gave free dinners and clothes to two.   Evidence from Police, S.P.C.C. branch, School Charity, Parish Sister, Employer, Headmistress, School Officer, and Doctors.

4. The father a complete wreck through intemperate and fast living; speculation first brought him down.   Was later moved to hospital where he died.   Had worked on railway a little time.   Mother hardworking, works out, home untidy owing to her being out so much.   She pays rent regularly, and does her best.   An elder boy groom, fed and clad by his master, sends home what he can.   Eldest boy does odd jobs, but seems a wastrel.   Parish gave 7/6 after father ill, and feeds four children now.   Winter of visit school dined five free daily, and clothed three, and previous winter three had free dinners and two had clothes.   A schoolboy earns.   The twins are delicate.   There are two lodgers.   The eldest child very dirty; the second, glands; the third, knock-kneed, pigeon chest, very feeble, enlarged radices.   Three children have died.   Housing: nine in three rooms.   Evidence from Police, Poor-law Officer, Parish Sister, School Charity, Army Charity, Children's Employment, School Officer, Factor, Pawnbroker, and Doctors.

5. The mother, a nice, clean, tidy woman, doing pretty well by the children.   They kept a little shop for a time, and she used to do a day's charring now and then, but has too many babies now.   Parents married at 21 and 18 respectively; two children

dead and another expected. He reads papers a good deal, gets them out of trains. This is his first spell of regular work. Two boys sell papers, and a mission gives cheap meal. Food none too plentiful. One child gets free dinners. The eldest child has glands; impetigo; thin and badly nourished. The second, glands, hair lice, and nits bad. The third boils on neck; glands; thin. The fourth, glands. Housing: eight in two rooms. They are in two thrift societies. Evidence from Schoolmaster, Police, Parish Sister, Club, Army Charity, Charity School, Pawnbroker, and Doctors.

6. Father works in one shop in daytime, and in a public house at night. Rather soft; but wife industrious and energetic and does her best. Children well-fed and regular at school. Two children have enlarged tonsils. They get no help, and belong to two thrift societies. One of six children dead in ten years of married life. Housing: seven in two rooms. Evidence from Police, Doctors, Society, Church, Mission, Club, Headmistress, Charity School, and Pawnbrokers.

7. A family where parents are much given to drink; father invalided and being helped by a Sick Society, 3/— a week, and Parish 5/— a week. Housing: five in two rooms. They are in a burying club. Children fleabitten. Two have died. Food is rather scanty. Wife *very* quarrelsome and drunken. The boys play truant often. Two were given free food and clothes two winters ago, and this winter one has free dinners and clothes given. A mission has given cheap clothes. Evidence from Schoolmaster, Police, Poor-law Officer, C.O.S. branch, Church, School Charity, Sick Society, Children's Employment, Factor, School Officer, Charity School, Pawnbroker, and Doctors.

8. Fairly decent family; mother washes out, and man has very early work. He drinks, and his employment is somewhat irregular. A son in the country on a farm, and two dead. They

D

were married at 21 and 18. The food is erratic, the children getting "pieces" at dinner-time, or free school dinners; or when mother comes home, soup with her. The children are rather neglected, and the police give the parents an indifferent character. The eldest child has eustacian catarrh and naso-pharyngitis; glands. The second, enlarged uvula. Housing: four in two very small rooms. Evidence from Schoolmaster, Police, Parish Sister, Church, Factor, and Doctors.

9. Father an old soldier without a pension, who reads novels. All the small children were found eating a large meal of ham and eggs and strong tea after 8 P.M., he in bed at the time. They have lapsed from thrift society membership. They are extremely filthy and the man drinks. A mission sells them meal cheap. Wife 18 at marriage and one child died. They feed pretty largely but unhealthily, and eat "pieces" at lunch time. At time of visit, though very dirty, they were tidier than ever found before. The eldest child has chronic suppuration and large perforation of ear. Housing: five in two rooms. Evidence from Police, Parish Sister, Factor, Soldiers' Society, Charity School, and Doctors.

10. The man a carter, who drank to a certain extent, and died some months after visit, when a Charity gave her help. She had an illegitimate child and two others. He was careless, and both neglected church going. No medical evidence. Housing: five in two rooms. Evidence from Police, two Churches, Parish Sister, Employer, and Charity School.

§ 2

Now to the Socialist, as to any one who has caught any tinge of the modern scientific spirit, these facts present themselves simply as an atrocious failure of states-

manship.   Indeed, a social system in which the mass of
the population is growing up under these conditions, he
scarcely recognizes as a state, rather it seems to him a
mere preliminary higgledy-piggledy aggregation of human beings, out of which a state has to be made.   It
seems to him that this wretched confusion of affairs which
repeats itself throughout the country, wherever population has gathered, must be due to more than individual
inadequacy; it must be due to some general and essential failure, some unsoundness in the broad principles
upon which the whole organization is conducted.

What is this general principle of failure beneath all
these particular cases?

In any given instance this or that reason for the
failure of a child may be given.   In one case it may be
the father or mother drinks, in another that the child is
an orphan neglected by aunt or stepmother, in another
that the mother is an invalid or a sweated worker too
overwrought to do much for him, or, though a good-
hearted soul, she is careless and dirty or ignorant, or
that she is immoral and reckless, and so on and so on.
Our haphazard sample of ten Scotch cases gives instances
of nearly all these alternatives.   And from these proxi-
mate causes one might work back to more general ones,
to the necessity of controlling the drink traffic, of abol-
ishing sweating, of shortening women's hours of labour,

of suppressing vice. But for the present argument it is not necessary to follow up these special causes. We can make a wider generalization. For our present analysis it is sufficient to say that one more general maladjustment covers every case of neglected or ill brought-up children in the world, and that is this, that with or without a decent excuse, the parent has not been equal to the task of rearing a civilized citizen. We have demanded too much from the parent, materially and morally, and the 10 cases we have quoted are just 10 out of 10,000,000 of the replies to that demand. Of 52 children born, 14 are dead; and of the remainder we can hardly regard more than 13 as being tolerably reared.

Is it not obvious then that, unless we are content that things should remain as they are, we must put the relations of parent to child on some securer and more wholesome footing than they are at the present time? We demand too much from the parent, and this being recognized, clearly there are only two courses open to us. The first is to relieve the parents by lowering the standard of our demand; the second is to relieve them by supplementing their efforts.

The first course, the Socialist holds, is not only cruel and unjust to the innocent child, but an entirely barbaric and retrogressive thing to do. It is a frank abandonment of all ideas of progress and world betterment. He puts it aside, therefore, and turns to the alternative. In doing that he comes at once into harmony with all the developmental tendencies of the last hundred years. For a hundred years there has been going on a process of supplementing and controlling parental effort.

A hundred years or so ago the parent was the supreme authority in the child's destiny — short only of direct murder. Parents were held responsible for their children's rearing to God alone; should they fail, individual, good-hearted people might, if they thought proper, step in, give food, give help — provided the parents consented, that is; but it was not admitted that the community as a whole was concerned in the matter. Parents (and guardians in the absence of parents) were allowed to starve their children, leave them naked, prey upon their children by making them work in factories or as chimney sweeps and the like; the law was silent, the state acquiesced. Good-hearted parents, on the other hand, who were unsuccessful in the world's affairs had the torment of seeing their children go short of food and garments, grow up ignorant and feeble, their only hope of help the chance kindliness of their more prosperous neighbours and the ill-organized charities left by the benevolent dead.

Through all the nineteenth century the irresistible logic of necessity has been forcing people out of the belief in that state of affairs, has been making them see the impossibility of leaving things so absolutely to parental discretion and conscience, has been forcing them toward a constructive and organizing; that is to say, toward a Socialist attitude. Essentially the Socialist attitude is this: an insistence that parentage can no longer be regarded as an isolated private matter; that the welfare of the children is of universal importance, and must, therefore, be finally a matter of collective concern. The state, which a hundred years ago was utterly careless of children, is now every year becoming more and more their guardian, their over-parent.

To-day the power of the parents is limited in ways that would have seemed incredible a hundred years ago. In the first place they must no longer unrestrictedly use their very young children to earn money for them in toil and suffering. A great mass of labour legislation forbids them. In the next place their right to inflict punishment or to hurt wantonly has been limited in many ways. The private enterprises of charitable organizations for the prevention of cruelty and neglect has led to a growing system of law in this direction also. Nor may a parent now prevent a child getting some rudiments of an education.

Between the parent and Heaven now, in addition to the more or less legalized voluntary interference of well-disposed private people, there do appear certain rare functionaries who — while they interfere not at all between good and competent parents and their children — do in certain instances save a parental default from its complete fruition. There are the school inspector and the sanitary officer. Then there are, in the London City Council area, the "Ringworm" nurses who examine the children systematically, and by means of certain white and red cards of remonstrance and warning, intimidate the parent into good behaviour or pave the way for a prosecution, and there is the factory inspector — and in certain cases the police. All these functionaries and "accessory consciences" have been thrust in between the supremacy of the parent and the child within the century.

So much the Socialist regards as all to the good, as all in the direction of that great constructive plan of organized human welfare at which he aims. And they all amount to a destruction, so much with this and so much with that, of the independence of the family, an invasion of the old moral isolation of parent and child.

But while a number of people (who haven't read the Edinburgh Charity Organization Society's Report) are content to regard these interventions as "going far enough," the Socialist considers these things as only the

beginning of the organization of the welfare of the
nation's children. You will notice that all these laws
and regulations at which we have glanced are in the
nature of prohibitions or compulsions; few have any
element of aid. By virtue of them we have diminished
the power of the inferior sort of parents to do evil by
their child, but we have done little or nothing to increase and stimulate their powers to do good. We may
prevent them doing some sorts of evil things to the child;
they may not give it poisonous things, or let it live in
morally or physically contagious places, but we do not
insure that they shall give it wholesome things — better
than they had themselves. We must, if our work is ever
to reach effectual fruition, go on to the logical comple-
tion of that process of supplementing the parent that
the nineteenth century began.

Consider, for instance, the circumstances of parentage
among the large section of the working classes whose
girls and women engage in factory labour. In many
cases the earnings of the woman are vitally necessary to
the solvency of the family budget, the father's wages do
not nearly cover the common expenditure. In some
cases the women are unmarried, or the man is an invalid or out of work. Consider such a woman on the
verge of motherhood. Either she must work in a factory right up to the birth of her child — and so damage

its health through her strain and fatigue,[1] — or she must give up her work, lose money, and go short of food and necessities and *so* damage the coming citizen. Moreover, after the child is born, either she must feed it artificially and return to work (and prosperity) soon, with a very great risk indeed that the child will die, or she must stay at home to nourish and tend it — until her landlord sells her furniture and turns her out!

Now it does not need that you should be a Socialist to see how cruel and ridiculous it is to have mothers in such a dilemma.   But while people who are not Socialists have no remedy to suggest, or only immediate and partial remedies, such, for example, as the forbidding of factory work to women who are about to be or have recently been mothers, — an expedient which is bound to produce a plentiful crop of "concealment of birth" and infanticide convictions, — the Socialist does proffer a general principle to guide the community in dealing not only with this particular hardship, but with all the kindred hardships which form a system with it.   He declares that we are here in the presence of an unsound and harmful way of regarding parentage; that we treat it as a *private affair*, that we are still disposed to assume that

---

[1] The hard facts of the case are put very clearly and quite invincibly, by Miss Margaret Macmillan in *Infant Mortality*. See also *The Babies' Tribute to the Modern Moloch*, by F. Victor Fisher. (Twentieth Century Press. 1*d*.)

people's children are almost as much their private concern as their cats, and as little entitled to public protection and assistance. The right view, he maintains, is altogether opposed to this; parentage is a public service and a public duty; a good mother is the most precious type of common individual a community can have, and to let a woman on the one hand earn a living as we do, by sewing tennis-balls or making cardboard boxes or calico, and on the other, not simply not to pay her, but to impoverish her because she bears and makes sacrifices to rear children, is the most irrational aspect of all the evolved and chancy ideas and institutions that make up the modern state. It is as if we believed our civilization existed to make cheap cotton and tennis-balls instead of fine human lives.

The Socialist takes all that the nineteenth century has done in remedial legislation as a mere earnest of all that it has still to do. He works for a consistent application of the principles that England, for example, tacitly admitted when she opened her public elementary schools and compelled the children to come in; the principle that the Community as a whole is the general Over-Parent of all its children; that the parents must be made answerable to the community for the welfare of their children, for their clear minds and clean bodies, their eyesight and weight and training; and that, on the other hand, the parents who do their duty well are as much entitled to payment and economic security as a soldier, a judge, or any other sort of public servant.

§ 3

Now do not imagine the case for the state being regarded as the Over-Parent and for the payment and financial support of parents is based simply upon the consideration of neglected, underfed, under-educated, and poverty-blighted children. No doubt in every one of the great civilized countries of the world at the present time such children are to be counted by the hundred thousand, by the million; but there is a much stronger case to be stated in regard to that possibly greater multitude of parents who are not in default, those common people, the mass of our huge populations, the wives of the moderately skilled workers or the reasonably comfortable employees, of the middling sort of people, the two, three, and four hundred pounds a year families, who toil and deny themselves for love of their children, and do contrive to rear them cleanly, passably well-grown, decent-minded, taught, and intelligent to serve the future. Consider the enormous unfairness with which we treat them, the way in which the modern state trades upon their instincts, their affections, their sense of duty and self-respect, to get from them for nothing the greatest social service in the world.

For while the least fortunate sort of children have at any rate the protection of the police and school inspectors, and the baser sort of parent has all sorts of public and quasi-public helps and doles, the families that make the middle mass of our population are still in the position of the families of a hundred years ago, and have no help under heaven against the world. It matters not how well the home of the skilled artisan's wife or the small business man's wife has been managed, she may have educated her children marvellously, they may be clean, strong, courteous, intelligent — if the husband gets out of work or suffers from business ill-luck or trade depression or chances to be killed uninsured, down they all go to want. Such insurance as they are able to make — and it needs a tremendously heavy premium to secure an insurance that will not mean a heavy fall of income with the bread-winner's death — must needs be in a private insurance office, and there is no effectual guarantee for either honesty or solvency in that. In most of the petty insurance business the thrifty poor are enormously overcharged and overreached. Rumour has been busy, and I fear only too justly, with the financial outlook of the great Friendly Societies upon which the scanty security of so many working-class families depends. Such investments as the lower and middle-class father makes of surplus profits and savings must be made in ignorance of the manœuvres of the big and often quite ruthless financiers who control the world of prices. If he builds or trades, he does so as a small investor, at the highest cost and lowest profit. Half the big businesses in the world have been made out of the lost savings of the small investor, a point to which I shall return later. People talk as though Socialism proposed to rob the thrifty industrious man of his savings. He could not be more systematically robbed of his savings than he is at the present time. Nowhere is there security, not even in the gilt-edged respectability of Consols which in the last ten years have fallen from 114 to under 85. Consider the adventure of the thrifty, well-meaning citizen who used his savings-bank hoard to buy Consols at the former price and now finds himself the poorer for not having buried his savings in his garden. The middling sort of man saves for the sake of wife and child; our state not only fails to protect him from the adventures of the manipulating financier, but it deliberately avoids competition with banker, insurance agent, and promoter. In no way can the middle-class or artisan parent escape the financiers' power and get real security for his home or his children's upbringing.

Not only is every parent of any but the richest classes worried and discouraged by the universal insecurity of outlook in this private adventure world, but at every turn his efforts to do his best for his children are discouraged. If he has no children, he will have all his income to spend on his own pleasure; he needs only live in a little house; he pays nothing for school, less for doctor, less for all the needs of life; and he is taxed less, his income tax is the same, no bigger; his rent, his rates, his household bills are all less.

The state will not even help him to a tolerable home, to wholesome food, to needed fuel for the new citizens he is training for it. The state nowadays in its slow awakening does show a certain concern in the housing of the lowest classes, a concern alike stimulated and supplemented by such fine charities as Peabody's, for example; but no one stands between the two hundred a year man and his landlord in the pitiless struggle to get. For every need of his children whom he toils to make into good men and women, he must pay a toll of owner's profits, he must trust to the anything but intelligent greed of private enterprise.

The state will not even insist there is built for his class a sufficiency of comfortable, sanitary homes; if he wants the elementary convenience of a bathroom, he must pay extra toll to the water shareholder; his gas is as cheap in quality and dear in price as it can be; his bread and milk, under the laws of supply and demand, are at the legal minimum of wholesomeness; the coal trade cheerfully raises his coal in midwinter to ruinous prices. He buys clothes of shoddy and boots of brown paper. To get any other is nearly impossible for a man with three hundred pounds a year. His newspapers, which are supported by advertisers and financiers, in order to hide the obvious injustice of this one-man fight against the allied forces of property, din in his ears that his one grievance is local taxation, his one remedy "to keep down the rates" — the "rates" which do at least repair his roadway, police his streets, give him open spaces for his babies, and help educate his children, and which, moreover, constitute a burthen he might by a little intelligent political action shift quite easily from his own shoulders to the broad support of capital and land.

If the children of the decent skilled artisan and middle class suffer less obviously than the poorer sort of children, assuredly the parents, in wearing anxiety, in toil and limitation and disappointment, suffer more. And in less intense and dramatic, but perhaps even more melancholy ways, the children of this class do suffer. They do not die so abundantly in infancy, but they grow up, too many of them, to shabby and limited lives. In

Britain they are still, as a class, extraordinarily ill-educated — many of them still go to incompetent, under-staffed, and ill-equipped private adventure schools; they are sent into business prematurely, often at four-teen or fifteen; they become mechanical, "respectable" drudges in processes they do not understand. They may escape want and squalor for a while perhaps, but they cannot escape narrowness and limitation and a cramped and anxious life. If they get to anything better than that, it is chiefly through almost heroic parental effort and sacrifice.

The plain fact is that the better middle-class parents serve the state in this matter of child-rearing, the less is their reward, the less is their security, the greater their toil and anxiety. Is it any wonder then that throughout this more comfortable but more refined and exacting class, the skilled artisan and middle class, there goes on something even more disastrous from the point of view of the state than the squalor, despair, and neglect of the lower levels, and that is a very evident strike against parentage? While the very poor con-tinue to have many children who die or grow up under-sized, crippled, or half-civilized, the middle mass, which *can* contrive, with a struggle and sacrifice, to rear fairly well-grown and well-equipped offspring, which has a conscience for the well-being and happiness of the young, manifests a diminishing spirit for parentage, its families fall to four, to three, to two, and in an increasing number of instances there are no children at all.

With regard to the struggling middle-class and skilled-artisan-class parent, even more than to the lower poor, does the Socialist insist upon the plain need, if only that our state and nation should continue, of endowment and help.   He deems it not simply unreasonable but ridiculous that in a world of limitless resources, of vast expenditure, of unparalleled luxury, in which two-million-pound battleships and multi-millionaires are common objects, the supremely important business of rearing the bulk of the next generation of the middling sort of people should be left almost entirely to the unaided, unguided efforts of impoverished and struggling women and men.   It seems to him almost beyond sanity to suppose that so things must or can continue.

§ 4

And what I have said of the middle-class parent is true with certain modifications of all the classes above it, except that in a monarchy you reach at last one state-subsidized family, — in the case of Britain a very healthy and active group, the royal family, which is not only state-supported, but also, beyond the requirements of any modern Socialist, state-bred.   There are enormous

E

handicaps at every other social level upon efficient parentage, and upon the training of children for any public
and generous end. Parentage is treated as a private
foible, and those who undertake its solemn responsi-
bilities are put at every sort of disadvantage against
those who lead sterile lives, who give all their strength
and resources to vanity and socially harmful personal
indulgence. These latter, with an ampler leisure and
ampler means, determine the forms of pleasure and
social usage, they "set the fashion" and bar pride, distinction, or relaxation to the devoted parent. The typical British aristocrat is not parent-bred, but class-bred,
— a person with a lively sense of social influences and
no social ideas. The one class that is economically capable of making all that can be made of its children is
demoralized by the very irresponsibility of the wealth
that creates this opportunity. This is still more apparent in the American plutocracy, where perhaps half
the women appear to be artificially sterilized spenders
of money upon frivolous ends.

No doubt there is in the richer strata of the community a certain proportion of families with a real tradition of upbringing and service; such English families
as the Cecils, Balfours, and Trevelyans, for example,
produce, generation after generation, public-spirited and
highly competent men. But the family tradition in

these cases is an excess of virtue rather than any necessary consequence of a social advantage; it is a defiance rather than a necessity of our economic system. It is natural that such men as Lord Hugh and Lord Robert Cecil, highly trained, highly capable, but without that gift of sympathetic imagination which releases a man from the subtle mental habituations of his upbringing, should idealize every family in the world to the likeness of their own — and find the Socialist's over-parent of the state, not simply a needless but a mischievous and wicked innovation. They think, they will I fear continue to think, of England as a world of happy Hatfields, cottage Hatfields, villa Hatfields, Hatfields over the shop, and Hatfields behind the farmyard, wickedly and wantonly assailed and interfered with by a band of weirdly discontented men. It is a dream that the reader must not share. Even in the case of the rich and really prosperous it is an illusion. In no class at the present time is there a real inducement to the effectual rearing of trained and educated citizens; in every class are difficulties and discouragements.

This state of affairs, says the Socialist, is chaotic and socially wasteful. It means a world-wide failure in health, vigour, order, and beauty. Such pleasure as it permits is a gaudy indulgence filched from children and duty; such beauty, a hectic beauty stained with injustice; such happiness, a happiness that can only continue so long as it remains blind or indifferent to a sea of wretchednesses and failure. Our present system of isolated and unsupported families keeps the mass of the world beyond all necessity painful, ugly, and squalid. It stands condemned, and it must end.

§ 5

Let me summarize what has been said in this chapter in a compact proposition, and so complete the statement of the First Main Generalization of Socialism.

The ideas of the private individual rights of the parent and of his isolated responsibility for his children are harmfully exaggerated in the contemporary world. We do not sufficiently protect children from negligent, incompetent, selfish, or wicked parents, and we do not sufficiently aid and encourage good parents; parentage is altogether too much a matter of private adventure, and the individual family is altogether too irresponsible. As a consequence there is a huge amount of avoidable privation, suffering, and sorrow, and a large proportion of the generation that grows up, grows up stunted, limited, badly educated, and incompetent in comparison with the strength, training, and beauty with which a better social organization could endow it.

The Socialist holds that the community as a whole should be responsible, and every individual in the community, married or single, parent or childless, should be responsible, for the welfare and upbringing of every child born into that community. This responsibility may be delegated in whole or in part to parent, teacher, or other guardian — but it is not simply the right but the duty of the state — that is to say, of the organized power and intelligence of the community — to direct, to inquire, and to intervene in any default for the child's welfare.

Parentage rightly undertaken is a service as well as a duty to the world, carrying with it not only obligations but a claim, the strongest of claims, upon the whole community. It must be paid for like any other public service; in any completely civilized state it must be sustained, rewarded, and controlled. And this is to be done not to supersede the love, pride, and conscience of the parent, but to supplement, encourage, and maintain it.

§ 6

This is the first of the twin generalizations upon which the whole edifice of modern Socialism rests. Its fellow-generalization we must consider in the chapter immediately to follow.

But at this point the reader unaccustomed to social questions will experience a difficulty. He will naturally think of this much of change we have broached, as if it was to happen in a world that otherwise was to remain just as the world is now, with merchants, landowners, rich and poor, and all the rest of it. You are proposing, he may say, what is no doubt a highly desirable but which is also a quite impossible thing. You propose practically to educate all the young of the country and to pay at least sufficient to support them and their mothers in decency—out of what? Where will you get the money?

That is a perfectly legitimate question and one that must be answered fully if our whole project is not to fall to the ground.

So we come to the discussion of material means, of the wherewithal, that is to say, to the "Economics" of Socialism. The reader will see very speedily that this great social revolution we propose necessarily involves a revolution in business and industry that will be equally far-reaching. The two revolutions are indeed inseparable, two sides of one wheel, and it is scarcely possible that one could happen without the other.

Of course the community supports all its children now; the only point is that it does not support them in its collective character as a state "as a whole." All the children in the world are supported by all the people in the world, but very unfairly and irregularly, through the intervention of that great multitude of small private proprietors, the parents. When the parents fail,

Charity and the Parish step in.   If the reader will refer to those ten cases from Edinburgh I have already quoted in Chapter III, § 1, he will note that in eight out of the ten there comes in the eleemosynary element; in the seventh case especially he will get an inkling of its waste. A change in the system that diminished (though it by no means abolished) this separate dependence of children upon parents, each child depending upon these "pieces" from the parental feast, need not necessarily diminish the amount of wheat, or leather, or milk in the world; the children would still get the bread and milk and boots, but through different channels and in a different spirit. They might even get more.   The method of making and distribution will evidently have to be a different one and run counter to currently accepted notions; that is all. Not only is it true that a change of system need not diminish the amount of food in the world; it might even increase it.   The Socialist declares that his system would increase it.   He proposes a method of making and distribution, a change in industrial conditions and in the conventions of property, that he declares will not only not diminish, but will greatly increase, the production of the world, and changes in the administration that he is equally convinced will insure a far juster and better use of all that is produced.

   This side of his proposals we will proceed to consider in our next chapter.

CHAPTER IV

THE SECOND MAIN GENERALIZATION OF SOCIALISM

§ 1

WE have considered the Socialist criticism of the present state of affairs in relation to the most important of all public questions, the question of the welfare and upbringing of the next generation. We have stated the general principle of social reconstruction that emerges from that criticism. We have now to enter upon the question of ways and means, the economic question. We have to ask whether the vision we have conjured up of a whole population well-fed, well-clad, well-educated — in a word well-brought up — is, after all, only an amiable dream. Is it true that humanity is producing all that it can produce at the present time, and managing everything about as well as it can be managed; that, as a matter of fact, there isn't enough of food and care to go round, and hence the unavoidable anxiety in the life of every one (except in the case of a small minority of exceptionally secure people) and the absolute wretchedness of vast myriads of the poorer sort?

The Socialist says, No ! He asserts that our economic system is as chaotic and wasteful as our system of rearing children — is only another aspect of the same planlessness — that it does its work with a needless excess of friction, that it might be far simpler and almost infinitely more productive than it is.

Let us detach ourselves a little from our everyday habits of thinking in these matters; let us cease to take customary things for granted, and let us try to consider how our economic arrangements would strike a disinterested intelligence that looked at them freshly for the first time. Let us take some matter of primary economic importance, such as the housing of the population, and do our best to criticise it in this spirit of personal aloofness. In order to do that, let us try to detach ourselves a little from our own personal interest in these affairs. Imagine a mind ignorant of our history and traditions, coming from some other sphere, from some world more civilized, from some other planet perhaps, to this earth. Would our system of housing strike it as the very wisest and most practical possible, would it really seem to be the attainable maximum of outcome for human exertion, or would it seem confused, disorderly, wasteful, and bad? The Socialist holds that the latter would certainly be the verdict of such an impartial examination.

What would our visitor find in such a country as England, for example? He would find a few thousand people housed with conspicuous comfort and sumptuousness, in large, airy, and often extremely beautiful homes equipped with every convenience — except such as economize labour — and waited on by many thousands of attendants. He would find next, several hundreds of thousands in houses reasonably well built, but for the most part ill-designed and unpleasant to the eye, houses passably sanitary and convenient, fitted with bathrooms, with properly equipped kitchens, usually with a certain space of air and garden about them. And the rest of our millions he would find crowded into houses evidently too small for a decent life, and often dreadfully dirty and insanitary, without proper space or appliances to cook properly, wash properly, or, indeed, perform any of the fundamental operations of a civilized life tolerably well, — without, indeed, even the privacy needed for common decency. In the towns he would find most of the houses occupied by people for whose needs they were obviously not designed, and in many cases extraordinarily crowded, ramshackle, and unclean; in the country he would be amazed to find still denser congestion, sometimes a dozen people in one miserable, tumbledown, outwardly picturesque and inwardly abominable two-roomed cottage, — people living up against pigstyes and drawing water from wells they could not help but contaminate. Think of how the intimate glimpses from the railway train one gets into people's homes upon the outskirts of any of our large towns would impress him. And being, as we assume, clear minded and able to trace cause and effect, he would see all this disorder working out in mortality, disease, misery, and intellectual and moral failure.

All this would strike our visitor as a very remarkable state of affairs for reasonable creatures to endure, and probably he would not understand at first that millions of people were content to regard all this disorder as the permanent lot of humanity. He would assume that this must be a temporary state of affairs due to some causes unknown to him, some great migration, for example. He would suppose we were all busy putting things right. He would see on the one hand unemployed labour and unemployed material; on the other, great areas of suitable land and the crying need for more and better homes than the people had, and it would seem the most natural thing in the world that the directing intelligence of the community should set the unemployed people to work with the unemployed material upon the land to house the whole population fairly and well. There exist all that is needed to house the whole population admirably: the building material, the room, the unoccupied hands. Why is it not being done?

Our answer would be, of course, that he did not understand our difficulties; the land was not ours to do as we liked with,— it did not belong to the community but to certain persons, the Owners, who either refused to let us build upon it or buy it or have anything to do with it, or demanded money we could not produce for it; that equally the material was not ours, but belonged to certain other Owners, and that, thirdly, the community had insufficient money or credit to pay the wages and maintenance and equipment of the workers who starved and degenerated in our streets — for that money too was privately owned.

This would puzzle our visitor considerably. "Why do you have Owners?" he would ask.

We might find that difficult to answer.

"But why do you let the land be owned?" he would go on. "You don't let people own the air. And these bricks and timber you mustn't touch, the mortar you need and the gold you need, they all came out of the ground — they all belonged to everybody or nobody a little while ago!"

You would say something indistinct about Property.

"But why?"

"Somebody must own the things."

"Well, let the state own the things and use them for the common good. It owns the roads, it owns the foreshores, and the territorial seas — nobody owns the air !"

If you entered upon historical explanations with him, you would soon be in difficulties. You would find that so recently as the Feudal System — which was still living, so to speak, yesterday — the King, who stood for the State, held the land as the Realm, and the predecessors of the present owners held under him merely as the administrative officials who performed all sorts of public services and had all sorts of privileges thereby. They have dropped the services and stuck to the land and the privileges; that is all.

"I begin to perceive," our visitor would say as this became clear; "your world is under the spell of an exaggerated idea, this preposterous idea there must be an individual Owner for everything in the world. Obviously you can't get on while you are under the spell of that ! So long as you have this private Ownership in everything, there's no help for you. You cut up your land and material in parcels of all sorts and sizes among this multitude of irresponsible little monarchs; you let all the material you need get distributed among another small swarm of owners, and clearly you can only get them to work for public ends in the most roundabout, tedious, and wasteful way. Why should they? They're very well satisfied as they are ! But if the community

as a whole insisted that this idea of private ownership
you have in regard to land and natural things was all
nonsense — and it *is* all nonsense! — just think what
you might not do with it now that you have all the new
powers and lights that science has given you. You
might turn all your towns into garden cities, put an end
to overcrowding, abolish smoky skies."

"Hush!" I should have to interrupt; "if you talk of
the things that are clearly possible in the world to-day,
they will say you are an Utopian dreamer!"

But at least one thing would have become clear, the
little swarm of Owners and their claim standing in the
way of any bold collective dealing with housing or any
such public concern. The real work to be done here is
to change an idea, that idea of ownership, to so modify
it that it will cease to obstruct the rational development
of life, — and that is what the Socialist seeks to do.

§ 2

Now the argument that the civilized housing of the
masses of our population now is impossible because if
you set out to do it, you come against the veto of the
private owner at every stage, can be applied to almost
every general public service. Some little while ago I
wrote a tract for the Fabian Society about boots [1];

[1] *This Misery of Boots.* It is intended as an introductory
tract explaining the central idea of Socialism for propaganda pur-

and I will not apologize for repeating here a passage from that. To begin with, this tract pointed out the badness, unhealthfulness, and discomfort of people's footwear as one saw it in every poor quarter, and asked why it was things were in so disagreeable a state. There was plenty of leather in the world, plenty of labour.

" Here on the one hand — you can see for yourself in any un-fashionable part of Great Britain — are people badly, uncom-fortably, painfully shod, in old boots, rotten boots, sham boots; and on the other great stretches of land in the world, with un-limited possibilities of cattle and leather and great numbers of people who, either through wealth or trade disorder, are doing no work. And our question is, 'Why cannot the latter set to work and make and distribute boots?'

"Imagine yourself trying to organize something of this kind of Free Booting expedition; and consider the difficulties you would meet with. You would begin by looking for a lot of leather. Imagine yourself setting off to South America, for example, to get leather; beginning at the very beginning by setting to work to kill and flay a herd of cattle. You find at once you are interrupted. Along comes your first obstacle in the shape of a man who tells you the cattle and the leather belong to him. You explain that the leather is wanted for people who have no decent boots in England. He says he does not care a rap what you want it for, before you may take it from him you have to buy him off; it is his private property, this leather, and

poses, and it is published by the Fabian Society of 3 Clements Inn, London, W.C., at 3d. That together with my tract *Socialism and the Family* (A. C. Fifield, 44 Fleet Street, E.C. 6d.), gives the whole broad outline of the Socialist attitude pretty completely.

the herd and the land over which the herd ranges. You ask him how much he wants for his leather, and he tells you frankly just as much as he can induce you to give.

"If he chanced to be a person of exceptional sweetness of disposition, you might perhaps argue with him. You might point out to him that this project of giving people splendid boots was a fine one that would put an end to much human misery. He might even sympathize with your generous enthusiasm; but you would, I think, find him adamantine in his resolve to get just as much out of you for his leather as you could with the utmost effort pay.

"Suppose now you said to him, 'But how did you come by this land and these herds, so that you can stand between them and the people who have need of them, exacting this profit?' He would probably either embark upon a long rigmarole or, what is much more probable, lose his temper and decline to argue. Pursuing your doubt as to the rightfulness of his property in these things, you might admit he deserved a certain reasonable fee for the rough care he had taken of the land and herds. But cattle breeders are a rude, violent race, and it is doubtful if you would get far beyond your proposition of a reasonable fee. You would in fact have to buy off this owner of the leather at a good thumping price — he exacting just as much as he could get from you — if you wanted to go on with your project.

"Well, then you would have to get your leather here; and to do that, you would have to bring it by railway and ship to this country. And here again you would find people without any desire or intention of helping your project, standing in your course resolved to make every possible penny out of you on your way to provide sound boots for every one. You would find the railway was private property and had owner or owners; you would find the ship was private property, with an owner or owners; and that none of these would be satisfied for a moment with a mere fee adequate to their services. They too would be resolved to make every penny of profit out of you. If you made inquiries about the matter, you would probably find the real owners of railway and ship were companies of shareholders, and that the profit squeezed out of your poor people's boots at this stage went to fill the pockets of old ladies at Torquay, spend-thrifts in Paris, well-booted gentlemen in London clubs, all sorts of glossy people. . . .

"Well, you get the leather to England at last, and now you want to make it into boots. You take it to a centre of popula-tion, invite workers to come to you, erect sheds and machinery upon a vacant piece of ground, and start off in a sort of fury of generous industry, boot-making. . . . Do you? There comes along an owner for that vacant piece of ground, declares it is his property, demands an enormous sum for rent. And your work-ers all round you, you find, cannot get house room until they too have paid rent — every inch of the country is somebody's prop-erty, and a man may not shut his eyes for an hour without the consent of some owner or other. And the food your shoe-makers eat, the clothes they wear, have all paid tribute and profit to landowners, cart owners, house owners, — endless tribute over and above the fair pay for work that has been done upon them. . . .

"So one might go on. But you begin to see now one set of reasons at least why every one has not good comfortable boots. There could be plenty of leather; and there is certainly plenty of labour and quite enough intelligence in the world to manage that and a thousand other desirable things. But this institu-tion of Private Property in land and naturally produced things, these obstructive claims that prevent you using ground or moving material and that have to be bought out at exorbitant

F

prices, stand in the way. All these owners hang like parasites
upon your enterprise at its every stage; and by the time you
get your sound boots well made in England, you will find them
costing about a pound a pair, high out of the reach of the general
mass of people. And you will perhaps not think me fanciful
and extravagant when I confess that when I realize this and
look at poor people's boots in the street, and see them cracked
and misshapen and altogether nasty, I seem to see also a lot of
little phantom landowners, cattle owners, house owners, owners
of all sorts, swarming over their pinched and weary feet like
leeches, taking much and giving nothing and being the real cause
of all such miseries."

§ 3

Our visitor would not only be struck by the obstruction of our social activities through our system of
leaving everything to private enterprise; he would also
be struck by the immense wastefulness. Everywhere
he would see things in duplicate and triplicate; down
the High Street of any small town he would find
three or four butchers — all selling New Zealand
mutton and Argentine beef as English; five or six
grocers, three or four milk shops, one or two big
drapers, and three or four small haberdashers, milliners, and "fancy shops," two or three fishmongers, all
very poor, all rather bad, most of them in debt and
with their assistants all insecure and underpaid. He
would find in spite of this wealth of competition that
every one who could contrive it, all the really pros-

perous people in fact, bought most of their food and drapery from big London firms.

But why should I go on writing fresh arguments when we have Elihu's classic tract[1] to quote?

"Observe how private enterprise supplies the street with milk. At 7.30 a milk cart comes lumbering along and delivers milk at one house and away again. Half an hour later another milk cart arrives and delivers milk first on this side the street and then on that, until seven houses have been supplied, and then he departs. During the next three hours four other milk carts put in an appearance at varying intervals, supplying a house here and another there, until finally, as it draws toward noon, their task is accomplished and the street supplied with milk.

"The time actually occupied by one and another of these distributors of milk makes in all about an hour and forty minutes, six men and six horses and carts being required for the purpose, and these equipages rattle along, one after the other, all over the district, through the greater part of the day in the same erratic and extraordinary manner."

§ 4

Our imaginary visitor would probably quite fail to grasp the reasons why we do not forthwith shake off this obstructive and harmful idea of Private Ownership, dispossess our landowners, and so forth, as gently as

[1] Elihu's tracts are published by the I.L.P., 23 Bride Lane, Fleet Street, London, E.C., at one penny each. The best are: *Whose Dog art Thou? A Nation of Slaves; Milk and Postage Stamps; A Corner in Flesh and Blood;* and *Simple Division.*

possible, and set to work upon collective housing and the rest of it.   And so he would "exit wondering."

But that would be only the opening of the real argument.   A competent anti-Socialist of a more terrestrial experience would have a great many very effectual and very sound considerations to advance in defence of the present system.

He might urge that our present way of doing things, though it was sometimes almost as wasteful as Nature when fresh spawn or pollen germs are scattered, was in many ways singularly congenial to the infirmities of humanity.   The idea of property is a spontaneous product of the mortal mind; children develop it in the nursery, and are passionately alive to the difference of *meum* and *tuum*, and its extension to land, subterranean products, and wild free things, even if it is under analysis a little unreasonable, was at least singularly acceptable to humanity.

And there would be admirable soundness in all this. There can be little or no doubt that the conception of personal ownership has in the past contributed elements to human progress that could have come through no other means.   It has allowed private individuals in odd corners to try experiments in new methods and new appliances, that the general intelligence, such as it was, of the community could not have understood.   For all its faults our present individualistic order, compared not simply with the communism of primitive tribes, but even with the personal and largely illiterate control of the mediæval feudal governments, is a good efficient working method. I don't think a Socialist need quarrel with the facts of history or human nature. But he would urge that Private Ownership is only a phase, though no doubt quite a necessary phase, in human development. The world has needed Private Ownership just as (Lester F. Ward declares [1]) it once needed slavery to discipline men and women to agriculture and habits of industry, and just as it needed autocratic kings to weld warring tribes into nations and nations into empires, to build high-roads, end private war, and establish the idea of law, and a wider than tribal loyalty. But just as Western Europe has passed out of the phases of slavery and of autocracy (which is national slavery) into constitutionalism, so, he would hold, we are passing out of the phase of private ownership of land and material and food. We are doing so not because we reject it, but because we have worked it out, because we have learnt its lessons and can now go on to a higher and finer organization.

There the anti-Socialist would join issue with a lesser

[1] *Pure Sociology*, pp. 271–272, by Lester F. Ward.   (The Macmillan Company, New York.)

advantage. He would have to show not only that Private Ownership has been serviceable and justifiable in the past,— which many Socialists admit quite cheerfully, — but that it is the crown and perfection of human method, which the Socialists flatly deny. Universal Private Ownership, an extreme development of the sentiment of individual autonomy and of the limitation of the state to the merest police functions, were a necessary outcome of the breakdown of the unprogressive authoritative Feudal System in alliance with a dogmatic church. It reached its maximum in the eighteenth century, when even some of the prisons and workhouses were run by private contract, when people issued a private money, the old token coinage, and even regiments of soldiers were raised by private enterprise. It was, the Socialist alleges, a mere phase of that breaking-up of the old social edifice, a wrecking of the old circle of ideas that had to precede the new constructive effort. But with land, with all sorts of property and all sorts of businesses and public services, *just as with the old isolated private family,* the old separateness and independence is giving way to a new synthesis. The idea of Private Ownership, albeit still the ruling idea of our civilization, does not rule nearly so absolutely as it did. It weakens and falters before the inexorable demands of social necessity, manifestly under our eyes.

The Socialist would be able to appeal to a far greater number of laws in the nature of limitation of the owner of property than could be quoted to show the limitation of the old supremacy of the head of the family.   In the first place he would be able to point to a constantly increasing interference with the right of the landowner to do what he liked with his own, building regulations, intervention to create allotments, and so forth.   Then there would be a vast mass of factory and industrial legislation, controlling, directing, prohibiting, fencing machinery, interfering on behalf of health, justice, and public necessity with the owner's free bargain with his work people.   His business undertakings would be under limitations his grandfather never knew, even harmless adulterations that merely intensify profit forbidden him !

And in the next place and still more significant is the manifest determination to keep in public hands many things that would once inevitably have become private property.   For example, in the middle Victorian period, a water-supply, a gas-supply, a railway or tramway was inevitably a private enterprise, the creation of a new property; now, this is the exception rather than the rule.   While gas and water and trains were supplied by speculative owners for profit, electric light and power, new tramways and light railways are created in an increasing number of cases by public bodies who retain them for the public good. Nobody who travels to London as I do regularly in the dirty, overcrowded carriages of the infrequent and unpunctual trains of the South Eastern Company and who then transfers to the cleanly, speedy, frequent, in a word, "civilized" electric cars of the London County Council, can fail to estimate the value and significance of this supersession of the private owner by the commonweal.

All these things, the Socialists insist, are but a beginning. They point to a new phase in social development, to the appearance of a collective intelligence and a sense of public service taking over appliances, powers, enterprises, with a growing confidence that must end finally in the substitution of collective for private ownership and enterprise throughout the whole area of the common business of life.

§ 5

In relation to quite a number of large public services it can be shown that even under contemporary conditions Private Ownership does work with an enormous waste and inefficiency. Necessarily it seeks for profit; necessarily it seeks to do as little as possible for as much as possible. The prosperity of all Kent is crippled by a "combine" of two ill-managed and unenterprising railway companies, with no funds for new developments, grinding out an uncertain dividend by clipping expenditure.

I happen to see this organization pretty closely, and I can imagine no state enterprise west of Turkey or Persia presenting even to the passing eye so deplorable a spectacle of ruin and inefficiency. The South Eastern Company's estate at Seabrook presents the dreariest spectacle of incompetent development conceivable; one can see its failure three miles away; it is a waste with an embryo slum in one corner protected by an extravagant sea-wall, already partly shattered, from the sea.

To-day (January 15, 1907) the price of the ordinary South Eastern stock is 86 and its deferred stock 48; of the London, Chatham, and Dover ordinary stock 15½; an eloquent testimony to the disheartened state of the owners who now cling reluctantly to this disappointing monopoly. Spite of this impoverishment of the ordinary shareholder, this railway system has evidently paid too much profit in the past for efficiency; the rolling-stock is old and aging, much of it is by modern standards abominable; the trains are infrequent and the shunting operations at local stations, with insufficient sidings and insufficient staffs, produce a chronic dislocation and unpunctuality in the traffic that is exaggerated by the defects of direction evident even in the very time-tables. The trains are not well planned, the connections with branch lines are often extremely ill-managed. The service is bad to its details. It is the exception rather than the rule to find a ticket-office in the morning with change for a five-pound note, and, as a little indication of the spirit of the whole machine, I discovered the other day that the conductors upon the South Eastern trams at Hythe start their morning with absolutely no change at all. Recently the roof of the station at Charing Cross fell in through sheer decay. A whole rich county now stagnates hopelessly under the grip of this sample of private enterprise; towns fail to grow, trade flows sluggishly from point to point. No population in the world would stand such a management as it endures at the hands of the South Eastern Railway, from any responsible public body. Out would go the whole board of managers at the next election. Consider what would have happened if the London County Council had owned Charing Cross station two years ago. But manifestly there is nothing better to be done under private ownership conditions. The common shareholders are scattered and practically powerless, and their collective aim is, at any expense to the public welfare, to keep the price of the shares from going still lower.

The South Eastern Railway is only one striking instance of the general unserviceableness of private ownership for public services. Nearly all the British railway companies, in greater or less degree, present now a similar degenerative process. Years of profit-sweating, of high dividends, have left them with old stations, old rolling-stock, old staffs, bad habits, and diminishing borrowing power. Only a few of these corporations make any attempt to keep pace with invention. It is remarkable now in an epoch of almost universal progress how stagnant the British privately owned railways are. One travels nowadays if anything with a decrease of comfort from the 1880 accommodation, because of the greater overcrowding; and there has been no general increase of speed, no increase in smooth running, no increase in immunity from accident now for quite a number of years. One travels in a dingy box of a compartment that is too ill-lit at night for reading and full of invincible draughts. In winter the only warmth is too often an insufficient footwarmer of battered tin for which the passengers fight fiercely with their feet. An observant person cannot fail to be struck by the shabby-looking porters on so many of our lines — they represent the standard of good clothing for the year 1848 or thereabouts — and by the bleak misery of many of the stations, the universal dirt that electricity might even now abolish. You dare not drop a parcel on any British railway cushion for fear of the cloud of horrible dust you would raise; you have to put it down softly. Consider, too, the congested infrequent suburban trains that ply round any large centre of population, the inefficient goods and parcel distribution that hangs up the trade of the local shopman everywhere. Not only in the arrested standard of comfort, but in the efficiency of working also, are our privately owned railways a hopeless discredit to private ownership.

None of them, hampered by their present equipment, are able to adapt themselves readily to the new and better mechanism science produces for them, electric traction, electric lighting, and so forth; and it seems to me highly probable that the last steam engines and the last oil lamps in the world will be found upon the southern railway lines of Great Britain. How can they go on borrowing money with their stock at the prices I have quoted, and how can they do anything without money? The conception of profit-raising that rules our railways takes rather an altogether different direction; it takes the form of attempts to procure a monopoly even of the minor traffic by resisting the development of light railways, and of keeping the standard of comfort, decency, and cleanliness low. As for the vast social ameliorations that could be wrought now and are urgently needed now, by redistributing population through enhanced and cheapened services scientifically planned, and by an efficient collection and carriage of horticultural and agricultural produce, these things lie outside the philosophy of the private owner altogether. They would probably not pay him, and there the matter ends; that they would pay the community enormously does not for one moment enter into his circle of ideas.

There can be little doubt that in the next decade or so the secular decay and lagging of the British railway services which is inevitable under existing conditions (in speed, in comfort, they have long been distanced by continental lines), the probable increase in accidents due to economically, administered permanent ways and aging stations and bridges, and the ever more perceptible checking of British economic development due to this clogging of the circulatory sytem, will be of immense value to the Socialist propaganda as an object-lesson in Private Ownership. In Italy the thing has already passed its inevitable climax, and the state is now struggling valiantly to put a disorganized, ill-equipped, and undisciplined network of railways, the legacy of a period of private enterprise, into tolerable working order.

§ 6

In a second great public service there is a perceptible, a growing recognition of the evil and danger of allowing

profit-seeking Private Ownership to prevail, and that is
the general food supply. A great quickening of the
public imagination in this matter has occurred through
the "boom" of Mr. Upton Sinclair's book, *The Jungle* —
a book every student of the elements of Socialism should
read. He accumulated a considerable mass of facts about
the Chicago stockyards, and incorporated them with his
story, and so enabled people to realize what they might
with a little imaginative effort have inferred before: that
the slaughtering of cattle and the preparation of meat,
when it is done wholly and solely for profit, that is to
say when it is done as rapidly and cheaply as possible,
is done *horribly;* that it is a business cruel to the beasts,
cruel to the workers, and dangerous to the public health.
The United States has long recognized the inadequacy
of private consciences in this concern, and while all the
vast profits of the business go to the meat-packers, the
community has maintained an insufficient supply of
underpaid and, it is said in some cases, bribable inspectors, to look after the public welfare.

In this country also, slaughtering is a private enterprise but slightly checked by inspection, and if we have
no Chicago, we probably have all its mean savings, its
dirt and carelessness and filth, scattered here and there
all over the country, a little in this privately owned
slaughter-house, a little in that. For what inducement

has a butcher to spend money and time in making his slaughter-house decent, sanitary, and humane above the standard of his fellows? To do that will only make him poor and insolvent. Anyhow, few of his customers will come to see their meat butchered, and as they say in the south of England, "What the eye don't see the heart don't grieve."

Many witnesses concur in declaring that our common jam, pickle, and preserve trade is carried on under equally filthy conditions. If it is not, it is a miracle, in view of the inducements the Private Owner has to cut his expenses, economize on premises and wages, and buy his fruit as near decay and his sugar as near dirt as he can. The scandal of our milk supply is an open one; it is more and more evident that so long as Private Ownership rules in the milk trade, we can never be sure that at every point in the course of the milk from cow to consumer there will not creep in harmful and dishonest profit-making elements. The milking is too often done dirtily from dirty cows and into dirty vessels — why should a business man fool away his profits in paying for scrupulous cleanliness when it is almost impossible to tell at sight whether milk is clean or dirty? — and there come more or less harmful dilutions and adulterations and exposures to infection at every handling, at every chance at profit-making. The unavoidable inefficiency of the private milk trade reflects itself in infant mortality; we pay our national tribute to private enterprise in milk — a tribute of many thousands of babies every year. We try to reduce this tribute by inspection. But why should the state pay money for inspection, upon keeping highly trained and competent persons merely to pry and persecute in order that private incompetent people should reap profits with something short of a maximum of child murder? It would be much simpler to set to work directly, employ and train these private persons, and run the dairies and milk distribution ourselves.

There is an equally strong case for a public handling of bakehouses and the bread supply. Already the public is put to great and entirely unremunerative expense in inspecting and checking weights and hunting down the grosser instances of adulteration, grubbiness, and dirt, and with it all the common bakehouse remains for the most part a subterranean haunt of rats, mice, and cockroaches, and the ordinary baker's bread is so insipid and unnutritious that a great number of more prosperous people nowadays find it advantageous to health and pocket alike to bake at home. A considerable amount of physical degeneration may be connected with the general poorness of our bread. The plain fact of the case is that our population will never get good wholesome bread from the private owner's bakehouse, until it employs one skilled official to watch every half dozen bakers, and another to watch him; and it seems altogether saner and cheaper to abolish the private owner in this business also and do the job cleanly, honestly, and straightforwardly in proper buildings with properly paid labour, as a public concern.

Now what has been said of the food supply is still truer of the trade in fuel. Between the consumer and the collier is a string of private persons each resolved to squeeze every penny of profit out of the coal on its way to the cheap and wasteful grate one finds in the jerry-built homes of the poor. In addition there is every winter now, either in Great Britain or America, a manipulation of the coal market and a more or less severe coal famine. Coal is jerked up to unprecedented prices, and the small consumer, who has no place for storage, who must buy, if not from day to day, from week to week, finds he must draw upon his food fund and his savings to meet the Private Owner's raised demands or freeze. Every such coal famine reaps its harvest for death of old people and young children, and wipes out so many thousands of savings-bank accounts and hoarded shillings. Consider the essential imbecility of allowing the nation's life and the nation's thrift to be preyed upon for profit in this way! Is it possible to doubt that the civilized community of the future will

G

have to resume possession of all its stores of fuel, will keep itself informed of the fluctuating needs of its population, and will distribute and sell coal, gas, and oil — not for the maximum profit, but the maximum general welfare ?[1]

Another great branch of trade in which private ownership and private freedom is manifestly antagonistic to the public welfare is the Drink Traffic. Here we have a commodity, essentially a drug, its use readily developing a vice, deleterious at its best, complex in composition and particularly susceptible to adulteration and the enhancement of its attraction by poisonous ingredients and indeed to every sort of mischievous secret manipulation. Probably nothing is more rarely found pure and honest than beer or whiskey; whiskey begins to be blended and doctored before it leaves the distillery. And we allow the production and distribution of this drug of alcoholic drink to be from first to last a source of private profit! We so contrive it that we put money prizes upon the propaganda of drink. Is it any wonder that drink is not only made by adulteration far more evil than it naturally is, but that it is forced upon the public in every possible way?

[1] In Dakota, 1906–1907, private enterprise led to a particularly severe coal famine in the bitterest weather, and the shortage was felt so severely that the population rose and attacked and stopped passing coal trains.

"He tempts them to drink," I have heard a clergyman say of his village publican. But what else did he think the publican was there for? — to preach total abstinence? Naturally, inevitably, the whole of the Trade is a propaganda, not of drunkenness, but of habitual heavy drinking. The more successful propagandists, the great brewers and distillers, grow rich just in the proportion that people consume beer and spirits; they gain honour and peerages in the measure of their success.

It is very interesting to the Socialist to trace the long struggle of the temperance movement against its initial ideas of freedom, and to see how inevitably the most reluctant and unlikely people have been forced to recognize private ownership in this trade and for profit as the ultimate evil. I am delighted to have at hand an excellent little tract by "A Ratepayer," *National Efficiency and the Drink Traffic.* It has a preface by Mr. Haldane, — who as one of our clearest-thinking statesmen *must* come to outright Socialism sooner or later in spite of his recent repudiations, and it is as satisfactory a demonstration of the absolute necessity of thoroughgoing Socialism in this particular field as any Socialist could wish. One encounters the Bishop of Chester, for example, in its pages talking the purest Socialism, and making the most luminous admissions of the impossibility of continued private control, in phrases that need but a few verbal changes to apply equally to milk, to meat, to bread, to housing, to bookselling.[1]

<h2 style="text-align:center">§ 7</h2>

Land and housing, railways, food, drink, coal, in each of these great general interests there is a separate strong case for the substitution of collective control for the private ownership methods of the present time. There is a great and growing number of people like "A Rate-payer" and Mr. Haldane, who do not call themselves Socialists, but who are yet strongly tinged with Socialist conceptions, who are convinced — some in the case of the land, some in the case of the drink trade or the milk — that private ownership and working for profit must cease. But they will not admit a general principle; they argue each case on its merits.

The Socialist maintains that, albeit the details of each problem must be studied apart, there does underlie all these cases and the whole economic situation at the present time one general fact, that through our whole social system, from top to base, we find things under the influence of a misleading idea that must be changed, and which, until it is changed, will continue to work out

[1] For a clear and admirable account of the Socialist attitude to the temperance question see the tract on *Municipal Drink Traffic*, published by the Fabian Society; price one penny.

in waste, unserviceableness, cramped lives, and suffering and death. Each man is for himself, that is this misleading idea, seeking, perforce, ends discordant with the general welfare. Who serves the community without exacting pay goes under; who exacts pay without service, prospers and continues; success is not to do well, it is to have and to get; failure is not to do ill, it is to lose and not have; and under these conditions how can we expect anything but dislocated, unsatisfying service at every turn?

The contemporary Christian moralist and the social satirist would appeal to the Owner's sense of duty; he would declare in a platitudinous tone that property had its duties as well as its rights and so forth. The Socialist, however, looks a little deeper, and puts the thing differently. He brings both rights and duties to a keener scrutiny. What underlies all these social disorders, he alleges, is one simple thing, a misconception of property, an unreasonable exaggeration, an accumulated inherited exaggeration of the idea of property. He says the idea of private property, which is just and reasonable in relation to intimate personal things, to clothes, appliances, books, one's home or apartments, the garden one loves, or the horse one rides, has become unreasonably exaggerated until it obsesses the world; that the freedom we have given men to claim and own and hold the land upon which we must live; the fuel we burn, the supplies of food and metal we require, the railways and ships upon which our business goes, and to fix what prices they like to exact for all these services, leads to the impoverishment and practical enslavement of the mass of mankind.

And so he comes to his second main generalization which I may perhaps set out in these words: —

The idea of the private ownership of things and the rights of owners is enormously and mischievously exaggerated in the contemporary world. The conception of private property has been extended to land, to material, to the values and resources accumulated by past generations, to a vast variety of things that are properly the inheritance of the whole race. As a result of this, there is an enormous obstruction and waste of human energy and an entire loss of opportunity and freedom for the mass of mankind; progress is retarded; there is a vast amount of avoidable wretchedness, cruelty, and injustice.

The Socialist holds that the community as a whole should be inalienably the owner and administrator of the land, of all raw materials, of all values and resources accumulated from the past, and that all private property must be of a terminable nature, reverting to the community, and subject to the general welfare.

This is the second of the twin generalizations upon which the edifice of modern Socialism rests. Like the first, and like the practical side of all sound religious teaching, it is a specific application of one general rule of conduct, and that is — the subordination of the individual motive to the happiness and welfare of the species.

§ 8

But now the reader unaccustomed to Socialist discussion will begin to see the crude form of the answer to the question raised by the previous chapter; he will see the resources from which the enlargement of human life we there contemplated is to be derived, and realize the economic methods to be pursued.   Collective ownership is the necessary corollary of collective responsibility. There are to be no private landowners, no private bankers and lenders of money, no private insurance adventurers, no private railway owners nor shipping owners, no private mine owners, oil kings, silver kings, coal and wheat forestallers, or the like.   All this realm of property is to be resumed by the state, is to be state-owned and state-managed, and the vast revenues that are now devoted to private ends will go steadily to feed, maintain, and educate a new and better generation, to promote research and advance science, to build new houses, develop fresh resources, plant, plan, beautify and reconstruct the world.

CHAPTER V

§ 1

WE have stated now how the constructive plan of Socialism aims to replace the accepted ideas about two almost fundamental human relations by broader and less fiercely egotistical conceptions; how it denies a man property in his wife and children, how it would secure their material welfare, — leaving, however, all his other relations with them intact, — and how it asserts that a vast range of inanimate things also which are now held as private property must be regarded as the inalienable possession of the whole community. This change in the circle of ideas (as the Herbartians put it) is the essence of the Socialist project.

It means no little change. It means a general change in the spirit of living; it means a change from the spirit of gain (which now necessarily rules our lives) to the spirit of service.

I have tried to show in the preceding chapter that Socialism seeks to make life less squalid and cruel, less degrading and dwarfing for the children that are born into it, and I have tried also to make clear that realization of, and revolt against, the bad management and waste and muddle which result from our present economic system. I want now to point out that Socialism seeks to ennoble the intimate personal life, by checking and discouraging passions that now run rampart, and by giving wider scope for passions that are now thwarted and subdued.   The Socialist declares that life is now needlessly dishonest, base, and mean, because our present social organization, such as it is, makes an altogether too powerful appeal to some of the very meanest elements in our nature.

Not perhaps to the lowest.   There can be no disputing that our present civilization does discourage much of the innate bestiality of man; that it helps people to a measure of continence, cleanliness, and mutual toleration; that it does much to suppress brute violence, the spirit of lawlessness, cruelty, and wanton destruction. But on the other hand it does also check and cripple generosity and frank truthfulness, any disinterested creative passion, the love of beauty, the passion for truth and research, and it stimulates avarice, parsimony, overreaching, usury, falsehood, and secrecy, by making money-getting its criterion of intercourse.

Whether we like it or not, we who live in this world

to-day find we must either devote a considerable amount of our attention to getting and keeping money and shape our activities, or, if you will, distort them, with a constant reference to that process, or we must accept futility. Whatever powers men want to exercise, whatever service they wish to do, it is a preliminary condition for most of them that they must by earning something or selling something, achieve opportunity. If they cannot turn their gift into some salable thing or get some propertied man to "patronize" them, they cannot exercise these gifts. The gift for getting is the supreme gift, all others bow before it.

Now this is not a thing that comes naturally out of the quality of man; it is the result of a blind and complex social growth, of this set of ideas working against that, and of these influences modifying those. The idea of property has run wild and become a choking universal weed. It is not the natural master-passion of a wholesome man to want constantly to own. People talk of Socialism as being a proposal "against human nature," and they would have us believe this life of anxiety, of parsimony and speculation, of mercenary considerations and forced toil we all lead, is the complete and final expression of the social possibilities of the human soul. But, indeed, it is only quite abnormal people, people of a narrow, limited, specialized intelligence, Rockefellers,

Morgans, and the like, people neither great nor beautiful, mere financial monomaniacs, who can keep themselves devoted to and concentrated upon gain. To the majority of capable good human stuff, buying and selling, saving and investing, insuring one's self and managing property, is a mass of uncongenial, irrational, and tiresome procedure, conflicting with the general trend of instinct and the finer interests of life. The great mass of men and women indeed find the whole process so against nature, that in spite of all the miseries of poverty, all the slavery of the economic disadvantage, they remain poor, they cannot urge themselves to this irksome cunning game of besting the world. Most, in a sort of despair, make no effort; many resort to that floundering endeavour to get by accident, gambling; many achieve a precarious and unsatisfactory gathering of possessions, a few houses, a claim on a field, a few hundred pounds in some investment as incalculable as a kite in a gale; just a small minority have and get — for the most part either inheritors of riches or energetic people who, through a real dulness toward the better and nobler aspects of life, can give themselves almost entirely to grabbing and accumulation. To such as these, all common men who are not Socialists, do in effect conspire to give the world.

The anti-Socialist argues that out of this evil of encouraged and stimulated avarice comes good, and that this peculiar meanly greedy type that predominates in the individualist world to-day, the Rockefeller-Harriman type, "creates" great businesses, exploits the possibilities of nature, gives mankind railways, power, commodities. As a matter of fact, a modern intelligent community is quite capable of doing all these things infinitely better for itself, and the beneficent influence of commerce may easily become, and does easily become, the basis of a cant. Exploitation by private persons is no doubt a necessary condition to economic development in an illiterate community of low intelligence, just as flint implements marked a necessary phase in the social development of mankind; but to-day the avaricious getter, like some obsolescent organ in the body, consumes strength and threatens health. And to-day he is far more mischievous than ever he was before, because of the weakened hold of the old religious organization upon his imagination. For the most part the great fortunes of the modern world have been built up by proceedings either not socially beneficial, or in some cases positively harmful. Consider some of the commoner methods of growing rich. There is first the selling of rubbish for money, exemplified by the great patent-medicine fortunes and the fortunes achieved by the debasement of journalism, the sale of prize-competition magazines and the like; next there is forestalling, the making of "corners" in such commodities as corn, nitrates, borax, and the like; then there is the capture of what Americans call "franchises," securing at low terms by expedients that usually will not bear examination, the right to run some profitable public service for private profit which would be better done in public hands — the various private enterprises for urban traffic, for example; then there are the various more or less complex financial operations, watering stock, "reconstructing," "shaking out" the ordinary shareholder, which transfer the savings of the common struggling person to the financial magnate. All the activities in this list are more or less anti-social, yet it is by practising them that the great successes of recent years have been achieved. Fortunes of a second rank have no doubt been made by building up manufactures and industries of various types by persons who have known how to buy labour cheap, organize it well, and sell its products dear; but even in these cases the social advantage of the new product is often largely discounted by the labour conditions. It is impossible, indeed, directly one faces current facts, to keep up the argument of the public good achieved by men under the incentive of gain and the necessity of that incentive to progress and economic development.

Now not only is it true that the subordination of our

affairs to this spirit of gain places our world in the hands of a peculiar, acquisitive, uncreative, wary type of person, and that the mass of people hate serving the spirit of gain and are forced to do so through the obsession of the whole community by this idea of Private Ownership; but it is also true that even now the real driving force that gets the world along is not that spirit at all, but the spirit of service. Even to-day it would be impossible for the world to get along if the mass of its population was really specialized for gain. A world of Rockefellers, Morgans, and Rothschilds would perish miserably after a vigorous campaign of mutual skinning; it is only because the common run of men is better than these profit-hunters that any real and human things are achieved.

Let us go into this aspect of the question a little more fully, because it is one that appears to be least clearly grasped by those who discuss Socialism to-day.

§ 2

This fact must be insisted upon that most of the work of the world and all the good work is done to-day for some other motive than gain; that profit-seeking not only is not the moving power of the world, but that it cannot be, that it runs counter to the doing of effectual work in every department of life.

It is hard to know how to set about proving a fact that is to the writer's perception so universally obvious. One can only appeal to the intelligent reader to use his own personal observation upon the people about him. Everywhere he will see the property-owner doing nothing, the profit-seeker busy with unproductive efforts, with the writing of advertisements, the mis-representation of goods, the concoction of a plausible prospectus, and the extraction of profits from the toil of others, while the real necessary work of the world,— I don't mean the labour and toil only, but the intelligent direction, the real planning and designing and inquiry, the management and the evolution of ideas and methods, — is in the enormous majority of cases done by salaried individuals working either for a fixed wage and the hope of increments having no proportional relation to the work done, or for a wage varying within definite limits. All the engineering design, all architecture, all our public services, the exquisite work of our museum control, for example, all the big wholesale and retail businesses, al-most all big industrial concerns, mines, estates,— all these things are really in the hands of salaried or quasi-salaried persons *now*, just as they would be under Socialism. They are only possible now because all these managers, officials, employees, are as a class unreasonably honest and loyal, are interested in their work and anxious to

do it well, and do not seek *profits* in every transaction
they handle. Give them even a small measure of security
and they are content with interesting work; they are glad
to set aside the urgent perpetual search for personal gain
that Individualists have persuaded themselves is the
ruling motive of mankind; they are glad to set these aside
altogether and, as the phrase goes, "get something
done." And this is true all up and down the social
scale. A bricklayer is no good unless he can be interested in laying bricks. One knows whenever a domestic servant becomes mercenary, when she ceases to
take, as people say, "a pride in her work" and thinks
only of "tips" and getting, she becomes impossible.
Does a signalman every time he pulls over a lever, or a
groom galloping a horse, think of his wages — or want to?

I will confess I find it hard to write with any patience
and civility of this argument that humanity will not
work except for greed or need of money and only in
proportion to the getting. It is so patently absurd. I
suppose the reasonable anti-Socialist will hardly maintain it seriously with that crudity. He will qualify. He
will say that although it may be true that good work is
always done for the interest of the doing or in the spirit
of service, yet in order to get and keep people at work and
to keep the standard high through periods of indolence
and distraction, there must be the dread of dismissal

and the stimulating eye of the owner. That certainly puts the case a good deal less basely and much more plausibly.

There is perhaps this much truth in that, that most people do need a certain stimulus to exertion and a certain standard of achievement to do their best, but to say that this is provided by private ownership and can only be provided by private ownership, is an altogether different thing. Is the British Telephone Service, for example, kept as efficient as it is — which isn't very much, by the bye, in the way of efficiency — by the protests of the shareholders or of the subscribers? Does the grocer's errand boy loiter any less than his brother who carries the Post-Office telegrams? In the matter of the public milk supply again, would not an intelligently critical public, anxious for its milk good and early, be a far more formidable master than a speculative proprietor in the back room of a creamery? And when one comes to large business organizations managed by officials and owned by dispersed shareholders, the contrast is all to the advantage of the community.

No! the only proper virtues in work, the ones that have to be relied upon, and developed and rewarded in the civilized state we Socialists are seeking to bring about, are the spirit of service and the passion for doing well, the honourable competition not to get but to *do*. By sweating and debasing urgency, we get meagrely

H

done what we might get handsomely done by the Good
Will of emancipated mankind.   For all who really make,
who really do, the imperative of gain is the inconvenience,
the enemy.   Every artist, every scientific investigator,
every organizer, every good workman knows that.
Every good architect knows that this is so and can tell
of time after time when he has sacrificed manifest profit
and taken a loss to get a thing done as he wanted it done,
right and well; every good doctor, too, has turned from
profit and high fees to the moving and interesting case,
to the demands of knowledge and the public health;
every teacher worth his or her salt can witness to the
perpetual struggle between business advantage and right
teaching; every writer has faced the alternative of his
æsthetic duty and the search for beauty on the one hand
and the "salable" on the other.   All this is as true of
ordinary making as of special creative work.   Every
plumber capable of his business hates to have to paint
his leadwork; every carpenter knows the disgust of
turning out unfinished "cheap" work, however well it
pays him; every tolerable cook can feel shame for an
unsatisfying dish, and none the less shame because by
making it, materials are saved and economies achieved.

And yet, with all the facts clear as day before any observant person, *we are content to live on in an economic
system that raises every man who subordinates these*

wholesome prides and desires to watchful, incessant getting, over the heads of every other type of character; that in effect gives all the power and influence in our state to successful getters; that subordinates art, direction, wisdom, and labour to these inferior narrow men, these men who clutch and keep.

Our social system, based on Private Ownership, encourages and glorifies this spirit of gain, and cripples and thwarts the spirit of service. You need but have your eyes once opened to its influence, and thereafter you will never cease to see how the needs and imperatives of Property taint the honour and dignity of human life. Just where life should flower most freely into splendour, this chill, malign obsession most nips and cripples. The law that makes getting and keeping an imperative necessity poisons and destroys the freedom of men and women in love, in art, and in every concern in which spiritual or physical beauty should be the inspiring and determining factor. Behind all the handsome professions of romantic natures the gaunt facts of monetary necessity remain the rulers of life. Every youth who must sell his art and capacity for gain, every girl who must sell herself for money, is one more sacrifice to the Minotaur of Private Ownership — before the Theseus of Socialism comes.

Opponents of Socialism, ignoring all these things and

inventing with that profusion which is so remarkable a trait of the Anti-Socialist campaign, are wont to declare that we, whose first and last thought is the honour and betterment of life, seek to destroy all beauty and freedom in love, accuse us of aiming at some "human stud farm." The reader will measure the justice of that by the next chapter, but here I would say that just as the private ownership of all that is necessary to humanity, except the air and sunlight and a few things that it has been difficult to appropriate, debases work and all the common services of life, so also it taints and thwarts the emotions, and degrades the intimate physical and emotional existence of an innumerable multitude of people.

All this amounts to a huge impoverishment of life, a loss of existence and discrimination of rich and subtle values. Human existence to-day is a mere tantalizing intimation of what it might be. It is frost-bitten and dwarfed from palace to slum. It is not only that a great mass of our population is deprived of space, beauty, and pleasure, but that a large proportion of such space, beauty, and pleasure as there are in the world, must necessarily have a meretricious taint and be in the nature of things bought and made for pay.

§ 3

If there is one profession more than another in which devotion is implied and assumed, it is that of the doctor.

It happens that on the morning when this chapter was drafted, I came upon the paragraph that follows; it seemed to me to supply just one striking concrete instance of how life is degraded by our present system, and to offer me a convenient text for a word or so more upon this question between gain and service. It's a little vague in its reference to Mr. Tompkins "of Birmingham," and I should not be surprised if it were a considerable exaggeration of what really happened. But it is true enough to life in this, that it is a common practice, a necessity with doctors in poor neighbourhoods to insist inexorably upon a fee before attendance.

"A case of medical inhumanity is reported from Birmingham. A poor man named Tompkins was taken seriously ill early on Christmas morning, and although snow was falling and the atmosphere was terribly raw, his wife left the house in search of a doctor. The nearest practitioner declined to leave the house without being paid his fee; a second imposed the same condition, and the woman then went to the police station. As the horse ambulance was out, they could not help her, and she tried other doctors. In all the poor woman called on eight, and the only one who did not decline to get up without his fee was down with influenza. Eventually a local chemist was persuaded to see the man, and he ordered his removal to the hospital."

That is the story. You note the charge of "inhumanity" in the very first line, and in much subsequent press comment there was the same note. Apparently

every one expects a doctor to be ready at any point in the
day or night to attend anybody for nothing. Most
Socialists are disposed to agree with the spirit of that
expectation. A practising doctor should be in life-long
perpetual war against pain and disease, just as a cam-
paigning soldier is continually alert and serving. But
existing conditions will not permit that. Existing conditions require the doctor to get his fee at any cost; if
he goes about doing work for nothing, they punish him
with shabbiness and incapacitating need, they forbid
his marriage or doom his wife and children to poverty
and unhappiness. A doctor *must* make money whatever
else he does or does not do, he *must* secure his fees. He
is a private adventurer, competing in a crowded market
for gain, and keeping his energies perforce for those who
can pay best for them. To expect him to behave like
a public servant whose income and outlook are secure, or
like a priest whose church will never let him want or
starve, is ridiculous. If you put him on a footing with
the green grocer and coal merchant, you must expect
him to behave like a tradesman. Why should the press
blame the poor doctor of a poor neighbourhood because
a moneyless man goes short of medical attendance,
when it does not for one moment blame Mr. J. D.
Rockefeller because a poor man goes short of oil, or
the Duke of Devonshire because tramps need lodgings

in Eastbourne? One never reads this sort of paragraph: —

"A case of commercial inhumanity is reported from Birmingham. A poor man named Tompkins was seriously hungry early on Christmas morning, and although snow was falling and the atmosphere was terribly raw, his wife left the house in search of food. The nearest grocer declined to supply provisions without being paid his price; a second imposed the same condition, and the woman then went to the police station. As that is not a soup kitchen, they could not help her and she tried other grocers and bread shops. In all the poor woman called on eight, and the only one who did not decline to supply food without payment was for some reason bankrupt and out of stock. Eventually a local overseer was persuaded to see the man, and he ordered his removal to the workhouse, where after considerable hardship, he was partly appeased with skilly."

I, myself, have known an overworked, financially worried doctor at his bedroom window call out, "Have you brought the fee?" and have pitied and understood his ugly alternatives. "Once I began that sort of thing," he explained to me a little apologetically, "they'd none of them pay — none."

The Socialists' remedy for this squalid state of affairs is plain and simple. Medicine is a public service, an honourable devotion, it should no more be a matter of profit-making than the food-supply service or the house-supply service, or salvation. It should be a part of the organization of a civilized state to have a public health service of well-paid, highly educated men distributed over the country and closely correlated with public research departments and a reserve of specialists, who would be as ready and eager to face dangers and to sacrifice themselves for honour and social necessity as soldiers or sailors. I believe every honourable man in the medical profession under forty now would rather it were so. It is indeed a transition from private enterprise to public organization that is already beginning. We have the first intimation of the change in the appearance of the medical officer of health, underpaid, overworked, and powerless though he is at the present time. It cannot be long before the manifest absurdity of our present conditions begins a process of socialization of the medical profession entirely analogous to that which has changed three-fourths of the teachers in Great Britain from private adventurers to public servants in the last forty years.

And that is the aim of Socialism all along the line, — to convert one public service after another from a chaotic profit scramble of proprietors amidst a mass of sweated employees into a secure and disciplined service in which every man will work for honour, promotion, achievement, and the commonweal.

I write a "secure and disciplined service," and I intend by that not simply an exterior but an interior discipline. Let us have done with this unnatural theory that men may submit unreservedly to the guidance of "self-interest." Self-interest never took a man or a community to any other end than damnation. For all services there is necessary a code of honour and devotion which a man must set up for himself and obey, to which he must subordinate a number of his impulses. The must is seconded by an internal imperative. Men and women *want* to have a code of honour. In the army, for example, there is among the officers particularly, a tradition of courage, cleanliness, and good form, more imperative than any law; in the little band of men who have given the world all that we mean by science, the little host of volunteers and underpaid workers who have achieved the triumphs of research, there is a tradition of self-abnegation and of an immense, painstaking, self-forgetful veracity. These traditions work. They add something to the worth of every man who comes under them.

Every writer, again, knows clearly the difference between gain-seeking and doing good work, and few there are who have not at times done something as they say "to please themselves." Then in the studio, for all the non-moral protests of Bohemia, there is a tradition, an admirable tradition, of disregard for mercenary imperatives, a scorn of shams and plagiarism that triumphs again and again over economic laws. The public services of

the coming civilization will demand, and will develop, a
far completer discipline and tradition of honour.   Against
the development and persistence of all such honourable
codes now, against every attempt at personal nobility,
at a new chivalry, at sincere artistry, our present individualist system wages pitiless warfare; says in effect:
"Fools you are!   Look at Rockefeller!   Look at Pier-
pont Morgan!   Look at Astor!   Get money!   All your
sacrifices only go to their enrichment.   You cannot serve
humanity, however much you seek to do so.   They block
your way, enormously receptive of all you give.   All the
increment of human achievement goes to them — they
own it *à priori* . . .   Get money!   Money is freedom to
do, to keep, to rule.   Do you care nothing for your wives
and children?   Are you content to breed servants and
dependents for these children of these men?   Make
things beautiful, make things abundant, make life glorious!   Fools!   if you work and sacrifice yourselves and
do not *get,* they will possess.   Your sons shall be the
loan-monger's employees, your daughters handmaidens
to the millionaire.   Or if you cannot face that, go childless, and let your life-work gild the palace of the millionaire's still more acquisitive descendants!"

Who can ignore the base scramble for money under
these alternatives?

§ 4

But let me here insert a very brief paragraph to point out one particular thing and that is that Socialism does not propose to "abolish competition" — as many hasty and foolish antagonists declare. If the reader has gone through what has preceded this he will know that this is not so. Socialism looks to competition, looks to competition for the service and improvement of the world. And in order that competition between man and man may have free play, Socialism seeks to abolish one particular form of competition, the competition to get and hold property that degrades our present world. But it would leave men free to compete for fame, for service, for salaries, for position and authority, for leisure, for love and honour.

§ 5

But now let me take up certain difficulties the student of Socialism encounters. He comes thus far perhaps with the Socialist argument, and then his imagination gets to work trying to picture a world in which a moiety of the population, perhaps even the larger moiety, is employed by the state, and in which the whole population is educated by the state and insured of a decent and comfortable care and subsistence during youth and old age. He then begins to think of how all this vast organization is to be managed, and with that his real difficulties begin.

Now I for one am prepared to take these difficulties very seriously, as the latter part of this book will show. I will even go so far as to say that, to my mind, the contemporary Socialist controversialist meets all this system of objections far too cavalierly. These difficulties are real difficulties for the convinced Socialist as for the inquirer; they open up problems that have still to be solved before the equipment of Socialism is complete. "How will you Socialists get the right men in the right place for the work that has to be done? How will you arrange promotion? how will you determine" — I put the argument in its crudest form — "who is to engage in historical research in the Bodleian, and who is to go out seaward in November and catch mackerel?" Such "posers" — they have a thousand variants — convey the spirit of the living resistance to Socialism; they explain why every rational man is not an enraptured Socialist at the present time.

Throughout the rest of this book I hope that the reader will be able to see growing together in this aspect and then in that, in this and that suggestion, the complex solution of this complex system of difficulties. My object in raising them now is not to dispose of them, but to give them the fullest recognition — and to ask the student to read on. In all these matters the world is imperfect now, and it will still be imperfect under Socialism — though, I firmly believe, with an infinitely lesser and altogether nobler imperfection.

But I do want to point out here that though these are reasonable and, to all undogmatic men, most helpful criticisms of the Socialist design, they are no sort of justification for things as they are. All the difficulties that the ordinary exposition of Socialism seems to leave unsolved are at least equally not solved now. Only rarely does the right man seem to struggle to his place of adequate opportunity. Men and women get their chance in various ways: some of implacable temper and versatile gifts thrust themselves to the position they need for the exercise of their powers; others display an astonishing facility in securing honours and occasions they can then only waste; others outside their specific gift are the creatures of luck or the victims of modesty, tactlessness, or incapacity. Most of the large businesses of the world now are in the hands of private proprietors and managed either directly by an owner or by directors or managers acting for directors. The quality of promotion or the recognition of capacity varies very much in these great concerns, but they are, on the whole, probably inferior to the public services. Even where the administration is keenest it must be remembered it is not

seeking the men who work the machine best, but the
men who can work it cheapest and with the maximum
of profit.   It is pure romancing to represent the ordinary
business magnate as being in perpetual search for capacity among the members of his staff.   He wants them
to get along and not make trouble.

Among the smaller businesses that still, I suppose,
constitute the bulk of the world's economic body,
capacity is enormously hampered.   I was once an apprentice in a chemist's shop, and also once in a draper's, —
I was a difficult son to "place"; two of my brothers have
been shop assistants, and so I am still able to talk un-
derstandingly with clerks and employees, and I know that
in all that world all sorts of minor considerations obstruct
the very beginnings of efficient selection.   Every shop
is riddled with jealousies; "sucking up to the gov'ner"
is the universal crime, and among the women in many
callings promotion is too often tainted by still baser
suspicions.   No doubt in a badly criticised public service there is such a thing as "sucking up to" the head
of the department, but at its worst it is not nearly so
bad as things may be in a small private concern under
a petty autocrat.

In America it is said that the public services are inferior in personal quality to the staffs of the great private
business organizations.   My own impression is that,

considering the salaries paid, they are, so far as Federal concerns go, immeasurably superior. In state and municipal affairs, American conditions offer no satisfactory criterion; the Americans are, for reasons I have discussed elsewhere,[1] a "state-blind" people concentrated upon private getting; they have been negligent of public concerns, and the public appointments have been left to the peculiarly ruffianly type of politician their unfortunate constitution and their unfortunate traditions have evolved. In England, too, public servants are systematically undersalaried so that the big businesses have merely to pay reasonably well to secure the pick of the national capacity. Moreover, it must be remembered by the reader that the public services do not advertise, and that the private businesses do; so that while there is the fullest ventilation of any defects in our military or naval organization, there is a very considerable check upon the discussion of individualist incapacity. An editor will rush into print with the flimsiest imputations upon the breach of the new field-gun or the housing of the militia at Aldershot, but he thinks twice before he proclaims that the preserved fruits that pay his proprietor a tribute of some hundreds a year are an unwholesome embalmment of decay. On the whole, it is probable that in spite of scandalously bad pay and

[1] *The Future in America*, Ch. IX. (Chapman and Hall, 1906.)

of the embarrassment of party considerations, the
British navy, post-office, and civil service generally, and
the educational work and much of the transit and building work of the London County Council and of many of
the greater English and Scotch municipalities, are as
well managed as any private businesses in the world.

On the other hand one must admit there are political
and social conditions that can carry the quality of the
state service almost as low as the lowest type of private
enterprise. It is little marvel that under the typical
eighteenth-century monarchy when the way to ship,
regiment and the apostolic succession alike lay through
the ante-chamber of the king's mistress, there was
begotten that absolute repudiation of state control to
which Herbert Spencer was destined at last to give the
complete expression, that irrational, passionate belief
that whatever else is right the state is necessarily incompetent and wrong.

The gist of this matter seems to be that where you have
honourable political institutions, free speech and a general high level of intelligence and education you will
have an efficient criticism of men and their work and
powers, and you will get a wholesome system of public
promotion and many right men in the right place. The
higher the collective intelligence, that is to say, the higher
is the collective possibility. Under Socialist institutions

which will give education and a sense of personal security
to every one, this necessity of criticism is likely to be
most freely, frankly and disinterestedly provided.   But
it is well to keep in mind the entire dependence of Socialism upon a high level of intelligence, education and
freedom.   Socialist institutions, as I understand them,
are only possible in a civilized state, in a state in which
the whole population can read, write, discuss, participate,
and in a considerable measure understand.   Education
must precede the Socialist state.   Socialism, modern
Socialism, that is to say, such as I am now concerned with,
is essentially an exposition of and training in certain general ideas; it is impossible in an illiterate community, a
basely selfish community, or in a community without the
capacity to use the machinery and the apparatus of
civilization.   At the best, and it is a poor best, a stupid,
illiterate population can but mock Socialism with a sort
of bureaucratic tyranny; for a barbaric population, too
large and various for the folk-meeting, there is nothing
but monarchy and the ownership of the king; for a savage tribe, tradition and the undocumented will of the
strongest males.   Socialism, I will admit, presupposes
intelligence, and demands as fundamental necessities,
schools, organized science, literature, and a sense of the
state.

ɪ

CHAPTER VI

WOULD SOCIALISM DESTROY THE HOME?

§ 1

FOR reasons that will become clearer when we tell something of the early history and development of Socialism, the Socialist propositions with regard to the family lie open to certain grave misconceptions. People are told — and told quite honestly and believingly — that Socialism will destroy the home, will substitute a sort of human stud-farm for that warm and intimate nest of human life, will bring up our children in incubators and creeches and — institutions generally.

It isn't so.

But before we come to what modern Socialists do desire in these matters, it may be well to consider something of the present reality of the home people are so concerned about. The reader must not idealize. He must not shut his eyes to facts, dream, as Lord Hugh Cecil and Lord Robert Cecil — those admirable champions of a bad cause — probably do, of a beautiful world of homes, orderly, virtuous, each a little human

114

fastness, each with its porch and creeper, each with its books and harmonium, its hymn-singing on Sunday night, its dear mother who makes such wonderful cakes, its strong and happy father — and then say, "These wicked Socialists want to destroy all this."   Because in the first place such homes are being destroyed and made impossible now by the very causes against which Socialism fights, and because in this world at the present time very few homes are at all like this ideal.   In reality every poor home is haunted by the spectre of irregular employment and undermined by untrustworthy insurance; it must shelter in insanitary dwellings and its children eat adulterated food because none other can be got.   And that, I am sorry to say, it is only too easy to prove — by a second appeal to a document of which I have already made use.

One hears at times still of the austere, virtuous, kindly, poor Scotch home; one has a vision of the "Cottar's Saturday Night."   "Perish all other dreams," one cries, "rather than that such goodness and simplicity should end."   But now let us look at the average poor Scotch home, and compare it with our dream.

Here is the reality.

These entries come from the recently published Edinburgh Charity Organization Society's report upon the homes of about fourteen hundred school children, that is to say, about eight hundred Scotch homes. Remember they are *sample homes*. They are, as I have already suggested by quoting authorities for London and York — and as any district visitor will recognize — little worse and little better than the bulk of poor people's homes in Scotland and England at the present time. I am just going to copy down — not a selection, mind, but a series of consecutive entries taken haphazard from this implacable list. My last quotation was from cases 1, 2, 3, and so on; I've now thrust my finger among the pages and come upon numbers 191 and 192, etc. Here they are, one after the other, just as they come in the list: —

191. A widow and child lodging with a married son. Three grown-up people and three children occupy one room and bed-closet. The widow leads a wandering life and is intemperate. The house is thoroughly bad and insanitary. The child is pallid and delicate looking and receives little attention, for the mother is usually out working. He plays in the streets. Five children are dead. Boy has glands and is fleabitten. Evidence from Police, School Officer, and Employer.

192. A miserable home. Father dead. Mother and eldest son careless and indifferent. Of the five children, the two eldest are grown up. The elder girl is working, and she is of a better type and might do well under better circumstances; she looks overworked. The mother is supposed to char; she gets parish relief, and one child earns out of school hours. Four children are dead. The children at school are dirty and ragged. The mother could work if she did not drink. The children at school get free

dinners and clothing, and the family is favourably reported on by the church. The second child, impetigo; neck glands; body dirty; the third, glands; dirty and fleabitten. Housing: six in two small rooms. Evidence from Parish Sister, Parish Council, School Charity, Police, Teacher, Children's Employment, and School Officer.

193. A widow, apparently respectable and well-doing, but may drink. She must in any case have a struggle to maintain her family, though she has much help from Parish, Church, etc. She works out. The children at school are fed, and all together a large amount of charity must be received as two churches have interested themselves in the matter. Three children dead. Housing: three in two tiny rooms. Evidence from Church, Parish Council, School Charity, Police, Parish Sister, Teacher, Insurance, and Factor.

194. The father drinks, and, to a certain extent, the mother; but the home is tidy and clean, and the rent is regularly paid. Indeed, there is no sign of poverty. There is a daughter who has got into trouble. Only two children out of nine are alive. The father comes from the country and seems intelligent enough, but he appears to have degenerated. They go to a mission, it is believed, for what they can get from it. Housing: four in two rooms. Evidence from Club, Church, Factor, and Police.

195. The husband is intemperate. The mother is quiet, but it is feared that she drinks also. She seems to have lost control of her little boy of seven. The parents married very young, and the first child was born before the marriage. The man's work is not regular, and probably things are not improving with him. Still, the house is fairly comfortable, and they pay Club money regularly, and have a good police report. One child has died. Housing: five in two rooms. Evidence from Parish Sister, Police, Club, Employer, Schoolmistress, and Factor.

196. A filthy, dirty house. The most elementary notions of cleanliness seem disregarded. The father's earnings are not large, and the house is insanitary, but more might be made of things if there were sobriety and thrift. There does not, however, appear to be *great* drunkenness, and five small children must be difficult to bring up on the money coming in. There are two women in the house. The eldest child dirty and fleabitten. Housing: seven in two rooms. Evidence from Police, Club, Employer, Schoolmistress, and School Officer.

197. The parents are thoroughly drunken and dissolute. They have sunk almost to the lowest depths of social degradation. There is no furniture in the house, and the five children are neglected and starved. One boy earns a trifle out of school hours. All accounts agree as to the character of the father and mother, though they have not been in the hands of the police. Second child has ricketts, bronchitis, slight glands, and is bow-legged. Two children have died. Housing: seven in two rooms. Evidence from Police, Parish Sister, Employer, and Schoolmistress.

198. This house is fairly comfortable, and there is no evidence of drink, but the surroundings have a bad and depressing effect on the parents. The children are sent to school very untidy and dirty, and are certainly underfed. The father's wages are very small, and only one boy is working; there are six all together. The mother chars occasionally. Food and clothing is given to school children. The man is in a saving club. The eldest child fleabitten; body unwashed. The second, glands; fleabitten and dirty; cretinoid; much undergrown. Two have died. Housing: seven in two rooms. Evidence from School Charity, Factor, Police, and Schoolmistress.

199. The house was fairly comfortable, and the man appeared to be intelligent and the wife hardworking, but the police reports are very bad; there are several convictions against the

former. He has consequently been idle, and the burden of the family has rested on the wife. There are six children, two of them are working and earning a little, but a large amount of charity from school, church, and private generosity keeps the family going. The children are fearfully verminous. There is a suggestion that some baby farming is done, so many are about. Eldest child, anæmic; glands; head badly crusted; lice very bad. Second child, numerous glands; head covered with crusts; lice, very bad. Four have died. Housing: eight in two rooms Evidence from Police, Teacher, Church Parish Sister, and Factor.

200. The home is wretched and practically without furniture. The parents were married at ages 17 and 18. One child died and their mode of life has been reckless, if not worse. The present means of subsistence cannot be ascertained as the man is idle; however he recently joined the Salvation Army and signed the pledge. The child at school is helped with food and clothes. The girl very badly bitten; lice and fleas, hair nits. Housing: four in one room. Evidence from Church, School Charity, Coöperative, Employer, Parish Sister, Police, and Schoolmistress.

Total of children still living, 39.

Total of children dead, 27.

Need I go on? They are all after this fashion, 800 of them.

And if you turn from the congested town to the wholesome, simple country, here is the sort of home you have going on. This passage is a cutting from the *Daily News* of January 1, 1907, and its assertions have never been contradicted. It fills one with only the mildest enthusiasm for the return of our degenerate townsmen "back to the land." I came upon it as I read that morning's paper after drafting this chapter.

"Our attention has been called to a sordid Herefordshire tragedy recently revealed at an inquest on a child aged one year and nine months, who died in Weobly Workhouse of pneumonia. She entered the institution emaciated to half the proper weight of her age and with a broken arm — till then undiscovered — that the doctors found to be of about three weeks' standing. Her mother was shown to be in an advanced stage of consumption; one child had died at the age of seven months, and seven now remain. The father, whose work consists in tending eighty-nine head of cattle and ten pigs, is in receipt of eleven shillings a week, three pints of skim milk a day, and a cottage that has been condemned by the sanitary inspector and described as having no bedroom windows. We are not surprised to learn that the coroner before taking the verdict asked the house surgeon who gave evidence, whether he could say that death 'was accelerated by anything.' Our wonder is that the reply was in the negative. The cottage is in the possession of the farmer who employs the man, but his landlord is said to be liable for repairs. That landlord is a clergyman of the Church of England, a J.P., a preserver of game, and owner of three or four thousand acres of land."

And here, again, in the *Times*, by no means a Socialist organ, generalizing from official statements: —

"Houses unfit for human habitation, rooms destitute of light and ventilation, overcrowding in rural cottages, contaminated water supplies, accumulations of every description of filth and refuse, a total absence of drainage, a reign of unbelievable dirt in milk shops and slaughter houses, a total neglect of by-laws, and an inadequate supervision by officials who are frequently incompetent; such, in a general way, is the picture that is commonly presented — in the reports of inquiries in certain rural districts made by medical officers of the Local Government Board."

And even of such homes as this there is an insufficiency. In 1891–1895 more than a quarter of the deaths in London occurred in workhouses and other charitable institutions.[1] Now, suppose the modern Socialist did want to destroy the home; suppose that some Socialists have in the past really wanted to do so, remember that that is the reality they wanted to destroy.

But does the modern Socialist want to destroy the home? Rather, I hold he wants to save it from a destruction that is even now going on, to — I won't say restore it, because I have very grave doubts if the world has ever yet held a high percentage of good homes — but raise it to the level of its better realizations of happiness and security. And it is not only I say this but all my fellow-Socialists say it, too. Read, for example, that admirable paper "Economic and Social Justice" in Dr. Alfred Russel Wallace's *Studies, Scientific and Social*, and you will have the clearest statement of the attitude of a representative modern Socialist to this question.

[1] *Studies, Scientific and Social*, Vol. II, Ch. XXIV, by Dr. Alfred Russel Wallace.   (Macmillan and Co. 1900.)

§ 2

The reader must get quite out of his head the idea that the present system maintains the home and social purity.

In London at the present time there are thousands of prostitutes; in Paris, in Berlin, in every great city of Europe or America, thousands; in the whole of Christendom there cannot be less than a million of these ultimate instances of our civilization. They are the logical extremity of a civilization based on cash payments. Each of these women represents a smashed and ruined home and wasted possibilities of honour, service and love, each one is so much sheer waste. For the food they consume, their clothing, their lodging, they render back nothing to the community as a whole, and only a gross, dishonouring satisfaction to their casual employers. And don't imagine they are inferior women, that there has been any selection of the unfit in their sterilization; they are, one may see for oneself, well above the average in physical vigour, in spirit and beauty. Few of them have come freely to their trade, the most unnatural in the world; few of them have anything but shame and loathing for their life; and most of them must needs face their calling fortified by drink and drugs. For virtuous people do not begin to understand the things they endure. But it *pays* to be a prostitute, it does not pay to be a mother and a home maker, and the gist of the present system of individual property is that a thing *must pay* to exist. So much for one aspect of our present system of a "world of homes."

Consider next the great army of employed men and women, shop assistants, clerks, and so forth, living in, milliners, typists, teachers, servants who have practically no prospect whatever of marrying and experiencing those domestic blisses the Socialist is supposed to want to rob them of. They are involuntary monks and nuns, celibate not from any high or religious motive, but through economic hardship. Consider all that amount of pent-up, thwarted, or perverted emotional possibility, the sheer irrational waste of life implied.

We have glanced at the reality of the family among the poor; what is it among the rich? Does the wealthy mother of the upper middle class or upper class really sit among her teeming children, teaching them in an atmosphere of love and domestic exaltation? As a matter of fact she is a conspicuously devoted woman if she gives them an hour a day of her time; the rest of the time they spend with nurse or governess, and when they are ten or eleven off they go to board at the preparatory school. Whenever I find among my press-cuttings some particularly scathing denunciation of Socialists as home-destroyers, as people who want to snatch the tender child from the weeping mother to immure it in some terrible wholesale institution, I am apt to walk out into my garden, from which three boarding-schools for little children of the prosperous classes are visible, and rub my eyes and renew that sight and marvel at my kind.

Consider now, with these things in mind, the real drift of the first main Socialist proposition, and compare its tendency with these contemporary conditions. Socialism regards parentage under proper safeguards and good auspices, as "not only a duty but a service" to the state; that is to say, it proposes to pay for good parentage—in other words, to *endow the home.* Socialism comes not to destroy but to save.

And how will the endowment be done? Very probably it will be found that the most convenient and best method of doing this will be to pay the mother — who is or should be the principal person concerned in this affair — for her children; to assist her, not as a charity, but as a right in the period before the birth of her anticipated child, and afterwards to pay for that child so long as it is kept clean in a tolerable home, in good health, well taught, and properly clad. Frankly it will say to the sound mothering women, not typewriting, nor shirt-sewing, nor charring is your business, these children are. Neglect them, ill-treat them, prove incompetent, and your pay will cease, and we shall take them away from you and do what we can for them; love them, serve them, and, through them, the state, and you will serve yourself. Is that destroying the home? Is it not rather the rescue of the home from economic destruction?

Certain restrictions, it is true, upon our present way of doing things would follow almost necessarily from the adoption of these methods. It is manifest that no intelligent state would willingly endow the homes of hopelessly diseased parents, of imbecile fathers or mothers, of obstinately criminal persons or people incapable of education. It is evident, too, that the state would not tolerate chance fatherhood, that it would insist very emphatically upon marriage and the purity of the home, much more emphatically than we do now. Such a case as the one numbered 197, a beautiful instance of the sweet, old-fashioned, homely, simple life of the poor we Socialists are supposed to be vainly endeavouring to undermine, would certainly be dealt with in a drastic and conclusive spirit.

§ 3

So far Socialism goes toward regenerating the family and sustaining the home. But let there be no ambiguity on one point. It will be manifest that while it would reinvigorate and confirm the home, it does quite decidedly tend to destroy what has hitherto been the most typical form of the family throughout the world, that is to say, the family which is in effect the private property of the father, the patriarchal family. The tradition of the family in which we are still living, we must remember, has developed from a former state in which man owned the wife and child as completely as he owned horse or hut. He was its irresponsible owner. Socialism seeks to make him and his wife its jointly responsible heads. Until quite recently the husband might beat his wife and put all sorts of physical constraint upon her; he might starve her or turn her out of doors; her property was his; her earnings were his; her children were his. Under certain circumstances it was generally recognized he might kill her. To-day we live in a world that has faltered from the rigours of this position, but which still clings to its sentimental consequences. The wife nowadays is a sort of pampered and protected half-property. If she leaves her husband for another man, it is regarded not as a public offence on her part, but as a sort of mitigated theft on the part of the latter, entitling the former to damages. Politically she doesn't exist; the husband sees to all that. But on the other hand, he mustn't drive her by physical force, but only by the moral pressure of disagreeable behaviour. Nor has he the same large powers of violence over her children that once he had. He may beat — within limits. He may dictate their education so far as his religious eccentricities go, and be generous or meagre with the supplies. He may use his "authority" as a vague power far on into their adult life, if he is a forcible character. But it is at its best a shorn splendour he retains. He has ceased to be an autocrat and become a constitutional monarch; the state, sustained by the growing reasonableness of the world, intervenes more and more between him and the wife and children who were once powerless in his hands.

The Socialist would end that old predominance altogether. The woman, he declares, must be as important and responsible a citizen in the state as the man. She must cease to be in any sense or degree private property. The man must desist from tyrannizing in the nursery and do his proper work in the world. So far, therefore, as the family is a name for private property in a group of related human beings vesting in one of them, the head of the family, Socialism repudiates it altogether as unjust and uncivilized; but so far as the family is a grouping of children with their parents, in love and respect and mutual help, with the support and consent and approval of the whole community, Socialism advocates it, would make it for the first time, so far as a very large moiety of our population is concerned, a possible and efficient thing.

Moreover, as the present writer has pointed out elsewhere,[1] this putting of the home upon a public basis destroys its autonomy. Just as the Socialist and all who have the cause of civilization at heart, would substitute for the inefficient, wasteful, irresponsible, unqualified "private adventure school" that did such infinite injury to middle class education in Great Britain during the Victorian period, a public school, publicly and richly endowed and responsible and controlled, so the Socialist would put an end to the uncivilized go-as-you-please of the private adventure family, "Socialism, in fact, is the state family. The old family of the private individual must vanish before it just as the old water works of private enterprise or the old gas company."[1] To any one not idiotic nor blind with a passionate desire to lie about Socialism, the meaning of this passage is perfectly plain. Socialism seeks to broaden the basis of the family and to make the once irresponsible parent responsible to the state for its welfare; Socialism creates parental responsibility.

§ 4

And here we may give a few words to certain questions that are in reality outside the scope of Socialists altogether, special questions involving the most subtle ethical and psychological decisions. Upon them So-

[1] *Socialism and the Family.* (A. C. Fifield. 6d.)

cialists are as widely divergent as people who are not Socialists, and Socialism as a whole presents nothing but an open mind. They are questions that would be equally open to discussion in relation to an Individualist state or to any sort of state. Certain religious organizations have given clear and imperative answers to some or all of these questions, and so far as the reader is a member of such an organization he may rest assured that Socialism, as an authoritative whole, has nothing to say for or against his convictions. This cannot be made too plain by Socialists, nor too frequently repeated by them. A very large part of the so-called arguments against them arise out of deliberate misrepresentations and misconceptions of some alleged Socialist position in these indifferent matters.

I refer more particularly to the numerous problems in private morality and social organization arising from sexual conduct. May a man love one woman only in his life, or more, and may a woman love only one man? Should marriage be an irrevocable life union or not? Is sterile physical love possible, permissible, moral, honourable, or intolerable? Upon all these matters individual Socialists, like most other people, have their doubts and convictions, but it is no more just to saddle all Socialism with their private utterances and actions upon these issues than it would be to declare that the Roman Catholic Communion is hostile to beauty because wor-

K

shippers coming and going have knocked the noses off the figures on the bronze doors of the church of San Zeno at Verona, or that Christianity involves the cultivation of private vermin, because of the condition of Saint Thomas à Becket's hair shirt.[1] To argue in that way is to give up one's birthright as a reasonable being.

Upon certain points modern Socialism is emphatic; women and children must not be dealt with as private property; women must be citizens equally with men; children must not be casually born; their parents must be known and worthy, that is to say, there must be deliberation in begetting children, marriage under conditions. And there Socialism stops.

[1] "The haircloth encased the whole body down to the knees; the hair drawers as well as the rest of the dress being covered on the outside with white linen so as to escape observation; and the whole so fastened together as to admit of being readily taken off for his daily scourgings, of which yesterday's portion was still apparent in the stripes on his body. Such austerity had hitherto been unknown to English saints, and the marvel was increased by the sight — to our notions so revolting — of the innumerable vermin with which the haircloth abounded, boiling over with them, as one account describes it, like water in a simmering cauldron. At the dreadful sight all the enthusiasm of the previous night revived with double ardour. They looked at each other in silent wonder, then exclaimed, 'See, see what a true monk he was, and we knew it not !' and burst into alternate fits of weeping and laughter, between the sorrow of having lost such a head, and the joy of having found such a saint." — *Historical Memorials of Canterbury*, by the Rev. Arthur Penryn Stanley, D.D.

Socialism has not even worked out what are the reasonable conditions of a state marriage contract, and it would be ridiculous to pretend it had. This is not a defect in Socialism particularly, but a defect in human knowledge. At countless points in the tangle of questions involved, the facts are not clearly known. Socialism does not present any theory whatever about the duration of marriage, whether, as among the Roman Catholics, it should be absolutely for life, or, as some hold, forever, or as among the various divorce-permitting Protestant bodies, until this or that eventuality, or, even as Mr. George Meredith suggested some years ago, for a term of ten years. In these matters Socialism does not decide, and it is quite reasonable to argue that Socialism need not decide. The state is not urgently concerned with these questions. So long as a marriage contract provides for the health and sanity of the contracting parties, and for their proper behaviour so far as their offspring is concerned, and for so long as their offspring need it, the demands of the community, as the guardian of the children, are satisfied. That certainly would be the minimum marriage, the state marriage, and I, for my own part, would exact nothing more *in the legal contract.* But a number of more representative Socialists than I are for a legally compulsory life marriage. Some — but they are mostly of the older, less definite, Socialist teaching —

are for a looser tie.   Let us clearly understand that we
are here talking of the legal marriage only — the state's
share.   What was needed more than that minimum
would be provided, I believe, — always has been provided hitherto, even to excess, — by custom, religion,
social influence, public opinion.

For it may not be altogether superfluous to remind
the reader how little of our present moral code is ruled by
law.   We have in England, it is true, certain laws pre-
scribing the conditions of the marriage contract, penalties of a quite ferocious kind to prevent bigamy, and a
few quite trivial disabilities put upon those illegitimately
born.   But there is no legal compulsion upon any one to
marry now, and far less legal restriction upon irregular
and careless parentage than would be put in any scientifically organized Socialism.   Do let us get it out of our
heads that monogamy is enforced by law at the present
time.   It is not.   You are only forbidden to enter into
normal marriage with more than one person.   If a man
of means chooses to have as many concubines as King
Solomon and live with them all openly, the law (I am
speaking of Great Britain) will do nothing to prevent him.
If he chooses to go through any sort of nuptial ceremony,
provided it does not simulate a legal marriage, with
some or all of them, he may.   And to any one who evades
the legal marriage bond, there is a vast range of betrayal

and baseness as open as anything can be. The real controlling force in these matters is social influence, public opinion, a sort of conscience and feeling for the judgment of others that is part of the normal human equipment. And the same motives and considerations that keep people's lives pure and discreet now will be all the more freely in operation under Socialism, when money will count for less and reputation for more than they do now. Modern Socialism is a project to change the organization of living and the circle of human ideas — but it is no sort of scheme to attempt the impossible, to change human nature and to destroy the social sensitiveness of man.

I do not deny the intense human interest of these open questions, the imperative need there is to get the truth, whether it be one's own truth or the universal truth, upon them. But my point is that they are to be discussed apart from Socialist theory. It is no doubt interesting to discuss the benefits of vaccination and the justice and policy of its public compulsion, to debate whether one should eat meat or confine oneself to a vegetable dietary, whether the overhead or the slot system is preferable for tramway traction, whether steamboats are needed on the Thames in winter, and whether it is wiser to use metal or paper for money; but none of these things have anything to do with the principles of Socialism. Nor need we decide whether Whistler, Raphael, or Carpaccio has left us the most satisfying beauty, or which was the greater musician, Wagner, Scarlatti, or Beethoven, nor pronounce on the Bacon-Shakespeare controversy in any prescribed way, because we accept Socialism.

Coming to graver matters there are ardent theologians who would create an absolute antagonism between Socialism and Christianity, who would tie up Socialism with some extraordinary doctrine of Predestination, or deny the possibility of a Christian being a Socialist or a Socialist being a Christian. But these are matters on different planes. In a sense Socialism is a religion, to me it is a religion, in the sense, that is, that it gives a work to do that is not self-seeking, that it determines one in a thousand indecisions, that it supplies that imperative craving of so many human souls, a devotion. But I do not see why a believer in any of the accepted creeds of Christianity, from the Apostles' Creed upward, should not also whole-heartedly give himself to this great work of social reconstruction. To believe in a real and personal heaven is surely not to deny earth with its tragedy, its sorrows, its splendid possibilities. It is simply to believe a little more concretely than I do, that is all. To assert the brotherhood of man under God seems to me to lead logically to a repudiation of the severities of private

ownership — that is, to Socialism.   When the rich young
man was told to give up his property to follow Christ,
when the disciples were told to leave father and mother
— it seems to me ridiculous to present Christianity as
opposed to the self-abnegation of the two main generalizations of Socialism, — that relating to property in
things, and that relating to property in persons.   It is
true that the Church of Rome has taken the deplorable
step of forbidding Socialism (or at least *Socialismus*) to
its adherents; but there is no need for Socialists to
commit a reciprocal stupidity.   Let us Socialists at any
rate keep our intellectual partitions up.   The church that
now quarrels with Socialism once quarrelled with as-
tronomy and geology, and astronomers and geologists
went on with their own business.   Both religion and as-
tronomy are still alive and in the same world together.
And the Vatican observatory, by the bye, is honourably
distinguished for its excellent stellar photographs.   Perhaps, after all, the church does not mean by *Socialismus*
Socialism as it is understood in English; perhaps it
simply means the openly anti-Christian Socialism of the
Continental type.

I am not advocating indifference to any interest I
have here set aside as irrelevant to Socialism.   Men
have discussed and will, I hope, continue to discuss such
questions as I have instanced with passionate zeal; but

Socialism need not be entangled by their decisions. We can go on our road to Socialism, we can get to Socialism, to the civilized state, whichever answer is given to any of these questions, great or small.

CHAPTER VII

WOULD MODERN SOCIALISM ABOLISH ALL PROPERTY?

§ 1

AND having in the previous chapter cleared up a considerable mass of misconception and possibility of misrepresentation about the attitude of Socialism to the home, let us now devote a little more attention to the current theory of property and say just exactly where modern Socialism stands in that matter.

The plain fact of the case is that the Socialist, whether he wanted to or no, would no more be able to abolish personal property altogether than he would be able to abolish the human liver. The extension of one's personality to things outside oneself is indeed as natural and instinctive a thing as eating. But because the liver is necessary and inevitable, there is no reason why it should be enlarged to uncomfortable proportions, and because eating is an unconquerable instinct there is no excuse for repletion. The position of the modern Socialist is that the contemporary idea of personal property is enormously exaggerated and improperly extended to things that ought not to be "private"; not that it is not a socially most useful and desirable idea within its legitimate range.

There can be no doubt that many of those older writers who were "Socialists before Socialism," Plato, for instance, and Sir Thomas More, did very roundly abolish private property altogether. They were extreme Communists, and so were many of the earlier Socialists; in More's *Utopia*, doors might not be fastened, they stood open; one hadn't even a private room. These earlier writers wished to insist upon the need of self-abnegation in the ideal state, and to startle and confound, they insisted overmuch. The early Christians, one gathers, were almost completely communistic, and that interesting experiment in Christian Socialism (of a rather unorthodox type of Christianity), the American Oneida community, was successfully communistic in every respect for many years. But the modern Socialist is not a Communist; the modern Socialist, making his scheme of social reconstruction for the whole world and for every type of character, recognizes the entire impracticability of such dreams, recognizing too, it may be, the sacrifice of human personality and distinction such ideals involve.

The word "property," one must remember, is a slightly evasive word. Absolute property hardly exists, absolute, that is to say, in the sense of unlimited right of disposal;

almost all property is incomplete and relative. A man, under our present laws, has no absolute property even in his own life; he is restrained from suicide and punished if he attempt it. He may not go offensively filthy nor indecently clad; there are limits to his free use of his body. The owner of a house, of land, of a factory, is subject to all sorts of limitations, building regulations, for example, and so is the owner of horse or dog. Nor again is any property exempt from taxation. Even now property is a limited thing, and it is well to bear that much in mind. It can only be defined as something one may do "what one likes with," subject only to this or that specific restriction, and at any time it would seem, the state is at least legally entitled to increase the quantity and modify the nature of the restriction. The extremest private property is limited to a certain sanity and humanity in its use.

In that sense every adult nowadays has private property in his or her own person, in clothes, in such personal implements as hand-tools, as a bicycle, as a cricket bat or golf sticks. In quite the same sense would he have it under Socialism so far as these selfsame things go. The sense of property in such things is almost instinctive; my little boys of five and three have the keenest sense of *mine* and (almost, if not quite so vividly) *thine* in the matter of toys and garments. The disposition of modern Socialism is certainly no more to override these natural tendencies than it is to fly in the face of human nature in regard to the home. The disposition of modern Socialism is indeed far more in the direction of confirming and insuring this natural property. And again modern Socialism has no designs upon the money in a man's pocket. It is quite true that the earlier and extreme Socialist theorists did in their communism find no use for money, but I do not think there are any representative Socialists now who do not agree that the state must pay and receive in money, that money is indispensable to human freedom. The featurelessness of money, its universal convertibility, gives human beings a latitude of choice and self-expression in its spending that is inconceivable without its use.

All such property Socialism will ungrudgingly sustain, and it will equally sustain property in books and objects of æsthetic satisfaction, in furnishing, in the apartments or dwelling-house a man or woman occupies and in their household implements. It will sustain far more property than the average working-class man has to-day. Nor will it prevent savings or accumulations, if men do not choose to expend their earnings, — nor need it interfere with lending. How far it will permit or countenance usury is another question altogether. There will no doubt remain, after all the workaday needs of the world

have been met by a scientific public organization of the
general property in Nature, a great number of businesses
and enterprises and new and doubtful experiments
outside the range of legitimate state activity. In these,
interested and prosperous people will embark their
surplus money as shareholders in a limited liability
company, making partnership profits or losses in an entirely proper manner. But whether there should be debentures and mortgages or preference shares or such like
manipulatory distinctions, or interest in any shape or
form, I am inclined to doubt. A money-lender should
share risk as well as profit — that is surely the moral
law in lending that forbids usury; he should not be
allowed to bleed a failing business with his inexorable
percentage and so eat up the ordinary shareholder or
partner any more than the landlord should be allowed to
eat up the failing tenant for rent. That was once the
teaching of Christianity, and I do not know enough of
the history or spiritual development of the Catholic
Church to tell when she became what she now appears to
be — the champion of the rent-exacting landlord and the
usurer against Socialism. It is the present teaching of
Socialism. If usury obtains at all under the Socialist
state, if inexorable repayments are to be made in certain
cases, it will, I conceive, be a state monopoly. The state
will be the sole banker for every hoard and every enter-

prise, just as it will be the universal landlord and the universal fire and accident and old-age insurance office. In money matters as in public service and administration, it will stand for the species, the permanent thing behind every individual accident and adventure.

Posthumous property, that is to say, the power to bequeath and the right to inherit things will also persist in a mitigated state under Socialism. There is no reason whatever why it should not do so. There is a strong natural sentiment in favour of the institution of heirlooms, for example; one feels a son might well own — though he should certainly not sell — the intimate things his father desires to leave him. The pride of descent is an honourable one, the love for one's blood, and I hope that a thousand years from now some descendant will still treasure an obsolete weapon here, a picture there, or a piece of faint and faded needlework, from our days and the days before our own. One may hate inherited privileges and still respect a family tree.

Widows and widowers again have clearly a kind of natural property in the goods they have shared with the dead; in the home, in the garden close, in the musical instruments and books and pleasant homelike things. Now in nine cases out of ten we do in effect bundle the widow out; she remains nominally owner of the former home, but she has to let it furnished or sell it, to go and live in a boarding-house or an exiguous flat.

Even perhaps a proportion of accumulated money may reasonably go to friend or kin.   It is a question of public utility; Socialism has done with absolute propositions in all such things, and views these problems now as questions of detail, matters for fine discriminations.   We want to be quit of pedantry.   All that property which is an enlargement of personality, the modern Socialist seeks to preserve; it is that exaggerated property that gives power over the food and needs of one's fellow-creatures, property and inheritance in land, in industrial machinery, in the homes of others, and in the usurer's grip upon others, that he seeks to destroy.   The most doctrinaire Socialists will tell you they do not object to property for use and consumption but only to property in "the means of production," but I do not choose to resort to over-precise definitions.   The general intention is clear enough, the particular instance requires particular application. . . .   But it is just because we modern Socialists want every one to have play for choice and individual expression in all those realities of property that we object to this monstrous property of a comparatively small body of individuals expropriating the world.

§ 2

I am inclined to think — but here I speak beyond the text of contemporary Socialist literature — that in certain directions Socialism, while destroying property, will introduce a compensatory element by creating rights. For example, Socialism will certainly destroy all private property in land and in natural material and accumulated industrial resources; it will be the universal landlord and the universal capitalist, but that does not mean that we shall all be the State's Tenants-at-will. There can be little doubt that the Socialist state will recognize the rights of the improving occupier and the beneficial hirer. It is manifestly in accordance both with justice and public policy that a man who takes a piece of land and creates a value on it — by making a vineyard, let us say — is entitled to security of tenure, is to be dispossessed only in exceptional circumstances and with ample atonement. If a man who takes an agricultural or horticultural holding comes to feel that there he will toil and there later he will rest upon his labours, I do not think a rational Socialism will war against this passion for the vine and fig tree. If it absolutely refuses the idea of freehold, it will certainly not repudiate leasehold. I think the state may prove a far more generous and sentimental landlord in many things than any private person.

In another correlated direction, too, Socialism is quite reconcilable with a finer quality of property than our landowner-ridden Britain allows to any but the smallest minority.   I mean property in the house one occupies. . . . If I may indulge in a quite unauthorized speculation, I am inclined to think there may be two collateral methods of home-building in the future.   For many people always there will need to be houses to which they may come and go for longer and shorter tenancies and which they will in no manner own.   Nowadays such people are housed in the exploits of the jerry builder — all England is unsightly with their meagre pretentious villas and miserable cottages and tenement houses. Such homes in the Socialist future will certainly be sup- plied by the local authority, but they will be fair, decent houses by good architects, fitted to be clean and lit, airy and convenient, the homes of civilized people, sightly things altogether in a generous and orderly world.   But in addition there will be the prosperous private person with a taste that way, building himself a home as a lease- holder under the public landlord.   For him, too, there will be a considerable measure of property, a measure of property that might even extend to a right, if not of be- quest, then at any rate of indicating a preference among his possible successors in the occupying tenancy. . . .

Then there is a whole field of proprietary sensations in

L

relation to official duties and responsibility. Men who
have done good work in any field are not to be lightly
torn from it. A medical officer of health who has done
well in his district, a teacher who has taught a generation of a town, a man who has made a public garden,
have a moral lien upon their work for all their lives.
They do not get it under our present conditions. I
know that it will be quite easy to say all this is a question of administration and detail. It is. But it is
nevertheless important to state it clearly here, to make
it evident that the coming of Socialism involves no
destruction of this sort of identification of a man with
the thing he does; this identification that is so natural
and desirable — that this living and legitimate sense of
property will if anything be encouraged and its claims
strengthened under Socialism. To-day that particularly
living sort of property-sense is often altogether disregarded. Every day one hears of men who have worked
up departments in businesses, men who have created
values for employers, men who have put their lives into
an industrial machine, being flung aside because their
usefulness is over, or out of personal pique, or to make
way for favourites, for the employer's son or cousin or
what not, without any sort of appeal or compensation.
Ownership is autocracy, at the best it is latent injustice
in all such matters of employment.

Then again, consider the case of the artist and the inventor who are too often forced by poverty now to sell their early inventions for the barest immediate subsistence. Speculators secure these initial efforts — sometimes to find them worthless, sometimes to discover in them the sources of enormous wealth. In no matter is it more difficult to estimate value than in the case of creative work; few geniuses are immediately recognized, and the history of art, literature, and invention is full of Chattertons and Savages who perished before recognition came, and of Dickenses who sold themselves unwisely. Consider the immense social benefit if the creator even now possessed an inalienable right to share in the appreciation of his work. Under Socialism it would for all his life be his — and the world's, and controllable by him. He would be free to add, to modify, to repeat.

In all these respects modern Socialism tends to create and confirm property and rights, the property of the user, the rights of the creator. It is quite other property it tends to destroy,— the property, the claim, of the creditor, the mortgager, the landlord, and usurer, the forestaller, gambling speculator, monopolizer, and absentee. . . . In very truth Socialism would destroy no property at all, but only that sham property that, like some wizard-cast illusion, robs us all.

§ 3

And now we are discussing the truth about the Socialist attitude toward property, it may be well to consider a little group of objections that are often made in Anti-Socialist tracts. I refer more particularly to a certain hard case, the hard case of the Savings of the Virtuous Small Man.

The reader, if he is at all familiar with this branch of controversial literature, probably knows how that distressing case is put. One is presented with a poor man of inconceivable industry, goodness, and virtue; he has worked, he has saved; at last, for the security of his old age, he holds a few shares in a business, a "bit of land" or, perhaps through a building society, house property. Would we — the Anti-Socialist chokes with emotion — so alter the world as to rob him of *that?* . . . The Anti-Socialist gathers himself together with an effort and goes on to a still more touching thought . . . the widow !

Well, I think there are assurances in the previous section to disabuse the reader's mind a little in this matter. This solicitude for the Saving Small Man and for the widow and orphan seems to me one of the least honest of all the Anti-Socialist arguments. The man "who has saved a few pounds," the poor widow woman and her children clinging to some scrap of freehold, are thrust forward to defend the harvest of the landlord and the financier.   Let us look at the facts of the case and see how this present economic system of ours really does treat the "stocking" of the poor.

In the first place it does not guarantee to the small investor any security for his little hoard at all.   He comes into the world of investment ill-informed, credulous, or only unintelligently suspicious — and he is, as a class, continually and systematically deprived of his little accumulations.   One great financial operation after another in the modern world, as any well-informed person can witness, eats up the small investor.   Some huge, vastly respectable-looking enterprise is floated with a capital of so many scores or hundreds of thousands, divided into so many thousands of ordinary shares, so many five or six per cent preference, so much debentures.   It begins its career with a flourish of prosperity; the ordinary shares for a few years pay seven, eight, ten per cent.   The Virtuous Small Man provides for his widow and his old age by buying this estimable security.   Its price clambers to a premium, and so it passes slowly and steadily from its first speculative holders into the hands of the investing public.   Then comes a slow, quiet, downward movement, a check at the interim dividend, a rapid contraction.   Consider such a case as that of the great British Electric Traction Company which began with ordinary shares at ten, which clambered to above twenty-one ($21\frac{7}{8}$), which is now (March, 1907) fluctuating about three and a half. Its six per cent preference shares have moved between fourteen and seven and a half. Its ordinary shares represent a total capital of £1,333,010, and its preference £1,614,370; so that here in this one concern we have a phantom appearance and disappearance of over two million pounds' worth of value and a real disappearance of perhaps half that amount. It requires only a very slight knowledge of the world to convince one that the bulk of that sum was contributed by the modest investments of mediocre and small people out of touch with the real conditions of the world of finance.

These little investors, it is said, are the bitter champions of private finance against the municipalities and Socialists. One wonders why.

One can find a score of parallels and worse instances representing in the end many scores of millions of pounds taken from the investing public in the last few years. I will, however, content myself with one sober quotation from the New York *Journal of Commerce*, which the reader will admit is not likely to be a willing witness for Socialism. Commenting on the testimony of the principal witness, Mr. Harriman, of the Illinois Central Railroad, before the Interstate Commerce Commission (March, 1907), it says: —

"On his own admission he was one of a 'combine' of four who got possession of the Chicago and Alton Railroad, and immediately issued bonds for $40,000,000, out of the proceeds of which they paid themselves a dividend of 30 per cent on the stock they held besides taking the bonds at 65 and subsequently selling them at 90 or more, some of them to life insurance companies with which Mr. Harriman had some kind of relation. There were no earnings or surplus out of which the dividend could be paid, but the books of the company were juggled by transferring some $12,000,000 expended for betterments to capital account as a sort of bookkeeping basis for the performance.

"Besides this, the Chicago and Alton Railroad was transformed into a 'railway' and a capitalization of a little under $40,000,000 was swollen to nearly $123,000,000 to cover an actual expenditure in improvements of $22,500,000. In the process there was an injection of about $60,000,000 of 'water' into the stock held by the four, some of which was sold to the Union Pacific, of which Mr. Harriman was president, and more was unloaded upon the Rock Island. Mr. Harriman refused to tell how much he made out of that operation.

"It shows how some of our enormous fortunes are made as well as what motives and purposes sometimes prevail in the use of the power intrusted to the directors and officers of corporations. It is a simple and elementary principle that all values are created by the productive activity of capital, labour, and ability in industrial operations of one kind and another. No wealth comes out of nothing, but all must be produced and distributed, and what one gets by indirection another loses or fails to get. The personal profit of these speculative operations in which the capital, credit, and power of corporations are used by those intrusted with their direction come out of the general body of stockholders whose interests are sacrificed, or out of the public investors who are lured and deceived, or out of shippers who are overtaxed, for the service for which railroads are chartered, or out of all these in varying proportions. In other words they are the fruits of robbery."

So that you see it is not only untrue that Socialism would rob a poor man of his virtuously acquired "bit of property," but the direct contrary is the truth, that the present system, non-Socialism, is now constantly *butchering thrift!* Simple people believe the great financiers win and lose money to each other. They are not, to put it plainly, such fools. They use the public, and the public goes on being used, as a perpetual source of freshly accumulated wealth. I know one case of a man of fifty who serves in a shop, a most industrious, competent man, who has been saving and investing money all his life in what he had every reason to believe were safe and sober businesses; he has been denying himself pleasures, cramping his life to put by about a third of his wages every year since he was two and twenty, and to-day he has not got his keep for a couple of years, and his only security against disablement and old age is his subscription to a Friendly Society, a society which I have a very strong suspicion is no better off than most other Friendly Societies — and that is by no means well off, and by no means confident of the future.

It is possible to argue that the small man ought to take more pains about his investments; but, as a matter of fact, investing money securely and profitably is a special occupation of extraordinary complexity, and the common man with a few hundred pounds has no more chance in that market than he would have under water in Sydney Harbour amidst a shoal of sharks. It may be said that he is greedy, wants too much interest, but that is nonsense. One of the cruellest gulfs into which small savings have gone, in the case of the British public, has been the trap of Consols which pay even at the present price less than three per cent. Servants and working men with Post-office Savings' Bank accounts were urged, tempted, and assisted to invest in this solemn security, even when it stood at 114. Those who did so have now (March, 1907) lost a quarter of their money.

It is scarcely too much to say that a very large proportion of our modern great properties, tramway systems, railways, gasworks, bread companies, have been created for their present owners, — the debenture-holders and mortgagers, the great capitalists, — by the unintentional altruism of that voluntary martyr, the Saving Small Man.

Of course the habitual saver can insure with an insurance company for his old age and against all sorts of misadventures, and because of the government interference with "private enterprise" in that sort of business be reasonably secure; but under Socialism he would be able to do that with absolute security in the State Insurance Office if the universal old-age pension did not satisfy him. That, however, is beside our present discussion. I am writing now only of the sort of property that Socialism would destroy, and to show how little benefit or safety it brings to the small owner now. The unthinking rich prate "thrift" to the poor, and grow richer by a half-judicious, half-unconscious absorption of the resultant savings; that, in brief, is the grim humour of our present financial method.

It is not only in relation to investments that this absorption of small parcels of savings goes on. In every town the intelligent and sympathetic observer may see, vivid before the eyes of all who are not blind by use and wont, the slow subsidence of petty accumulations. The lodging-house and the small retail shop are, as it were, social "destructors"; all over the country they are converting hopeful, enterprising, ill-advised people with a few score or hundreds of pounds, slowly, inevitably into broken-hearted failures. It is to my mind the cruellest aspect of our economic struggle. In the little High Street of Sandgate over which my house looks, I should say between a quarter and a third of the shops are such downward channels from decency to despair; they are sanctioned, inevitable citizen-breakers. Now it is a

couple of old servants opening a "fancy" shop or a to-
bacco shop, now it is a young couple plunging into the
haberdashery, now it is a new butcher or a new fishmonger
or a grocer. This perpetual proce sion of bankruptcies
has made me lately shun that pleasant-looking street,
that in my unthinking days I walked through cheerfully
enough. The doomed victims have a way of coming to
the doors at first and looking out politely and hopefully.
There is a rich and lucrative business done by certain
wholesale firms in starting the small dealer in almost
every branch of retail trade; they fit up his shop, stock
him, take his one or two hundred pounds and give him
credit for forty or fifty. The rest of his story is an impossible struggle to pay rent and get that debt down.
Things go on for a time quite bravely.

I go furtively and examine the goods in the window
with a dim hope that this time something really will
come off; I learn reluctantly from my wife that they
are no better than any one else's and rather dearer than
those of the one or two solid and persistent shops that
do the steady business of the place. Perhaps I see the
new people going to church once or twice very respect-
ably, as I set out for a Sunday walk, and if they are a
young couple, the husband usually wears a silk hat.
Presently the stock in the window begins to deteriorate
in quantity and quality, and then I know that credit is

tightening. The proprietor no longer comes to the door, and his first bright confidence is gone. He regards one now through the darkling panes with a gloomy animosity. He suspects one all too truly of dealing with the "Stores." . . . Then suddenly he has gone; the savings are gone, and the shop, like a hungry maw, waits for a new victim. There is the simple common tragedy of the little shop; the landlord of the house has *his* money all right, the ground landlord has, of course, every penny of his money; the kindly wholesalers are well out of it, and the young couple or the old people, as the case may be, are looking for work or the nearest casual ward — just as though there was no such virtue as thrift in the world.

The particular function of the British lodging-house — though the science of economics is silent on this point — is to use up the last strength of the trusty old servant and the plucky widow. These people will invest from two or three hundred to a thousand pounds in order to gain a bare subsistence by toiling for boarders and lodgers. It is their idea of a safe investment. They can see it all the time. All over England this process goes on. The curious inquirer may see every phase for himself by simply looking for rooms among the apartment houses of such a region as Camden Town, London; he will realize more and more surely as he goes about that none of these people gain money, none of them ever recover the capital they sink, they are happy if they die before their inevitable financial extinction. It is so habitual with people to think of classes as stable, of a butcher or a baker as a man who keeps a shop of a certain sort at a certain level throughout a long and indeterminate life, that it may seem incredible to many readers that those two typically thrifty classes, the lodging-letting householder and the small retailer, are maintained by a steady supply of failing individuals; the fact remains that it is so. Their little savings are no good to them, investments and business beginnings mock them alike; steadily, relentlessly, our competitive system eats them up.

It is said that no class of people in the community is more hostile to Socialism and Socialistic legislation than these small owners and petty investors, these small rate-payers. They do not understand. Rent they consider in the nature of things like hunger and thirst; the economic process that dooms the weak enterprise to ruin is beyond the scope of their intelligence; but the rate-collector who calls and calls again for money, for more money, to educate "other people's children," to "keep paupers in luxury," to "waste upon roads and light and trams," seems the agent of an unendurable wrong. So the poor creatures go out pallidly angry to vote down that hated thing, municipal enterprise, and to make still more scope for that big finance that crushes them in the wine-press of its exploitation. It is a wretched and tragic antagonism, for which every intelligent Socialist must needs have sympathy, which he must meet with patience — and lucid explanations. If the public authority took rent, there would be no need of rates; that is the more obvious proposition. But the ampler one is the cruelty, the absurdity, and the social injury of the constant consumption of unprotected savings which is integral in our present system.

It is a doctrinaire and old-fashioned Socialism that quarrels with the little hoard; the quarrel of modern Socialism is with the landowner and the great capitalist who devour it.

§ 4

While we are discussing the true attitude of modern Socialism to property, it will be well to explain quite clearly the secular change of opinion that is going on in the Socialist ranks in regard to the process of expropriation. Even in the case of those sorts of property that Socialism repudiates, property in land, natural productions, inherited business capital, and the like, Socialism has become humanized and rational from its first extreme and harsh positions.

The earlier Socialism was fierce and unjust to owners.

"Property is Robbery," said Proudhon, and right down to the nineties Socialism kept too much of the spirit of that proposition. The property-owner was to be promptly and entirely deprived of his goods and to think himself lucky he was not lynched forthwith as an abominable rascal. The first Basis of the Fabian Society framed so lately as 1884 repudiates "compensation" — even a partial compensation of property-owners — though in its practical proposals the Fabian Society has always been saner than its creed.

Now property is not robbery. It may be a mistake, it may be unjust and socially disadvantageous to recognize private property in these great common interests; but every one concerned, and the majority of the property-owners certainly, held and hold in good faith, and do their best by the light they have. We live to-day in a vast tradition of relationships in which the rightfulness of that kind of private property is assumed, and suddenly, instantly, to deny and abolish it would be — I write this as a convinced and thorough Socialist — quite the most dreadful catastrophe human society could experience. For what sort of provisional government should we have in that confusion?

Expropriation must be a gradual process, a process of economic and political readjustment, accompanied at every step by an explanatory educational advance.

There is no reason why a cultivated property-owner should not welcome and hasten its coming. Modern Socialism is prepared to compensate him, not perhaps "fully" but reasonably, for his renunciations and to avail itself of his help, to relieve him of his administrative duties, his excess of responsibility for estate and business. It does not grudge him a compensating annuity nor terminating rights of user. It has no intention of obliterating him nor the things he cares for. It wants not only to socialize his possessions, but to socialize his achievement in culture and all that leisure has taught him of the possibilities of life. It wants all men to become as fine as he. Its enemy is not the rich man but the aggressive rich man, the usurer, the sweater, the giant plunderer, who are developing the latent evil of riches. It repudiates altogether the conception of a bitter class-war between those who Have and those who Have Not.

But this new tolerant spirit in method involves no weakening of the ultimate conception. Modern Socialism sets itself absolutely against the creation of new private property out of land, or rights or concessions not yet assigned. All new great monopolistic enterprises in transit, building, and cultivation, for example, must from the first be under public ownership. And the chief work of social statesmanship, the secular process of government, must be the steady, orderly resumption by the community, without violence and without delay, of the land, of the apparatus of transit, of communication, of food distribution, and of all the great common services of mankind, and the care and training of a new generation in their collective use and in more civilized conceptions of living.

CHAPTER VIII

THE MIDDLE-CLASS MAN AND SOCIALISM

AND let me here insert a few remarks upon a question that arises naturally out of the preceding sections, and that is the future of that miscellaneous section of the community known as the middle class. It is one that I happen to know with a special intimacy.

For a century or more the grinding out of the middle class has been going on. I began to find it interesting — altogether too interesting indeed — when I was still only a little boy. My father was one of that multitude of small shopkeepers which has been caught between the "Stores" and such-like big distributors above and the rising rates below, and from the knickerbocker stage onward I was acutely aware of the question hanging over us. "This isn't going on" was the proposition. "This shop in which our capital is invested will never return it. Nobody seems to understand what is happening, and there is nobody to advise or help us. What are we going to do?"

Except that people are beginning to understand a little now what it all means, exactly the same ques-

tion hangs over many hundreds of thousands of households to-day, not only over the hundreds of small
shopkeepers, but of small professional men, of people
living upon small parcels of investments, of clerks and
such-like who find themselves growing old and their value
depreciated by the competition of a new, better-educated
generation, of private schoolmasters, of boarding and
lodging house keepers, and the like.   They are all vaguely
aware of something more than personal failure, of a drift
and process which is against all their kind, of the need of
"doing something" for themselves and their children,
something different from just sticking to the shop or the
"situation" — and they don't know what to do !   What
ought they to do ?

Well, first, before one answers that, let us ask what it
is exactly that is grinding the middle class in this way.
Is it a process we can stop?   Can we direct the millstones?   If we can, ought we to do so?   And if we cannot, or decide that it isn't worth while, then what can
we do to mitigate this cruelty of slowly impoverishing
and taxing out of existence a class that was once the
backbone of the community?   It is not mere humanity
dictates this much, it is a question that affects the state
as a whole.   It must be extremely bad for the spirit
of the nation and for our national future that its middle
mass should be in a state of increasing financial worry

and stress, irritated, depressed, and broken in courage. One effect is manifest in our British politics now. Each fresh election turns upon expenditure more evidently than the last, and the promise to reduce taxation or lower the rates overrides more and more certainly any other consideration. What are Empire or Education to men who feel themselves drifting helplessly into debt? What chance has any constructive scheme with an electorate of men who are being slowly submerged in an economic bog?

The process that has brought the middle class into these troubles is a complex one, but the essential thing about it seems to be this, that there is a *change of scale* going on in most human affairs, a substitution of big organizations for detached individual effort almost everywhere. A hundred and fifty years ago or so the only very rich people in the community were a handful of great landowners and a few bankers; the rest of the world's business was being done by small prosperous independent men. The labourers and poor were often very poor and wretched, ill-clad, bootless, badly housed, and short of food, but there was nevertheless a great deal of middle-class comfort and prosperity. The country was covered with flourishing farmers; every country town was a little world in itself, with busy tradespeople and professional men; manufacturing was still done mainly by small people employing a few hands, master and apprentice worked together; in every town you found a parish school or so, an independent doctor and the like, doing well in a mediocre, comfortable fashion. All the carrying trade was in the hands of small independent carriers; the shipping was held by hundreds of small shipowners. And London itself was only a larger country town. It was, in effect, a middle-class world ruled over by aristocrats; the millstones had as yet scarcely stirred.

Then machinery came into the lives of men, and steam power, and there began that change of scale which is going on still to-day, making an ever widening separation of master and man and an ever enlarging organization of industry and social method. Its most striking manifestation was at first the substitution of organized manufacture in factories for the half-domestic hand-industrialism of the earlier period; the growth of the fortunes of some of the merchants and manufacturers to dimensions comparable with the wealth of the great landowners, and the sinking of the rest of their class toward the status of wage-earners. The development of joint-stock enterprise arose concurrently with this to create a new sort of partnership capable of handling far greater concerns than any single wealthy person, as wealth was measured by the old scale, could do. There followed a great development of transit, culminating for a time in the coming of the railways and steamships, which abolished the isolation of the old towns and brought men at the remotest quarters of the earth into business competition. Big towns of the modern type, with half a million inhabitants or more, grew up rapidly all over Europe and America. For the European big towns are as modern as New York, and the East End and south side of London scarcely older than Chicago. Shop-keeping, like manufactures, began to concentrate in large establishments, and big wholesale distribution to replace individual buying and selling. As the need for public education under the changing conditions of life grew more and more urgent, the individual enterprise of this schoolmaster and that gave place to the organized effort of such giant societies as (in Britain) the old National School Society and the British School Society, and at last to state education. And one after another the old prosperous middle-class callings fell under the stress of the new development.

The process still goes on, and there can be little doubt of the ultimate issue. The old small manufacturers are either ruined or driven into sweating and the slums; the old coaching innkeeper and common carrier have been impoverished or altogether superseded by the railways and big carrier companies; the once flourishing shopkeeper lives to-day on the mere remnants of the trade that great distributing stores or the branches of great companies have left him. Tea companies, provision-dealing companies, tobacconist companies, make the position of the old-established private shop unstable and the chances of the new beginner hopeless. Railways and tramways take the custom more and more effectually past the door of the small draper and outfitter to the well-stocked establishments at the centre of things; telephone and telegraph assist that shopping at the centre more and more. The small "middle-class" schoolmaster finds himself beaten by revived endowed schools and by new public endowments; the small doctor, the local dentist, find Harley Street always nearer to them and practitioners in motor-cars from the great centres playing havoc with their practices. And while the small men are more and more distressed, the great organizations of trade, of production, of public science, continue to grow and coalesce, until at last they grow into national or even world trusts, or into publicly owned monopolies. In America slaughtering and selling meat has grown into a trust, steel and iron are trustified, mineral oil is all gathered into a few hands. All through the trades and professions and sciences and all over the world the big eats up the small, the new enlarged scale replaces the old.

And this is equally true, though it is only now beginning

to be recognized, of the securities of that other section of the middle class, the section which lives upon invested money. There, too, big eats little. There, too, the small man is more and more manifestly at the mercy of the large organization. It was a pleasant illusion of the Victorian time that one put one's hundred pounds or thousand pounds "into something," beside the rich man's tens of thousands, and drew one's secure and satisfying dividends. The intelligent reader of Mr. Lawson's *Frenzied Finance* or of the bankruptcy proceedings of Mr. Hooley realizes this idyll is scarcely true to nature. Through the seas and shallows of investment flow great tides and depressions, on which the big fortunes ride to harbour while the little accumulations, capsized and swamped, quiver down to the bottom. It becomes more and more true that the small man saves his money for the rich man's pocket. Only by drastic state intervention is a certain measure of safety secured for insurance, and in America recently we have had the spectacle of the people's insurance-money used as a till by the rich financiers.

And when the middle-class man turns in his desperation from the advance of the big competitor who is consuming him, as a big codfish eats its little brother, to the state, he meets a tax-paper; he sees as the state's most immediate aspect the rate-collector and inexorable demands. The burden of taxation certainly falls upon him, and it falls upon him because he is collectively the weakest class that possesses any property to be taxed. Below him are classes either too poor to tax or too politically effective to stand taxation.   Above him is the class which owns a large part of the property in the world; but it also owns the newspapers and periodicals that are necessary for an adequate discussion of social justice, and it finds it cheaper to pay a voluntary tax to the hoardings at election time than to take over the small man's burdens.   He rolls about between these two parties, antagonized first to one and then the other, and altogether helpless and ineffectual.   So the millstones grind, and so it would seem they will continue to grind until there is nothing between them; until organized property in the hands of the few on the one hand and the proletariat on the other grind face to face.   So, at least, Karl Marx taught in *Das Kapital.*

But when one says the middle class will disappear, one means that it will disappear as a class.   Its individuals and its children will survive, and the whole process is not nearly so fatalistic as the Marxists would have us believe. The new great organizations that are replacing the little private enterprises of the world before machinery are not all private property.   There are alternatives in the matter of handling a great business.   To the exact nature of these alternatives the middle-class mind needs to direct itself if it is to exert any control whatever over its future. Take the case of the butcher. It is manifestly written on the scroll of destiny that the little private slaughter-house, the little independent butcher's shop, buying and selling locally, must disappear. The meat will all be slaughtered at some great, conveniently organized centre, and distributed thence to shops that will necessarily be mere agencies for distributing meat. Now, this great slaughtering and distributing business may either be owned by one or a group of owners working for profit — in which case it will be necessary for the state to employ an unremunerative army of inspectors to see that the business is kept decently clean and honest — or it may be run by the public authority. In the former case the present-day butcher or his son will be a slaughterman or shopkeeper employed by the private owners; in the latter case by the public authority. This is equally true of a milk-seller, of a small manufacturer, of a builder, of a hundred and one other trades. They are bound to be incorporated in a larger organization; they are bound to become salaried men where formerly they were independent men, and it is no good struggling against that. It is doubtful, indeed, whether from the standpoint of welfare it would be worth the middle-class man's while to struggle against that. But in the case of very many great public services — meat, milk, bread, transit, housing, and land administration, education and research, and the public health — it is still an open question whether the big organization is to be publicly owned, publicly controlled, and constantly refreshed by public scrutiny and comment, or whether it is to be privately owned, and conducted solely for the profit of a small group of very rich owners. The alternatives are Plutocracy or Socialism, and between these the middle-class man remains weakly undecided and ineffectual, lending no weight to and getting small consideration therefore from either side. He remains so because he has not grasped the real nature of his problem, because he clings in the face of overwhelming fate to the belief that in some way the wheels of change may be arrested and his present method of living preserved.

I think, if he could shake himself free from that impossible conservatism, he would realize that his interests lie with the interests of the intelligent working-class man — that is to say, in the direction of Socialism rather than in the direction of capitalistic competition; that the best use he can make of such educational and social advantages as still remain for him is to become the willing leader instead of the panic-fierce antagonist of the Socialist movement. His place, I hold, is to forward the development of that state and municipal machinery the Socialist foreshadows, and to secure for himself and his sons and daughters an adequate position and voice in the administration. Instead of struggling to diminish that burthen of public expenditure which educates and houses, conveys and protects him and his children, he ought rather to increase it joyfully, while at the same time working manfully to transfer its pressure to the broad shoulders of those very rich people who have hitherto evaded their legitimate share of it. The other course is to continue his present policy of obstinate resistance to the extension of public property and public services. In which case these things will necessarily become that basis of monopolistic property on which the coming Plutocracy will establish itself. The middle-class man will be taxed and competed out of independence just the same, and he will become a salaried officer just the same, but with a different sort of master and under different social conditions according as one or other of these alternatives prevails.

Which is the better master — the democratic state or a "combine" of millionaires? Which will give the best social atmosphere for one's children to breathe — a Plutocracy or a Socialism? That is the real question to which the middle-class man should address himself.

No doubt to many minds a Plutocracy presents many attractions. In the works of Thomas Love Peacock, and still more clearly in the works of Mr. W. H. Mallock, you will find an agreeable rendering of that conception. The bulk of the people will be organized out of sight in a state of industrious and productive congestion, and a wealthy, leisurely, and refined minority will live in spacious homes, with excellent museums, libraries, and all the equipments of culture; will go to town, concentrate in Paris, London, and Rome, and travel about the world. It is to these large, luxurious, powerful lives that the idealist naturally turns. Their motor-cars, their aeroplanes, their steam yachts, will awaken terror and respect in every corner of the globe. Their handsome doings will fill the papers. They will patronize the arts and literature, while at the same time mellowing them by eliminating that too urgent insistence upon contemporary fact which makes so much of what is done to-day harsh and displeasing. The middle-class tradition will be continued by a class of stewards, tenants, managers and foremen, secretaries, and the like, respected and respectful. The writer, the artist, will lead lives of comfortable dependence, a link between class and class, the lowest of the rich man's guests, the highest of his servants. As for the masses, they will be fed with a sort of careless vigour and considerable economy from the Chicago stockyards, and by agricultural produce trusts, big breweries, fresh-water companies, and the like; they will be organized industrially and carefully controlled.

Their spiritual needs will be provided for by churches endowed by the wealthy, their physical distresses alleviated by the hope of getting charitable aid, their lives made bright and adventurous by the crumbs of sport that fall from the rich man's table. They will crowd to see the motor-car races, the aeroplane competitions. It will be a world rich in contrasts and not without its bright gleam of pure adventure. Every bright young fellow of capacity will have the hope of catching the eye of some powerful personage, of being advanced to some high position of trust, of even ending his days as a partner, a subordinate assistant Plutocrat. Or he may win a quite agreeable position by literary or artistic merit. A pretty girl, a clever woman of the middle class, would have before her even more brilliant and romantic possibilities.

There can be no denying the promises of colour and eventfulness a Plutocracy holds out, and though they do not attract me, I can quite understand their appeal to the more ductile and appreciative mind of Mr. Mallock. But there are countervailing considerations. There is, it is said, a tendency in Plutocracies either to become unprogressive, unenterprising, and stagnantly autocratic, or to develop states of stress and discontent, and so drift toward Cæsarism. The latter was the fate of the Roman Republic, and may perhaps be the destiny of the budding young Plutocracy of America.   But the developing British Plutocracy, like the Carthaginian, will be largely Semitic in blood, and like the Carthaginian may resist these insurgent tendencies.

So much for the Plutocratic possibility.   If the middle-class man on any account does not like that outlook, he can turn in the other direction; and then he will find fine promises indeed, but much more uncertainty than toward Plutocracy.   Plutocracies the world has seen before, but a democratic civilization organized upon the lines laid down by modern Socialists would be a new beginning in the world's history.   It is not a thing that will come about by itself; it will have to be the outcome of a sustained moral and intellectual effort in the community.   If there is not that effort, if things go on as they are going now, the coming of a Plutocracy is inevitable.   That effort, I am convinced, cannot be successfully made by the lower-class man alone; from him, unaided and unguided, there is nothing to be expected but wild convulsive attempts at social upheaval, which, whether they succeed (as the French Revolution did) or fail (as did the insurrectionary outbreaks of the Republic in Rome), lead ultimately to a Napoleon or a Cæsar.   But our contemporary civilization is unprecedented in the fact that the whole population now reads, and that intelligence and free discussion saturate the whole mass. Only time can show what possibilities of understanding, leadership, and political action lie in our new generation of the better-educated middle class. Will it presently begin to define a line for itself? Will it remain disorganized and passive, or will it become intelligent and decisive between these millstones of the organized property and the organizing state, between Plutocracy and Socialism, whose opposition is the supreme social and political fact in the world at the present time?

CHAPTER IX

SOME OBJECTIONS TO SOCIALISM

§ 1

IN the preceding eight chapters I have sought to give as plain and full an account of the great generalizations of Socialism as I can and to make it clear exactly what these generalizations convey, and how far they go in this direction and that. Before we go on to a brief historical and anticipatory account of the actual Socialist movement, it may be worth while to take up and consider compactly the chief objections that are urged against the general propositions of Socialism in popular discussion.

Now a very large proportion of these arise out of the commonest vice of the human mind, its disposition to see everything as "yes" or "no," as "black" or "white," its impatience, its incapacity for a fine discrimination of intermediate shades.[1] The queer old scholastic logic still prevails remarkably in our modern world; you find Mr. Mallock, for example, going about arranging

[1] See *Scepticism of the Instrument,* the Appendix to *A Modern Utopia.* (Chapman and Hall.)

his syllogisms, extracting his opponent's "self-contra-
dictions," and disposing with stupendous self-satisfac-
tion of Socialism in all the magazines. He disposes
of Socialism quite in the spirit of the young mediæval
scholar returning home to prove beyond dispute that
"my cat has ten tails" and, given a yard's start, that a
tortoise can always keep ahead of a running man. The
essential fallacy is always to declare that either a thing
is A or it is not A; either a thing is green or it is not
green; either a thing is heavy or it is not heavy. Unthinking people, and some who ought to know better,
fall into that trap. They dismiss from their minds the
fact that there is a tinge of green in nearly every object
in the world, and that there is no such thing as pure
green, unless it be just one line or so in the long series
of the spectrum; they forget that the lightest thing has
weight and that the heaviest thing can be lifted. The
rest of the process is simple and has no relation whatever
to the realities of life. They agree to some hard and fast
impossible definition of Socialism, permit the exponent
to extract absurdities therefrom as a conjurer gets rabbits from a hat, and retire with a conviction that on the
whole it is well to have had this disturbing matter
settled once for all.

For example, the anti-Socialist declares that Socialism
"abolishes property." He makes believe there is a hard

absolute thing called "property," which must either be or not be, which is now and which will not be under Socialism. To any person with a philosophical education this is a ridiculous mental process, but it seems perfectly rational to an untrained mind — and that is the usual case with the anti-Socialist. Having achieved this initial absurdity, he then asks in a tone of bitter protest whether a man may not sleep in his own bed, and is he to do nothing if he finds a coal-heaver already in possession when he retires? This is the method of Mr. G. R. Sims, that delightful writer, who from altitudes of exhaustive misunderstanding tells the working-man that under Socialism he will have no money of his own, no home of his own, no wife of his own, no children of his own! It's effective nonsense in its way — but nonsense nevertheless. In my preceding chapters I hope I have made it clear that "property," even to-day, is a very qualified and uncertain thing, a natural vague instinct capable of perversion and morbid exaggeration and needing control, and that Socialism seeks simply to give it a sharper, juster, and rationally limited form in relation to the commonweal.

Or again, the opponent has it that Socialism "abolishes the family," and with it, of course, "every sacred and tender association," etc. To that also I have given a chapter.

I do not think much Anti-Socialism is dishonest in these matters. Anti-Socialism, as its name implies, is no alternative doctrine; it is a mental resistance, not a mental force. For the most part one is dealing with sheer intellectual incapacity; with people, muddle-headed perhaps, but quite well-meaning, who are really unable to grasp the quantitative element in things. They think with a simple flat certitude that if, for example, a doctor says quinine is good for a case, it means that he wishes to put every ounce of quinine that can be procured into his patient, to focus all the quinine in the world upon him; or that if a woman says she likes dancing, that thereby she declares her intention to dance until she drops. They are dear lumpish souls who like things "straightforward," as they say — all or nothing. They think qualifications or any quantitative treatment "quibbling," to be loudly scorned, bawled down, and set aside.

In controversy the temptations for a hot and generous temperament, eager for victory, to misstate and over-state the antagonist's position are enormous, and the sensible Socialist must allow for them unless he is to find discussion intolerable. The reader of the pre-ceding chapters should know exactly how Socialism stands to the family relations, the things it urges, the things it regards with impartiality or patient toleration, the things it leaves alone. The preceding chapters merely summarize a literature that has been accessible for years. Yet it is extraordinary how few antagonists of Socialism seem able even to approach these questions in a rational manner. One admirably typical critic of a pamphlet in which I propounded exactly the same opinions as are here set out in the third chapter found great comfort in the expression "brood mares." He took hold of my phrase "State family" and ran wild with it. He declared it to be my intention that women were no longer to be wives but "brood mares" for the state. Nothing would convince him that this was a glaring untruth. His mind was essentially equestrian. "Human stud-farm" was another of his expressions.[1] Ridicule and argument failed to touch him; I believe he would have gone to the stake to justify his faith that Socialists want to put women in haras. His thick-headedness had, indeed, a touch of the heroic.

Then a certain Father Phelan of St. Louis, no doubt in a state of mental exaltation as honest as it was indiscriminating, told the world through the columns of an American magazine that I wanted to tear the babe

---

[1] What makes the expression particularly inappropriate in my case is the fact that in my *Mankind in the Making* there is a clearly reasoned chapter (Chapter 2) which has never been answered in which I discuss and, I think, conclusively dispose of Mr. Francis Galton's ideas of Eugenics and deliberate stirpiculture.

from the mother's breast and thrust it into an "Institution." He said worse things than that, but I set them aside as pulpit eloquence. Some readers, no doubt, knew better and laughed, but many were quite sincerely shocked, and resolved after that to give Socialism a very wide berth indeed. *Honi soit qui mal y pense;* the revolting ideas that disgusted them were not mine, they came from some hot, dark reservoir of evil thoughts that years of chastity and discipline seem to have left intact in Father Phelan's soul.

The error in all these cases is the error of overstatement, of getting into a condition of confused intellectual excitement, and because a critic declares your window curtains too blue, saying therefore and usually with passion that he wants the whole universe, sky and sea included, painted bright orange. The inquirer into the question of Socialism will find that an almost incurable disease of these controversies. Again and again he will meet with it. If after that critic's little proposition about your window curtains he chances to say that on the whole he thinks an orange sky would be unpleasant, the common practice is to accuse him of not "sticking to his guns."

My friends Mr. G. K. Chesterton and Mr. Max Beerbohm, those brilliant ornaments of our age, when they chance to write about Socialism, confess this universal failing, albeit in a very different quality and measure. They are not, it is true, distressed by that unwashed coal-heaver who haunts the now private bed of the common anti-Socialist, nor have they any horrid vision of the fathers of the community being approved by a select committee of the County Council — no doubt wrapped in horse-cloths and led out by their grooms — such as troubles the spurred and quivering soul of that equestrian, — I forget his name, — the "brood-mare" gentleman who denounced me in the *Pall Mall Gazette;* but their souls fly out in a passion of protest against the hints of discipline and order the advancement of Socialism reveals.   Mr. G. K. Chesterton mocks valiantly and passionately, I know, against an oppressive and obstinately recurrent anticipation of himself in Socialist hands, hair clipped, meals of a strictly hygienic description at regular hours, a fine for laughing, not that he would want to laugh, and austere exercises in several of the more metallic virtues daily.   Mr. Max Beerbohm's conception is rather in the nature of a nightmare, a hopeless, horrid, frozen flight from the pursuit of Mr. Sidney Webb and myself, both of us, short, inelegant men, but for all that terribly resolute, indefatigable, incessant, to capture him, to drag him off to a mechanical Utopia, and there to take his thumb-mark and his name, number him distinctly in indelible ink, and

let him loose (under inspection) in a world of neat
round lakes of blue lime-water and vistas of white
sanitary tiling.

The method of reasoning in all these cases is the same:
it is to assume that whatever the Socialist postulates as
desirable is wanted without limit of qualification; to
imagine whatever proposal is chosen for the controversy
is to be carried out by uncontrolled monomaniacs, and
so to make a picture of the Socialist dream. This picture is presented to the simple-minded person in doubt
with, "This is Socialism. Surely! — SURELY! you
don't want this!"

And occasionally the poor, simple-minded person really
is overcome by these imagined terrors. He turns back
to our dingy realities again, to the good old grimy world
he knows, thanking God beyond measure that he will
never live to see the hateful day when one baby out of
every four ceases to die in our manufacturing towns,
when lives of sordid care are banished altogether from the
earth, and when the "sense of humour" and the cult of
Mark Tapley which flourishes so among these things will
be in danger of perishing from disuse.

But the reader sees now what Socialism is in its essentials, the tempered magnificence of the constructive
scheme to which it asks him to devote his life. It is a
laborious, immense project to make the world a world

of social justice, of opportunity and full living, to abolish
waste, to abolish the lavish unpremeditated cruelty of
our present social order.   Do not let the wit or perversity
of the adversary or, what is often a far worse influence,
the zeal and overstatement of the headlong advocate,
do not let the manifest personal deficiencies of this
spokesman or that, distract you from the living heart in
Socialism, its broad generosity of conception, its immense claim in kinship and direction upon your Good
Will.

§ 2

For the convenience of those readers who are in the
position of inquirers, I had designed at this point a section which was to contain a list of the chief objections to
Socialism other than mere misrepresentations, which are
current nowadays. I had meant at first to answer
each one fully and gravely, to clear them all up exhaustively and finally before proceeding. But I find
now upon jotting them down, that they are for the most
part already anticipated by the preceding chapters, and
so I will note them here very compactly indeed, and
make but the briefest comment upon each.

There is first the assertion, which effectually bars
a great number of people from further inquiry into
Socialism teaching, that *Socialism is contrary to Chris-*

tianity. I would urge that this is the absolute inversion of the truth. Christianity involves, I am convinced, a practical Socialism if it is honestly carried out. This is not only my conviction, but the reader, if he is a Nonconformist, can find it set out at length by Dr. Clifford in a Fabian tract, *Socialism and the Teaching of Christ,* and, if a Churchman, by the Rev. Stewart Headlam in another, *Christian Socialism.* It is said that a good Catholic of the Roman Communion cannot also be a Socialist. Even this very general persuasion may not be correct. I believe the papal prohibition was aimed entirely at a specific form of Socialism, the Socialism of Marx, Engels, and Bebel, which is, I must admit, unfortunately strongly anti-Christian in tone, as is the Socialism of the British Social Democratic Federation to this day. It is true that many leaders of the Socialist party have also been Secularists, and that they have mingled their theological prejudices with their political work. This is the case not only in Germany and America, but in Great Britain, where Mr. Robert Blatchford of the *Clarion,* for example, has also carried on a campaign against Christianity. But this is only the inevitable throwing together of two sets of ideas because they have this in common, that they run counter to generally received opinions; there is no *necessary* connection. Secularists and Socialists get thrown together

and classed together as early Christians and criminals and
rebels against the emperor were no doubt thrown together in the Roman jails. They had this much in
common, that they were in conflict with what most
people considered to be right. It is a confusion that
needs constant explaining away. It is to me a most
lamentable association of two entirely separate thought-
processes, one constructive and the other destructive,
and I have already, in Chapter VI, § 4, done my best to
disavow it.

*Socialism is pure materialism, it seeks only physical
well-being,* just as much as nursing lepers for pity and
the love of God is pure materialism that seeks only physical well-being.

Socialism advocates free love. This objection I have
also disposed of in Chapter VI, §§ 2 and 4.

*Socialism renders love impossible, and reduces humanity
to the condition of a stud-farm.* This, too, has been already dealt with; see Chapter III, §§ 2 and 5, and
Chapter VI, §§ 2, 3, and 4. These two objections
generally occur together in the same anti-Socialist speech
or tract.

Socialism would destroy parental responsibility. This
absurd perversion is altogether disposed of in Chapter
VI, § 3. It is a direct inversion of current Socialist
teaching.

§ 3

Socialism would open the way to vast public corruption.
This is flatly opposed to the experience of America,
where local administration has been as little Socialistic
and as corrupt as anywhere in the world.   Obviously, in
order that a public official should be bribed, there must
be some wealthy person outside the system to bribe him
and with an interest in bribing him.   When you have
a weak administration with feeble powers and resources
and strong, unscrupulous private corporations seeking to
override the law and public welfare, the possibilities of
bribing are at the highest point.   In a community given
over to the pursuit of gain, powerful private enterprises
will resort to corruption to get and protract franchises,
to evade penalties, to postpone expropriation, and they
will do it systematically and successfully.   And even
where there is partial public enterprise and a competition
among contractors, there will certainly be, at least,
attempts at corruption to get contracts.   But where the
whole process is in public hands, where can the bribery
creep in ?   Who is going to find the money for the bribes,
and why ?

It is urged that in another direction there is likely to be
a corruption of public life due to the organized voting of
the employees in this branch of the public service or that,

seeking some advantage for their own service.   This is
Lord Avebury's bogey.[1]   Frankly, such voting by services is highly probable.   The tramway men or the milk-
service men may think they are getting too long hours or
too low pay in comparison with the teachers or the men
on the ocean liners, and the thing may affect elections.
That is only human nature, and the point to bear in mind
is that this sort of thing goes on to-day, and goes on with
a vigour out of all proportion to the mild possibilities
of a Socialist régime.   The landowners of Great Britain,
for example, are organized in the most formidable manner against the general interests of the community, and
constantly subordinate the interests of the commonweal
to their conception of justice to their class; the big
railways are equally potent, and so are the legal profession and the brewers.   But to-day these political interventions of great organized services athwart the
path of statesmanship are sustained by enormous financial resources.   The state employees under Socialism
will be in the position of employing one another and
paying one another; the teacher, for example, will be
educating the sons of the tramway men up to the requirements of the public paymaster, and travelling in
the trams to and from his work; there will be close

[1] *On Municipal and National Trading*, by Lord Avebury.
(Macmillan and Co., 1907.)

mutual observation and criticism therefore, and a strong community of spirit, and that will put very definite limits indeed upon the possibly evil influence of class and service interests in politics.

Socialism would destroy incentive and efficiency. This is dealt with in Chapter V on the Spirit of Gain and the Spirit of Service.

§ 4

Socialism would destroy freedom. This is a more considerable difficulty. To begin with, it may be necessary to remind the reader that absolute freedom is an impossibility. As I have written in my *Modern Utopia:* —

"The idea of individual liberty is one that has grown in importance and grows with every development of modern thought. To the classical Utopists freedom was relatively trivial. Clearly they considered virtue and happiness as entirely separable from liberty, and as being altogether more important things. But the modern view, with its deepening insistence upon individuality and upon the significance of its uniqueness, steadily intensifies the value of freedom, until at last we begin to see liberty as the very substance of life, that indeed it is life, and that only the dead things, the choiceless things, live in absolute obedience to law. To have free play for one's individuality is, in the modern view, the subjective triumph of existence, as survival in creative work and offspring is its objective triumph. But for all men, since man is a social creature, the play of will must fall short of absolute freedom. Perfect human liberty is possible only to a despot who is abso-

lutely and universally obeyed. Then to will would be to com-
mand and achieve, and within the limits of natural law we could
at any moment do exactly as it pleased us to do. All other
liberty is a compromise between our own freedom of will and the
wills of those with whom we come in contact. In an organized
state each one of us has a more or less elaborate code of what
he may do to others and to himself, and what others may do to
him. He limits others by his rights and is limited by the rights
of others, and by considerations affecting the welfare of the
community as a whole.

"Individual liberty in a community is not, as mathemati-
cians would say, always of the same sign. To ignore this is
the essential fallacy of the cult called Individualism. But
in truth, a general prohibition in a state may increase the sum of
liberty, and a general permission may diminish it. It does not
follow, as these people would have us believe, that a man is more
free where there is least law and more restricted where there is
most law. A socialism or a communism is not necessarily a
slavery, and there is no freedom under anarchy. . . .

"It follows, therefore, in a modern Utopia, which finds the final
hope of the world in the evolving interplay of unique individuali-
ties, that the state will have effectually chipped away just all
those spendthrift liberties that waste liberty, and not one liberty
more, and so have attained the maximum general freedom."

That is the gist of the Socialist's answer to this accu-
sation. He asks what freedom is there to-day for the
vast majority of mankind? They are free to do nothing
but work for a bare subsistence all their lives, they may
not go freely about the earth even, but are prosecuted
for trespassing upon the health-giving breast of our uni-

versal mother.   Consider the clerks and girls who hurry
to their work of a morning across Brooklyn Bridge in
New York, or Hungerford Bridge in London, go and
see them, study their faces.   They are free, with a freedom Socialism would destroy.   Consider the poor painted
girls who pursue bread with nameless indignities through
our streets at night.   They are free by the current standard.   And the poor half-starved wretches struggling
with the impossible stint of oakum in a casual ward, they,
too, are free!   The nimble footman is free, the crushed
porter between the trucks is free, the woman in the mill,
the child in the mine.   Ask them!   They will tell you
how free they are.   They have happened to choose these
ways of living, that is all.   No doubt the piquancy of the
life attracts them in many such cases.

Let us be frank;—a form of Socialism might conceivably exist without much freedom, with hardly more freedom than that of a British worker to-day.   A State
Socialism tyrannized over by officials, who might be
almost as bad at times as uncontrolled small employers,
is so far possible that in Germany it is practically half-
existent now.   A bureaucratic Socialism might conceivably be a state of affairs scarcely less detestable than
our own.   I will not deny there is a clear necessity of
certain addenda to the wider formulæ of Socialism if we
are to be safeguarded effectually from the official.   We

need free speech, free discussion, free publication, as essentials for a wholesome Socialist state. How they may be maintained, I shall discuss in a later chapter. But these admissions do not justify the present system. Socialism, though it failed to give us freedom, would not destroy anything that we have in this way. We want freedom now, and we have it not. We speak of freedom of speech, but to-day, in innumerable positions, Socialist employees who declared their opinions openly would be dismissed. Then again in religious questions there is an immense amount of intolerance and suppression of social and religious discussion to-day, especially in our English villages. As for freedom of action, most of us from fourteen to the grave are chased from even the leisure to require freedom by the necessity of earning a living. . . .

Socialism, as I have stated it thus far, and as it is commonly stated, would give economic liberty to men and women alike, it would save them from the cruel urgency of need, and so far it would enormously enlarge freedom, but it does not guarantee them political or intellectual liberty. That I frankly admit and accept as one of the incompletenesses of contemporary Socialism. I conceive, therefore, as I shall explain at length in a later chapter, that it is necessary to supplement such Socialism as is currently received by certain new propositions. But to admit that Socialism does not guarantee freedom, is not to admit that Socialism will destroy it. It is possible, given certain conditions, for men to be nearly absolutely free in speech, in movement, in conduct, enormously free, that is, as compared with our present conditions, in a Socialist state established upon the two great propositions I have formulated in Chapters III and IV. So that the statement that Socialism will destroy freedom is a baseless one of no value as a general argument against the Socialist idea.

§ 5

Socialism would reduce life to one monotonous dead level! This in a world in which the majority of people live in cheap cottages, villa residences, and tenement houses, read halfpenny newspapers, and wear ready-made clothes!

Socialism would destroy art, invention, and literature. I do not know why this objection is made, unless it be that the objectors suppose that artists will not create, inventors will not think, and no one write or sing except to please a wealthy patron. Without his opulent smile where would they be? Well, do not let us be ungrateful; the arts owe much to patronage. Go to Venice, go to Florence, and you will find a glorious harvest of pictures

and architecture, sown and reaped by a mercantile plutocracy.   But then in Rome, in Athens, you will find an
equal accumulation made under very different conditions.   Reach a certain phase of civilization, a certain
leisure and wealth, and art will out, however the wealth
may be distributed.   In certain sumptuous directions
art flourishes now, and would certainly flourish less in a
Socialist state; in the gear of ostentatious luxury, in
private furniture of all sorts, in palace building, in the
exquisite confections of costly feminine adornment, in
the luxurious binding of books, in the cooking of larks, in
the distinguished portraiture of undistinguished persons,
in the various refinements of prostitution, in the subtle
accommodations of mystic theology, in jewellery.   It is
quite conceivable that in such departments Socialism will
discourage and limit æsthetic and intellectual effort.
But no mercantile plutocracy could ever have produced
a Gothic cathedral, a folk-lore, a gracious natural type
of cottage or beautiful clothing for the common people,
and no mercantile plutocracy will ever tolerate a literature of power.   If the coming of Socialism destroys art,
it will also create arts; the architecture of private palaces
will give place to an architecture of beautiful common
homes, cottages, and colleges, and to a splendid development of public buildings; the Sargents of Socialism will
paint famous people instead of millionaires' wives;

poetry and popular romantic literature will revive. For my own part I have no doubt where the balance of advantage lies.

It seems reasonable to look to the literary and artistic people themselves for a little guidance in this matter. Well, we had in the nineteenth century an absolute revolt of artists against Individualism. The proportion of open and declared Socialists among the great writers, artists, playwrights, critics, of the Victorian period was out of all proportion to the number of Socialists in the general population. Wilde in his *Soul of Man under Socialism*, Ruskin in many volumes of imperishable prose, Morris in all his later life, have witnessed to the unending protest of the artistic spirit against the rule of gain.

Even this Individualistic country of ours, after the shameful shock of the great exhibition of 1851, decided that it could no longer leave art to private enterprise, and organized that systematic government Art Teaching, that has, in spite of its many defects, revolutionized the æsthetic quality of this country. And so far as research and invention go, one may very reasonably appeal to such an authority on the other side, as the late Mr. Beit, of Wernher, Beit and Co. The outcome of his experience as an individualist financier was to convince him that the only way to raise the standard

of technical science in England was by the endowment
of public teaching, and the huge "London Charlottenburg" rises out of his conviction. Even Messrs.
Rockefeller and Carnegie admit the failure of Individualism in this matter by pouring money into public
universities and public libraries. All these heads
of the commercial process confess by these acts what
this objection of the inexperienced denies, the power
of the state to develop art, invention, and knowledge;
the necessity that this duty should be done if not by,
then at any rate through, the state.

Socialism may very seriously change the direction of
intellectual and æsthetic endeavour, that one admits.
But there is no reason whatever for supposing it will not,
and there are countless reasons for supposing that it
will, enormously increase the opportunities and en-
couragements for æsthetic and intellectual endeavour.

§ 6

Socialism would arrest the survival of the fittest. Here
is an objection from quite a new quarter. It is the
stock objection of the science student. Hitherto we
have considered religious and æsthetic difficulties, but
this is the difficulty of the mind that realizes clearly the
nature of the biological process, the secular change in

every species under the influence of its environment,
and is most concerned with that. Species, it is said,
change — and the student of the elements of science is
too apt to conclude that this change is always ascent in
the scale of being — by the killing off of the individuals
out of harmony with the circumstances under which the
species is living. This is not quite true. The truer
statement is that species change because, allowing for
chance and individual exceptions, only those individuals survive to reproduce themselves who are fairly well
adjusted to the conditions of life; so that in each generation there is only a small proportion of births out of
harmony with these conditions. This sounds very like
the previous proposition, but it differs in this that the
accent is shifted from the ''killing'' to the suppression
of births; that is the really important fact. In any case,
then, the believer in evolution believes that the qualities
encouraged by the environment increase in the species
and the qualities discouraged diminish. The qualities
that have survival value are not always what we human
beings consider admirable; that is a consideration many
science students fail to grasp. The remarkable habits
of all the degenerating crustacea, for example, the appe-
tite of the vulture, the unpleasing personality of the
common hyena, — all that less charming side of Mother
Nature that her scandalized children may read of in

Cobbold's *Human Parasites*, — are the result of survival under the pressure of environment, just as much as the human eye or the wing of an eagle. Let the objector therefore ask himself what sort of "fittest" are surviving now.

The plain answer is that under our present conditions the *Breeding-getter* wins, the man who can hold and keep and reproduce his kind. People with the instinct of owning stronger than any other instinct float out upon the top of our seething mass, and flourish there. Aggressive, intensely acquisitive, reproductive people — the ignoble sort of Jew is the very type of it — are the people who will prevail in a social system based on private property and mercantile competition. No creative power, no nobility, no courage can battle against them. And below in the slums and factories, what will be going on? The survival of a race of stunted toilers, with great resisting power to infection, contagion, and fatigue, omnivorous as rats.

Don't imagine that the high infantile deathrate of our manufacturing centres spares the fine big children. It does not. Here is the effectual answer to that. It is taken from the Report of the Education Committee of the London County Council for the year 1905, and it is part of an account of an inquiry conducted by the headmaster of one school in a poor neighbourhood.

" The object of the inquiry was to discover the causes of variation in the physical condition of children within the limits of this single school. Each of the 405 boys was carefully weighed and measured without boots, a note was made of the condition of the teeth, and a general estimate of the personal cleanliness and sufficiency of clothing as a basis for determining the home conditions of neglect or otherwise from external evidence. The teacher of each class added an estimate of mental capacity." [Here follow tabular arrangement of results, and height and weight charts.]

" . . . It may be noted in the heights and weights for each age that the curve is not a continuous line of growth, but that at some ages it springs nearer to, and at others sinks further from, the normal. The greatest effect upon the life capital of the population is produced by the infantile mortality, which in some years actually kills off during the first year one in five of all children born; the question naturally arises what is its effect upon the survivors — do the weakly ones get killed off and only the strong muddle through, or does the adverse environment which slaughters one in five have a maiming effect upon those left? . . . When the infantile mortality for the parish in which the school is situate was charted above the physique curve, an absolute correspondence is to be observed. The children born in a year when infantile mortality is low show an increased physique, rising nearest to the normal in the extraordinary good year 1892; and those born in the years of high mortality show a decreased physique. . . . It appears certain, therefore, that in years of high infantile mortality the conditions, to which one in five or six of the children born are sacrificed, have a maiming effect upon the other four or five."

The fine big children are born in periods of low infantile mortality, that is the essential point.

So that anyhow, since the fittest under present conditions is manifestly the ratlike, the survival of the fittest that is going on now is one that it is highly desirable to stop as soon as possible, and so far Socialism *will* arrest the survival of the fittest. But that does not mean that it will stop the development of the species altogether. It will merely shift the incidence of selection and rejection to a new set of qualities. I think I have already hinted (Chapter VI, § 2) that a state that pays for the children born into it will do its best to secure good births. That implies a distinct bar to the marriage and reproduction of the halt and the blind, the bearers of transmissible diseases, and the like. And women, being economically independent, will have a far freer choice in wedlock than they have now. Now they must in practice marry men who can more or less keep them, they must subordinate every other consideration to that. Under Socialism they will certainly look less to a man's means and acquisitive gifts, and more to the finer qualities of his personality. They will prefer prominent men, able men, fine, vigorous and attractive persons. There will indeed be far more freedom of choice on either side than under the sordid conditions of the present time. I submit that such a free choice is far more likely to produce a secular increase in the beauty, in intellectual and physical activity and in the capacity of the race, than our present haphazard mercenariness.

The science student will be interested to read in this connection *The Ethic of Free Thought, Socialism in Theory and Practice,* and *The Chances of Death and other Studies in Evolution,* by Karl Pearson.

§ 7

Socialism is against human nature. This objection I have left until last because firstly it is absolutely true, and secondly it leads naturally to the newer ideas that have already peeped out once or twice in my earlier chapters and which will now ride up to a predominance in what follows and particularly the idea that an educational process and a moral discipline are not only a necessary part, but the most fundamental part of any complete Socialist scheme. Socialism is against human nature. That is true, and it is equally true of everything else; capitalism is against human nature, competition is against human nature, cruelty, kindness, religion and doubt, monogamy, polygamy, celibacy, decency, indecency, piety, and sin are all against human nature. The present system in particular is against human nature, or what is the policeman for, the soldier, the debt-collector, the judge, the hangman? What means the glass along my neighbour's wall? Human nature is

against human nature. For human nature is in a perpetual conflict; it is the Ishmael of the Universe, against
everything, and with everything against it; and within,
no more and no less than a perpetual battleground of
passion, desire, cowardice, indolence, and good will.
So that our initial proposition, as it stands at the head
of this section, is as an argument against Socialism, just
worth nothing at all.

None the less valuable is it as a reminder of the essential constructive task of which the two primary generalizations of Socialism we have so far been developing
are but the outward and visible forms. There is no
naturalness in Socialism, no uneducated pristine force on
our side. I have tried to let it become apparent that
while I do firmly believe, not only in the splendour and
nobility of the Socialist dream, but in its ultimate practicality, I do also recognize quite clearly that with people
just as they are now, with their prejudices, their ig-
norances, their misapprehensions, their unchecked vani-
ties and greeds and jealousies, their untutored and mis-
guided instincts, their irrational traditions, no Socialist
state can exist, no better state can exist, than the one
we have now with all its squalor and cruelty. Every
change in human institutions must happen concurrently
with a change in ideas. Upon this plastic, uncertain,
teachable thing human nature, within us and without,

we have if we really contemplate Socialism as our achievement, to impose guiding ideas and guiding habits, we have to coördinate all the Good Will that is active or latent in our world in one constructive plan. To-day the spirit of humanity is lost to itself, divided, dispersed, and hidden in little narrow distorted circles of thought. These divided, misshapen circles of thought are not "human nature," but human nature has fallen into these forms and has to be released. Our fundamental business is to develop the human spirit. It is in the enlargement and enrichment of the average circle of thought that the essential work and method of Socialism is to be found.

CHAPTER X

SOCIALISM A DEVELOPING DOCTRINE

§ 1

So far we have been discussing the broad elementary propositions of modern Socialism. As we have dealt with them, they amount to little more than a sketch of the foundation for a great scheme of social reconstruction. It would be a poor service to Socialism to pretend that this scheme is complete. From this point onward one enters upon a series of less unanimous utterances and more questionable suggestions. Concerning much of what follows, Socialism has as yet not elaborated its teaching. It has to do so, it is doing so, but huge labours lie before its servants. Before it can achieve any full measure of realization, it has to overcome problems at present but half solved, problems at present scarcely touched, the dark unsettling suggestion of problems that still await formulation. The anti-Socialist is freely welcome to all these admissions. No doubt they will afford grounds for some cheap transitory triumph. They affect our great generalizations not at all; they detract nothing from the fact that Socialism is the most inspiring, creative scheme that ever came into the chaos of human affairs. The fact that it is not cut and dried, that the scheme lives and grows, that every honest adherent adds not only to its forces but to its thought and spirit, is itself inspiration.

The new adherent to Socialism in particular must bear this in mind, that Socialism is no garment cut and finished that we can reasonably ask the world to wear forthwith. It is not that its essentials remain in doubt, it is not that it does not stand for things supremely true, but that its proper method and its proper expedients have still to be established. Over and above the propaganda of its main constructive ideas and the political work for their more obvious and practical application, an immense amount of intellectual work remains to be done for Socialism. The battle of Socialism is to be fought not simply at the polls and in the market-place, but at the writing desk and in the study. To many questions, the attitude of Socialism to-day is one of confessed inquiring imperfection.[1] It would indeed be very remarkable if a proposition for changes so vast and com-

[1] The student will find very clear, informing, and suggestive reading in Kirkup's *History of Socialism*. (A. and C. Black, 1906.) A fine impartial account of these developments which may be used as a correction (or confirmation) for this book.

prehensive as Socialism advances was in any different state at this present time.

It is so recently as 1835 that the world first heard the word Socialism. It appeared then, with the vaguest implications and the most fluctuating definition, as a general term for a disconnected series of protests against the extreme theories of Individualism and Individualist Political Economy; against the cruel, race-destroying, industrial spirit that then dominated the world. Of these protests the sociological suggestions and experiments of Robert Owen were most prominent in the English community, and he it is, more than any other single person, whom we must regard as the father of Socialism. But in France, ideas essentially similar were appearing about such movements and personalities as those of Saint Simon, Proudhon, and Fourier. They were part of a vast system of questionings and repudiations, political doubts, social doubts, hesitating inquiries, and experiments.

It is only to be expected that early Socialism should now appear as not only an extremely imperfect but a very inconsistent system of proposals. Its value lay not so much in its plans as in its hopeful and confident denials. It had hold of one great truth, it moved one great amendment to the conception of practical human equality the French Revolution had formulated, and that was its clear indication of the evil of unrestricted private property and of the necessary antagonism of the interests of the individual to the commonweal that went with that. While most men had to go propertyless in a world that was privately owned, the assertion of equality was an empty lie. For the rest, primordial Socialism was entirely sketchy and experimental. It was wild as the talk of schoolboys. It disregarded the most obvious needs. It did not provide for any principle of government, or for the maintenance of collective thought and social determination; it offered no safeguards and guarantees for even the most elementary privacies and freedoms; it was extraordinarily not-constructive. It was extreme in its proposed abolition of the home, and it flatly ignored the huge process of transition needed for a change so profound and universal.

The early Socialism was immediately revolutionary. It had no patience. The idea was to be made into a definite project forthwith; Fourier drew up his compact scheme, arranged how many people should live in each *phalange*, and so forth, and all that remained to do, he thought, was to sow *phalanges* as one scatters poppy seed. With him it was to be Socialism by contagion; with many of his still hastier contemporaries it was to be Socialism by proclamation. All the evils of society were to crumble to ruins like the Walls of Jericho at the first onset of the Great Idea.

Our present generation is less buoyant, perhaps, but wiser. However young you may be as a reformer, you know you must face certain facts these early Socialists ignored. Whatever sort of community you dream of you realize that it has to be made of the sort of people you meet every day or of the children growing up under their influence. The damping words of the old philosopher to the ardent social reformer of seventeen were really the quintessence of our criticism of revolutionary Socialism: "Will your aunts join us, my dear? No! Well, is the grocer on our side? And the family solicitor? We shall have to provide for them all, you know, unless you suggest a lethal chamber."

For a generation Socialism, in the exaltation of its self-discovery, failed to measure these primary obstacles, failed to recognize the real necessity, the quality of the task of making these people understand. To this day the majority of Socialists still fail to grasp completely the Herbartian truth, the fact that every human soul moves within its *circle of ideas*, resisting enlargement, incapable indeed if once it is adult of any extensive enlargement, and that all effectual human progress can be achieved only through such enlargement. Only ideas cognate to a circle of ideas are assimilated or assimilable; ideas too alien, though you shout them in the ear, thrust them in the face, remain foreign and incomprehensible.

P

The early Socialists, arriving at last at their Great Idea, after toilsome questionings, after debates, disputations, studies, trials, *saw*, and instantly couldn't understand those others who did not see; they failed altogether to realize the leaps they had made, the brilliant omissions they had achieved, the difficulties they had evaded to get to this magnificent conception. I suppose such impatience is as natural and understandable as it is unfortunate. None of us escape it. Much of this early Socialism is as unreal as mathematics, has much the same relation to truth as the abstract absolute process of calculation has to concrete individual things; much of it more than justifies altogether that "black or white" method of criticism of which I wrote in the preceding chapter. They were as downright and unconsidering, as little capable of the reasoned middle attitude. Proudhon, perceiving that the world was obsessed by a misconception of the scope of property whereby the many were enslaved to the few, went off at a tangent to the announcement that "Property is Robbery," an exaggeration that, as I have already shown, still haunts Socialist discussion. The ultimate factor of all human affairs, the psychological factor, was disregarded. Like the classic mathematical problem, early Socialism was always "neglecting the weight of the elephant" or some other — from the practical point of view — equally essential factor. This was perhaps an unavoidable stage. It is probable that by no other means than such exaggeration and partial statement could Socialism have got itself begun. The world of 1830 was fatally wrong in its ideas of property; early Socialism rose up and gave those ideas a flat, extreme, outrageous contradiction. After that, analysis and discussion became possible.

The early Socialist literature teems with rash, suggestive schemes. It has the fertility, the confusion, the hopefulness, the promise of glowing youth. It is a quarry of ideas, a mine of crude expedients, a fountain of emotions. The abolition of money, the substitution of labour notes, the possibility, justice, and advantage of equalizing upon a time-basis the remuneration of the worker, the relation of the new community to the old family, a hundred such topics were ventilated — were not so much ventilated as tossed about in an impassioned gale.

Much of this earlier Socialist literature was like Cabet's book, actually Utopian in form; a still larger proportion was Utopian in spirit; its appeal was imaginative, and it aimed to be a plan of a new state as definite and detailed as the plan for the building of a house. It has been the fashion with a number of later Socialist writers and speakers, mind-struck with that blessed word "evolution," confusing "scientific," a popular epithet to which they aspired, with "unimaginative," to sneer at the Utopian method, to make a sort of ideal of a leaden practicality, but it does not follow because the Utopias produced and the experiments attempted were in many aspects unreasonable and absurd that the method itself is an unsound one. At a certain phase of every creative effort you must cease to study the thing that is, and plan the thing that is not. The early Socialisms were only premature plans and hasty working models that failed to work.

And it must be remembered when we consider Socialism's early extravagancies, that any idea or system of ideas which challenges the existing system is necessarily, in relation to that system, outcast. Mediocre men go soberly on the highroads, but saints and scoundrels meet in the jails. If A and B rebel against the government, they are apt, although they rebel for widely different reasons, to be classed together; they are apt, indeed, to be thrown together and tempted to sink even quite essential differences in making common cause against the enemy. So that from its very beginning Socialism was mixed up — to this day it remains mixed up — with other movements of revolt and criticism, with which it has no very natural connection. There is, for example, the unfortunate entanglement between the Socialist theory and that repudiation of any but subjective sexual limitations which is called "free love," and there is that still more unfortunate association of its rebellion against orthodox economic theories, with rebellion against this or that system of religious teaching. Several of the early Socialist communities again rebelled against orthodox clothing, and their women made short hair and bloomers the outward and visible associations of the communistic idea. I have done my very best (in Chapter VIII, § 2) to clear the exposition of Socialism from these entanglements, but it is well to recognize that these are no corruptions of its teaching, but an inevitable birth infection that has still to be completely overcome.

§ 2

The comprehensively constructive spirit of modern Socialism is very much to seek in these childhood phases that came before Marx. These early projects were for the most part developed by literary men (and by one philosophic business man, Owen) to whose circle of ideas the conception of state organization and administration was foreign. They took peace and order for granted — they left out the schoolmaster, the judge, and the policeman, as the amateur architect of the anecdote left out the staircase. They set out to contrive a better industrial organization, or a better social atmosphere within the present scheme of things. They wished to reform what they understood, and what was outside their circle of ideas they took for granted, as they took the sky and sea. Not only was their literature Utopian literature about little islands of things begun over again from the beginning, but their activities tended in the direction of Utopian experiments equally limited and isolated. Here again a just critic will differ from many contemporary Socialists in their depreciation of this sort of work. Owen's experiments in socialized production were of enormous educational and scientific value. They were, to use a mining expert's term, "hand specimens" of human welfare of the utmost value to promoters. They made factory legislation possible; they initiated the now immense coöperative movement; they stirred commonplace imaginations as only achievement can stir them; they initiated a process of amelioration in industrial conditions that will never, I believe, cease again until the Socialist State is attained.

But apart from Owen and the general advertisement given to Socialist ideas, it must be admitted that a great majority of Socialist communities have, by every material standard, failed rather than succeeded. Some went visibly insolvent and to pieces; others were changed by prosperity. Some were wrecked by the sudden lapse of the treasurer into an extreme individualism. Essentially, Socialism is a project for the species, but these communities made it a system of relationships within a little group; to the world without they had necessarily to turn a competitive face, to buy and sell and advertise on the lines of the system as it is. If they failed, they failed; if they succeeded, they presently found themselves landlords, employers, no more and no less than a corporate individualism. I have described elsewhere [1] the fate of the celebrated Oneida Community of New York State, and how it is now converted into an aggressive, wealthy, fighting corporation of the most modern type, employing immigrant labour.

Professed and conscious Socialism in its earliest stages, then, was an altogether extreme proposition; it was at once imperfect and over-emphatic, and it was confused with many quite irrelevant and inconsistent novelties with regard to diet, dress, medicine, and religion. Its first manifest, acknowledged, and labelled fruits were a series of futile "communities" — Noyes's *History of American Socialisms* gives their simple history of births and of fatal infantile ailments — Brook Farm, Fourierite "Phalanges," and the like. But correlated with these extreme efforts, drawing ideas and inspiration from them, was the great philanthropic movement for the amelioration of industrialism, that was, I insist, for all its absence of a definite Socialist label, in many cases, an equally legitimate factor in the mak-

[1] *The Future in America.* (Chapman and Hall, 1906.)

ing of the great conception of modern Socialism.
Socialism may be the child of the French Revolution,
but it certainly has one aristocratic Tory grandparent.
There can be little dispute of the close connection of Lord
Shaftesbury's Factory Acts, that commencement of
constructive statesmanship in industrialism, with the
work of Owen. The whole Victorian period marks a
steady development of social organization out of the
cruel economic anarchy of its commencement; the beginnings of public education, adulteration acts, and
similar checks upon the extremities of private enterprise,
the great successful experiments of coöperative distribution, and the first appearance of what has now become
a quasi-official representation of labour in the state
through the trades unions. Two great writers, Car-
lyle and Ruskin, the latter a professed Socialist, spent
their powers in a relentless campaign against the harsh
theories of the liberty of property, the gloomy supersti-
tions of political economy that barred the way to any
effectual constructive scheme. An enormous work was
done throughout the whole Victorian period by Socialists and Socialistic writers, in criticising and modifying
the average circle of ideas, in bringing conceptions that
had once seemed weird, outcast and altogether fantastic,
more and more within the range of acceptable practicality.

The first early Socialisms were most various and eccentric upon the question of government and control. They had no essential political teaching. Many, but by no means all, were inspired by the democratic idealism of the first French Revolution. They believed in a mystical something that was wiser and better than any individual, the People, the Common Man. But that was by no means the case with all of them. The Noyes community was a sort of theocratic autocracy; the Saint Simonian tendency was aristocratic. The English Socialism that in the middle Victorian period developed partly out of the suggestions of Owen's beginnings and partly as an independent fresh outpouring of the struggling Good Will in man, that English Socialism that found a voice in Ruskin and in Maurice and Kingsley and the Christian Socialists, was certainly not democratic. It kept much of what was best in "the public spirit" of contemporary English life, and it implied, if it did not postulate, a "governing class." Benevolent and even generous in conception, its exponents betray all too often the ties of social habituations, the limited circle of ideas of English upper and upper middle-class life, easy and cultivated, well served and distinctly, most unmistakably, authoritative.

While the experimental Utopian Socialisms gave a sort of variegated and conflicting pattern of a reorganized industrialism and (incidentally to that) a new heaven and earth, the benevolent Socialism, Socialistic liberalism, and Socialistic philanthropy of the middle Victorian period, really went very little farther in effect than a projected amelioration and moralization of the relations of rich and poor. It needed the impact of an entirely new type of mind before Socialism began to perceive its own significance as an ordered scheme for the entire reconstruction of the world, began to realize the gigantic breadth of its implications.

CHAPTER XI

REVOLUTIONARY SOCIALISM

§ 1

IT was Karl Marx who brought the second great influx of suggestion into the intellectual process of Socialism. Before his time there does not seem to have been any clear view of economic relationships- as having laws of development, as having interactions that began and went on and led toward new things. But Marx had visions. He had, as Darwin and the evolutionists had, as most men with a scientific training, and many educated men without that advantage now have, a sense of secular change. Instead of being content with the accepted picture of the world as a scene where men went on producing and distributing wealth and growing rich or poor, — it might be for endless ages, — he made an appeal to history and historical analogies, and for the first time viewed our age of individualist industrial development, not as a possible permanent condition of humanity, but as something unstable and in motion, as an economic process; that is to say, with a beginning, a middle, and as he saw it, an almost inevitable end.

The last thing men contrive to discern in every question is the familiar obvious, and it came as a great and shattering discovery to the economic and sociological thought of the latter half of the nineteenth century that there was going on not simply a production, but an immense concentration of wealth, a differentiation of a special wealthy class of landholder and capitalist, a diminution of small property owners and the development of a great and growing class of landless, nearly propertyless men, the *proletariat*. Marx showed — he showed so clearly that to-day it is recognized by every intelligent man — that, *given a continuance of our industrial and commercial system,* of uncontrolled gain seeking; that is, given a continuance of our present spirit and ideas of property, there must necessarily come a time when the owner and the proletarian will stand face to face, with nothing—if we accept a middle class of educated professionals dependent on the wealthy, who are after all no more than the upper stratum of the proletariat, to mask or mitigate their opposition. We shall have two classes, the class-conscious worker and the class-conscious owner, and they will be at war. And with a broad intellectual sweep he flung the light of this conception upon the whole contemporary history of mankind. His *Capital* has no sketch of Utopias, no limitation to the conditions or possibilities of this country or

that. "Here," he says in the widest way, "is what is
going on all over the world. So long as practically untrammelled private property, such as you conceive it
to-day, endures, this must go on. The worker gravi-
tates steadily everywhere to a bare subsistence; the rest
of the proceeds of his labour swells the power of the owners. So it will go on while gain and getting are the rule
of your system, until accumulated tensions between class
and class smash this present social organization and
inaugurate a new age."

In considering the thought and work of Karl Marx,
the reader must bear in mind the epoch in which that
work commenced. The intellectual world was then
under the sway of an organized mass of ideas known as
the Science of Political Economy, a mass of ideas that
has now not so much been examined and refuted as
slipped away imperceptibly from its hold upon the
minds of men. In the beginning, in the hands of Adam
Smith, — whose richly suggestive books are now all too
little read, — political economy was a broad-minded and
sane inquiry into the statecraft of trade based upon
current assumptions of private ownership and personal
motives, but from him it passed to men of, perhaps, in
some cases quite equal intellectual energy, but inferior
vision and range. The history of Political Economy is
indeed one of the most striking instances of the mis-

chief wrought by intellectual minds devoid of vision in
the entire history of human thought. Special definition,
technicality, are the stigmata of second-rate intellectual
men; they cannot work with the universal tool, they
cannot appeal to the general mind. They must abstract and separate. On such men fell the giant's robe
of Adam Smith, and they wore it after their manner.
Their arid atmospheres are intolerant of clouds, an
outline that is not harsh is abominable to them. They
criticised their master's vagueness, and must needs
mend it. They sought to give political economy a
precision and conviction such a subject will not stand.
They took such words as " *value*," an incurably and
necessarily vague word, " *rent*," the name of the specific
relation of landlord and tenant, and " *capital*," and
sought to define them with relentless exactness and use
them with inevitable effect. So doing they departed
more and more from reality. They developed a literature more abundant, more difficult and less real than all
the exercises of the schoolmen put together. To use
common words in uncommon meanings is to sow a
jungle of misunderstanding. It was only to be expected that the bulk of this economic literature resolves
upon analysis into a ponderous, intricate, often aston-
ishingly able and foolish wrangling about terminology.

Now in the early Victorian period in which Marx

planned his theorizing, political economy ruled the educated world. Ruskin had still to attack the primary
assumptions of that tyrannous and dogmatic edifice.
The duller sort of educated people talked of the "im-
mutable laws of political economy" in the blankest
ignorance that the basis of everything in this so-called
science was a plastic human convention. Humane
impulses were checked, creative effort tried and condemned by these mystical formulæ. Political economy
traded on the splendid achievements of physics and
chemistry and pretended to an equally inexorable authority. Only a man of supreme courage, intelligence and
power, a man resolved to give his lifetime to the task,
could afford in those days to combat the pretensions of
the political economist; to deny that his categories presented scientific truth, and to cast that jargon side. As
for Marx, he saw fit to accept the verbal instruments of
his time (albeit he bent them not a little in use), to
accommodate himself to their spirit, and to split and
reclassify and redefine them at his need. So that he has
become already difficult to follow, and his more specialized exponents among Socialists use terms that arouse
no echoes in the contemporary mind. The days when
Socialism need present its theories in terms of a science
whose fundamental propositions it repudiates, are at
an end. One hears less and less of "surplus value" now,

as one hears less and less of Ricardo's theory of Rent. It may crop up in the inquiries of some intelligent mechanic seeking knowledge among the obsolescent accumulations of a public library, or it may for a moment be touched upon by some veteran teacher. But the time when social and economic science had to choose between debatable and inexpressive technicalities on the one hand, or the stigma of empiricism on the other, is altogether past.

The language a man uses, however, is of far less importance than the thing he has to say, and it detracts little from the cardinal importance of Marx that his books will presently demand restatement in contemporary phraseology, and revision in the light of contemporary facts. He opened out Socialism. It is easy to quibble about Marx, and say he didn't see this or that, to produce this eddy in a backwater, or that as a triumphant refutation of his general theory. One may quibble about the greatness of Marx, as one may quibble about the greatness of Darwin, he remains great and cardinal. He first saw and enabled this world to see capitalistic production as a world process, passing by necessity through certain stages of social development, and unless some change of law and spirit came to modify it, moving toward an inevitable destiny. His followers are too apt to regard that as an absolutely inevitable destiny, but the fault of that lies not at his door. He saw that destiny as Socialism. It did not appear to him as it does to many that there is a possible alternative to Socialism, that the process may give us, not a triumph for the revolting proletariat, but their defeat, and the establishment of a plutocratic aristocracy culminating in Imperialism and ending in social disintegration. From his study, from the studious rotunda of the British Museum Reading Room, he made his prophecy of the growing class consciousness of the workers, of the inevitable class war, of the revolution and the millennium that was to follow it. He gathered his facts, elaborated his deductions, and waited for the dawn.

So far as his broad generalizations of economic development go, events have wonderfully confirmed Marx. The development of Trusts, the concentration of property that America in particular displays, he foretold. Given that men keep to the unmodified ideas of private property and individualism, and it seems absolutely true that so the world must go. And in the American *Appeal to Reason*, for example, which goes out weekly from Kansas to a quarter of a million of subscribers, one may, if one chooses, see the developing class consciousness of the workers, and the promise—and when strikers take to rifles and explosives, as they do in Pennsylvania

Q

and Colorado, something more than the promise of the class war.

But the modern Socialist considers that this generalization is a little too confident and comprehensive; he perceives that a change in custom, law, or public opinion may delay, arrest, or invert the economic process, that Socialism may arrive after all, not by a social convulsion, but by the gradual and detailed concession of its propositions. The Marxist presents dramatically what, after all, may come methodically and unromantically, a revolution as orderly and quiet as the procession of the Equinoxes. There may be a concentration of capital and a relative impoverishment of the general working mass of people, for example, and yet a general advance in the world's prosperity and a growing sense of social duty in the owners of capital and land may do much to mask this antagonism of class interests and ameliorate its miseries. Moreover, this antagonism itself may in the end find adequate expression through temperate discussion, and the class war come disguised beyond recognition, with hates mitigated by charity and swords beaten into pens, a mere constructive conference between two classes of fairly well-intentioned albeit perhaps still biassed men and women.

§ 2

The circle of ideas in which Marx moved was that of a student deeply tinged with the idealism of the renascent French Revolution. His life was the life of a recluse from affairs, an invalid's life; a large part of it was spent round and about the British Museum reading-room, and his conceptions of Socialism and the social process have at once the spacious vistas given by the historical habit and the abstract quality that comes with a divorce from practical experience of human government. Only in England and in the eighties did the expanding propositions of Socialism come under the influence of men essentially administrative. As a consequence Marx, and still more the early "Marxists" were and are negligent of the necessities of government and crude in their notions of class action. He saw the economic process with a perfect lucidity; practically he foretold the consolidation of the Trusts, and his statement of the necessary development of an entirely propertyless working-class with an intensifying class-consciousness is a magnificent generalization. He saw clearly up to that opposition of the many and the few, and then his vision failed because his experience and interests failed. There was to be a class-war, and numbers schooled to discipline by industrial organization were to win.

After that the teaching weakens in conviction. The proletariat was to win in the class-war; then classes would be abolished, property in the means of production and distribution would be abolished, all men would work reasonably, and the millennium would be with us.

The constructive part of the Marxist programme was too slight. It has no psychology. Contrasted, indeed, with the splendid destructive criticisms that preceded it, it seems indeed trivial. It diagnoses a disease admirably and then suggests rather an incantation than a plausible remedy. And as a consequence Marxist Socialism appeals only very feebly to the man of public affairs or business or social experience. It does not attract teachers or medical men or engineers. It arouses such men to a sense of social instability, but it offers no remedy. They do not believe in the mystical wisdom of the People. They find no satisfactory promise of a millennium in anything Marx foretold.

To the labouring man, however, accustomed to take direction and government as he takes air and sky, these difficulties of the administrative and constructive mind do not occur. His imagination raises no questioning in that picture of the proletariat triumphant after a class-war and quietly coming to its own. It does not occur to him for an instant to ask, " How? "

Question the common Marxist upon these difficulties

and he will relapse magnificently into the doctrine of *laissez-faire.* "That will be all right," he will tell you.

"How?"

"We'll take over the trusts and run them."

It is part of the inconveniences attending all powerful new movements of the human mind that the disciple bolts with the teacher, overstates him, underlines him, and it is no more than a tribute to the potency of Marx that he should have paralyzed the critical faculty in a number of very able men. To them Marx is a final form of truth. They talk with bated breath of a "classic socialism," to which no man may add one jot or one tittle, to which they are as uncritically pledged as extreme Bible Christians are bound to the letter of the "Word." . . .

The peculiar evil of the Marxist teaching is this: that it carries the conception of a necessary economic development to the pitch of fatalism; it declares, with all the solemnity of popular "science," that Socialism *must* prevail. Such a fatalism is morally bad for the adherent: it releases him from the inspiring sense of uncertain victory, it leads him to believe the stars in their courses will do his job for him. The common Marxist is apt to be sterile of effort therefore and intolerant — preaching predestination and salvation without works.

By a circuitous route, indeed, the Marxist reaches a moral position curiously analogous to that of the disciple of Herbert Spencer. Since all improvement will arrive by leaving things alone, the worse things get, the better; for so much the nearer one comes to the final exaspera- tion, to the class-war and the triumph of the proletariat. This certainty of victory in the nature of things makes the Marxists difficult in politics, pedantic sticklers for the letter of the teaching, obstinate opponents of what they call "Palliatives"—of any instalment system of re- form. They wait until they can make the whole journey in one stride and would, in the meanwhile, have no one set forth upon the way. In America the Marxist fatal- ism has found a sort of supreme simplification in the gospel of Mr. H. G. Wilshire. The trusts, one learns, are to consolidate all the industry in the country, own all the property. Then when they own everything, the nation will take them over. "Let the nation own the trusts!" The nation in the form of a public, reading capitalistic newspapers, inured to capitalistic methods, represented and ruled by capital-controlled politicians, will suddenly take over the trusts and begin a new system. . . .

It would be quite charmingly easy, if it were only in the remotest degree credible.

§ 3

The Marxist teaching tends to an unreasonable fatalism. Its conception of the world after the class-

war is over is equally antagonistic to intelligent constructive effort. It faces that Future, utters the word
"democracy," and veils its eyes.

The conception of democracy to which the Marxist ad-
heres is that same mystical democracy that was evolved
at the first French Revolution; it will sanction no analysis of the popular wisdom. It postulates a sort of spirit
hidden, as it were, in the masses and only revealed by a
universal suffrage of all adults or, according to some social
democratic federation, authorities who do not believe
in women, all adult males, at the ballot-box. Even a
large proportion of the adults will not do, — it must be all.
The mysterious spirit that thus peers out and vanishes
again at each election is the People, not any particular
person, but the quintessence, and it is supposed to be
infallible; it is supposed to be not only morally but
intellectually omniscient. It will not even countenance
the individuality of elected persons, they are to be mere
tools, *delegates*, from this diffused, intangible Oracle,
the Ultimate Wisdom.

Well, it may seem ungracious to sneer at the gro-
tesque formulation of an idea profoundly wise, at the
hurried, wrong, arithmetical method of rendering that
collective spirit a community undoubtedly can and
sometimes does possess, — I myself am the profoundest
believer in democracy, in a democracy awake intellec-

tually, conscious, and self-disciplined,—but so long as this mystic faith in the crowd, this vague, emotional, uncritical way of evading the immense difficulties of organizing just government and a collective will prevails, so long must the Socialist project remain not simply an impracticable, but, in an illiterate, badly organized community, even a dangerous suggestion. I as a Socialist am not blind to these possibilities, and it is foolish because a man is in many ways on one's side that one should not call attention to his careless handling of a loaded gun. Social-Democracy may conceivably become a force that in the sheer power of untutored faith may destroy government and not replace it. I do not know how far that is not already the case in Russia. I do not know how far this may not ultimately be the case in the United States of America.

The Marxist teaching, great as was its advance on the dispersed chaotic Socialism that preceded it, was defective in other directions as well as in its innocence of any scheme of state organization. About women and children, for example, it was ill-informed; its founders do not seem to have been inspired either by educational necessities or philoprogenitive passion. No biologist — indeed no scientific mind at all — seems to have tempered its severely "economic" tendencies. Indeed it so over-accentuates the economic side of life that at moments one might imagine it dealt solely with some world of purely "productive" immortals, who were never born and never aged, but only warred forever in a developing industrial process.

Now reproduction and not production is the more central fact of social life. Women and children and education are things in the background of the Marxist proposal — like a man's dog or his private reading or his pet rabbits. They are in the foreground of modern Socialism. The Social-Democrat's doctrines go little further in this direction than the liberalism that founded the United States, which ignored women, children, and niggers, and made the political unit the adult white man. They were blind to the supreme importance of making the next generation better than the present as the aim and effort of the whole community. Herr Bebel's book, *Woman*, is an ample statement of the evils of woman's lot under the existing régime, but the few pages upon the future of woman with which he concludes are eloquent of the jejune insufficiency of the Marxite outlook in this direction. Marriage as a social fact is to vanish; women are to count as men so far as the state is concerned. That is all. . . .

This disregard of the primary importance of births and upbringing in human affairs and this advocacy of

mystical democracy alike contribute to blind the Marxist
to the necessity of an educational process and of discipline
in the Socialist scheme. He can say with a light and
confident heart to untrained, ignorant, groping souls,
"destroy the government; expropriate the rich; establish manhood suffrage; elect delegates, strictly pledged,
— and you will be happy!"

A few modern Marxists stipulate in addition for a
referendum, by which the activities of the elected delegates can be further checked by referring disputed
matters to a general vote of all the adults in the community. . . .

§ 4

My memory, as I write these things of Marxism,
carries me to the dusky largeness of a great meeting in
Queen's Hall, and I see again the back of Mr. Hyndman's head moving quickly, as he receives and answers
questions. It was really one of the strangest and most
interesting meetings I have ever attended. It was a
great rally of the Social-Democratic federation, and the
place, floor, galleries and platform, was thick but by
no means overcrowded with dingy, earnest people.
There was a great display of red badges and red ties, and
many white faces, and I was struck by the presence of
girls and women with babies. It was more like the

Socialist meetings of the popular novel than any I had ever seen before. In the chair that night was Lady Warwick, that remarkable intruder into the class conflict; a blond lady rather expensively dressed, I should judge, about whom the atmosphere of class-consciousness seemed to thicken. Her fair hair, her floriferous hat, told out against the dim multitudinous values of the gathering unquenchably; there were moments when one might have fancied it was simply a gathering of village tradespeople about the lady patroness, and at the end of the proceedings, after the red flag had been waved, after the "Red Flag" had been sung by a choir and damply echoed by the audience, some one moved a vote of thanks to the Countess in terms of familiar respect that completed the illusion.

Mr. Hyndman's lecture was "In the Rapids of Revolution," and he had been explaining how inevitable the whole process was, how Russia drove ahead, and Germany and France and America, to the foretold crisis and the foretold millennium. But incidentally he also made a spirited exhortation for effort, for agitation, and he taunted England for lagging in the schemes of fate. Some one amidst the dim multitude discovered an inconsistency in that.

Now the questions were being handed in, written on strips of paper, and at last that listener's difficulty

cropped up. "What's this?" said Mr. Hyndman, un-
folded the slip and read out, "Why trouble to agitate or
work if the trusts are going to do it all for us?"

The veteran leader of the Social-Democratic federation paused only for a moment.

"Well, we've got to get *ready* for it, you know," he said,
rustling briskly with the folds of the question to follow,
and with these words, it seemed to me, that fatalistic
Marxism crumbled down to dust.

We *have* got to get ready for it. Indeed we have to
make it, by education and intention and set resolve.
Socialism is to be attained, not by fate, but by will.

§ 5

And here, as a sort of Eastern European gloss upon
Marxist Socialism, as an extreme and indeed ultimate
statement of this marriage of mystical democracy to
Socialism, we may say a word of Anarchism. Anarchism carries the administrative *laissez-faire* of Marx to
its logical extremity. "If the common, untutored man
is right anyhow — why these ballot-boxes? why these
intermediaries in the shape of law and representative?"

That is the perfectly logical outcome of ignoring
administration and reconstruction. The extreme Social-
Democrat and the extreme Individualist meet in a
doctrine of non-resistance to the forces of Evolution —

which in this connection they deify with a capital letter. Organization, control, design, the disciplined will, these are evil, they declare, *the* evil of life. So you come at the end of the process, if you are active-minded, to the bomb as the instrument of man's release to unimpeded virtue, and if you are pacific in disposition, to the Tolstoyan attitude of passive resistance to all rule and property.

Anarchism, then, is, as it were, a final perversion of the Socialist stream, a last meandering of Socialist thought, released from vitalizing association with an active, creative experience. Anarchism comes when the Socialist repudiation of property is dropped into the circles of thought of men habitually ruled and habitually irresponsible, men limited in action and temperamentally adverse to the toil, to the vexatious rebuffs, and insufficiencies, the dusty effort, fatigue, and friction of the practical pursuit of a complex ideal. So that it most flourishes eastwardly where men, it would seem are least energetic and constructive, and explodes or dies on American soil.

Anarchism, with its knife and bomb, is a miscarriage of Socialism, an acephalous birth from that fruitful mother. It is an unnatural offspring, opposed in nature to its parent, for always from the beginning the constructive spirit, the ordering and organizing spirit, has been strong among Socialists. It was by a fallacy, an oversight, that *laissez-faire* in politics crept into a movement that was before all things an organized denial of *laissez-faire* in economic and social life. . . .

I write this of the Anarchism that is opposed to contemporary Socialism, the political Anarchism. But there is also another sort of Anarchism, which the student of these schools of thought must keep clear in his mind from this, the Anarchism of Tolstoy and William Morris, which waves no flag of black, and counsels no violence; which is indeed, I hazard, the moral ideal of all right-thinking men. It is worth while to define very clearly the relation of the second sort of Anarchism, the nobler Anarchism, to the toiling constructive Socialism which many of us now make our practical guide in life's activities, to say just where they touch and where they are apart.

Now the ultimate ideal of human intercourse is surely a way of life that is not litigious and not based upon jealously guarded rights, which is free from property, free from jealousy, and "above the law." There, there shall not be "marriage or giving in marriage." The whole mass of Christian teaching points to such an ideal; Paul and Christ turn again and again to the ideal of a world of "just men made perfect," in which right and beauty come by instinct, in which just laws and regulations are unnecessary and unjust ones impossible. "Turn your attention," says my friend, the Rev. Stewart Headlam, in his admirable tract on Christian Socialism: —

"Turn your attention to that series of teachings of Christ's which we call parables — comparisons, that is to say, between what Christ saw going on in the everyday world around him and the Kingdom of Heaven. If by the Kingdom of Heaven in these parables is meant a place up in the clouds, or merely a state in which people will be after death, then I challenge you to get any kind of meaning out of them whatever. But if by the Kingdom of Heaven is meant (as it is clear from other parts of Christ's teaching is the case) the righteous Society to be established upon earth, then they all have a plain and beautiful meaning; a meaning well summed up in that saying so often quoted against us by the sceptic and the atheist, 'Seek ye first the Kingdom of God and His righteousness, and all these things shall be added unto you'; or in other words, live, Christ said, all of you together, not each of you by himself; live as members of the righteous society which I have come to found upon earth, and then you will be clothed as beautifully as the Eastern lily and fed as surely as the birds."

This is not simply the Christian ideal of society, it is the ideal of every right-thinking man, of every man with a full sense of beauty. You will find it rendered in two imperishably beautiful Utopias of our own time, both, I glory to write, by Englishmen: the *News from Nowhere* of William Morris and Hudson's exquisite *Crystal Age*. Both these present practically Anarchist states, both assume idealized human beings, beings finer, simpler, nobler than the heated, limited, and striving poor souls who thrust and suffer among the stresses of this present life. And the present writer too — I must mention him here to guard against a confusion in the future—when a little while ago he imagined humanity exalted morally and intellectually by the brush of a comet's tail,[1] presented not a Socialist state, but a glorious Anarchism, as the outcome of that rejuvenescence of the world.

But the business of Socialism lies at a lower level and concerns immediate things; our material is the world as it is, full of unjust laws, bad traditions, bad habits, inherited diseases and weaknesses, germs and poisons, filths and envies. We are not dealing with magnificent creatures such as one sees in ideal paintings and splendid sculpture, so beautiful they may face the world naked and unashamed; we are dealing with hot-eared, ill-kempt people, who are liable to indigestion, baldness, corpulence, and fluctuating tempers, who wear top hats and bowler hats or hats kept on by hatpins (and so with all the other necessary clothing); who are pitiful and weak and vain and touchy almost beyond measure, and very naughty and intemperate; who have, alas! to be bound over to be in any degree faithful and just to one another. To strip such people suddenly of law and

---

[1] *In the Days of the Comet.* (Macmillan and Co., 1906.)

restraint would be as dreadful and ugly as stripping the clothes from their poor bodies.

That Anarchist world, I admit, is our dream; we do believe—well, I, at any rate, believe—this present world, this planet, will some day bear a race beyond our most exalted and temerarious dreams, a race begotten of our wills and the substance of our bodies, a race, so I have said it, "who will stand upon the earth as one stands upon a footstool and laugh and reach out their hands amidst the stars," but the way to that is through education and discipline and law. Socialism is the preparation for that higher Anarchism; painfully, laboriously we mean to destroy false ideas of property and self, eliminate unjust laws and poisonous and hateful suggestions and prejudices, create a system of social right-dealing and a tradition of right feeling and acting. Socialism is the schoolroom of true and noble Anarchism, wherein by training and restraint we shall make free men.

There is a graceful and all too little known fable by Mr. Max Beerbohm, *The Happy Hypocrite*, which gives, I think, not only the relation of Socialism to philosophic Anarchism, but of all discipline to all idealism. It is the story of a beautiful mask that was worn by a man in love, until he tired even of that much of deceit and, a little desperately, threw it aside — to find his own face beneath changed to the likeness of the self he had

R

desired. So would we veil the greed, the suspicion of the self-seeking scramble of to-day under institutions and laws that will cry "duty and service" in the ears and eyes of all mankind, keep down the evil so long and so effectually that at last law will be habit, and greed and self-seeking cease forever from being the ruling impulse of the world. Socialism is the mask that will mould the world to that better Anarchism of good men's dreams.

But these are long views, glimpses beyond the Socialist horizon. The people who would set up Anarchism to-day are people without human experience or any tempering of humour, only one shade less impossible than the odd one-sided queer beings one meets, ridiculously inaccessible to laughter, who invite one to set up consciously with them in the business of being Overmen, to rule a world full of our betters, by fraud and force. It is a vile teaching saved only from being horrible by being utterly asinine. For us the best is faith and humility, truth and service; our utmost glory is to have seen the vision and to have failed — not altogether. . . . For ourselves and such as we are, let us not "deal in pride," let us be glad to learn a little of this spirit of service, to achieve a little humility, to give ourselves to the making of Socialism and the civilized State without presumption — as children who are glad they may help in a work greater than themselves, and the toys that have heretofore engaged them.

CHAPTER XII

§ 1

MARX gave to Socialism a theory of world-wide social development, and rescued it altogether from the eccentric and localized associations of its earliest phases; he brought it so near to reality that it could appear as a force in politics, embodied first as the International Association of Working Men, and then as the Social-Democratic movement of the continent of Europe that commands to-day over a third of the entire poll of German voters. So much Marx did for Socialism. But if he broadened its application to the world, he narrowed its range to only the economic aspect of life. He arrested for a time the discussion of its biological and moral aspects altogether. He left it an incomplete doctrine of merely economic reconstruction supplemented by mystical democracy, and both its mysticism and incompleteness, while they offered no difficulties to a labouring man ignorant of affairs, rendered

243

it unsubstantial and unattractive to people who had any real knowledge of administration.

It was left chiefly to the little group of English people who founded the Fabian Society to supply a third system of ideas to the amplifying conception of Socialism, to convert Revolutionary Socialism into administrative Socialism.

This new development was essentially the outcome of the reaction of its broad suggestions of economic reconstruction upon the circle of thought of one or two young officials of genius and of one or two members of that politic-social stratum of society, the English "governing class." I make this statement, I may say, in the loosest possible spirit. The reaction is one that was not confined to England; it was to some extent inevitable wherever the new movement in thought became accessible to intelligent administrators and officials. But in the peculiar atmosphere of British public life, with its remarkable blend of individual initiative and a lively sense of the state, this reaction has had the freest development. There was, indeed, Fabianism before the Fabian Society; it would be ingratitude to some of the most fruitful social work of the middle Victorian period to ignore the way in which it has contributed in suggestion and justification to the Socialist synthesis. The city of Birmingham, for example, developed the most exten-

sive process of municipalization as the mere common-
sense of local patriotism. But the movement was without formulæ and correlation until the Fabians came.

That unorganized, unpaid public service of public-
spirited aristocrats and wealthy financial and business
people, the "governing class," which dominated the
British Empire throughout the nineteenth century, has,
through the absence of definite class boundaries in
England and the readiness of each class to take its tone
from the class above, given a unique quality to
British thought upon public questions, and to British
conceptions of Socialism. It has made the British mind
as a whole "administrative." As compared with the
American mind, for example, the British is state-con-
scious, the American state-blind. The American is, no
doubt, intensely patriotic, but the nation and the state
to which his patriotism points is something overhead
and comprehensive like the sky, like a flag hoisted, something, indeed, that not only does not but must not interfere with his ordinary business occupations. To have
public spirit, to be aware of the state as a whole, and to
have an administrative feeling toward it, is necessarily
to be accessible to constructive ideas, — that is to say, to
Socialistic ideas. In the history of thought in Victorian
Great Britain, one sees a constant conflict of this administrative disposition with the individualistic com-

mercialism of the aggressively trading and manufacturing class, the class that in America reigns unchallenged to this day. In the latter country Individualism reigns unchallenged, it is assumed; in the former it has fought an uphill fight against the traditions of Church and State, and has never absolutely prevailed. The political economists and Herbert Spencer were its prophets, and they never at any time held the public mind in any invincible grip. Since the eighties that grip has weakened altogether. Socialistic thought and legislation, therefore, was going on in Great Britain through all the Victorian period. Nevertheless, it was the Fabian Society that, in the eighties and through the intellectual impetus of at most four or five personalities, really brought this obstinately administrative spirit in British affairs into relation with Socialism as such.

The dominant intelligence of this group was Mr. Sidney Webb, and as I think of him thus coming after Marx to develop the third phase of Socialism, I am struck by the contrast with the big-bearded Socialist leaders of the earlier school and this small, active figure with the finely shaped head, the little imperial under the lip, the glasses, the slightly lisping, insinuating voice. He emerged as a Colonial Office clerk of conspicuous energy and capacity, and he was already the leader and "idea factory" of the Fabian Society when he married Miss Beatrice Potter, a brilliant student of sociological questions. Both he and she are devotees to social service, living laborious, ordered, austere, incessant lives, making the employment of secretaries their one extravagance and alternations between research and affairs their change of occupation.

A new type of personality altogether they were in the Socialist movement, which had hitherto been richer in eloquence than discipline. And during the past twenty years of the work of the Fabian Society, through their influence, one dominant question has prevailed. Assuming the truth of the two main generalizations of Socialism, taking that statement of intention for granted, *how is the thing to be done?* They put aside the glib assurances of the revolutionary Socialists that everything would be all right when the People came to their own and so earned for themselves the undying resentment of all those who believe the world is to be effectually mended by a liberal use of chest notes and red flags. They insisted that the administrative and economic methods of the future must be a secular development of existing institutions, and inaugurated a process of study,— which has long passed beyond the range of the Fabian Society, broadening out with the organized work of the school of economics and of a growing volume of university study in England and America, — to the end that this "*how?*" should be answered.

The broad lines of the process of transition from the present state of affairs to the Socialist state of the future as they are developed by administrative Socialism lie along the following lines:—

1. The peaceful and systematic taking over from private enterprise, by purchase or otherwise, either by the national or by the municipal authorities, as may be most convenient, of the great common services of land, control, mining, transit, food-supply, the drink trade, lighting, force-supply, and the like.

2. Secular expropriation of private owners by death-duties and increased taxation.

3. The exploitation of all new social services by the public authorities and not by private enterprise, the prevention, that is to say, of any additions to the present bulk of privately owned property.

4. The building up of a great scientifically organized administrative machinery to carry on these enlarging public functions.

5. A steady increase and expansion of public education, research, museums, libraries, and all such public services. The systematic promotion of measures for raising the school-leaving age, for the public feeding of school children, for the provision of public baths, parks, playgrounds, and the like.

6. The systematic creation of a great service of public health to take over the disorganized confusion of hospitals and other charities, sanitary authorities, officers of health and private enterprise medical men.

7. The recognition of the claim of every citizen to welfare by measures for the support of mothers and children, and by the establishment of old-age pensions.

8. The systematic raising of the minimum standard of life by factory and labour legislation, and particularly by the establishment of a minimum wage. . . .

These are the broad forms of the Fabian Socialist's answer to the question of *how*, with which the revolutionary Socialist's were confronted. The diligent student of Socialism will find all these proposals worked out to a very practicable-looking pitch, indeed, in that Bible of Progressive Socialism, the collected tracts of the Fabian Society,[1] and to that volume I must refer him. The theory of the minimum standard and the minimum wage is explained, moreover, with the utmost lucidity in that Socialist classic, *Industrial Democracy*, by Sidney and Beatrice Webb.

§ 2

Every movement has the defects of its virtues, and it is not perhaps very remarkable that the Fabian Society

[1] *Fabian Tracts.* (Fabian Society, 4/6.)

of the eighties and nineties, having introduced the conception of the historical continuity of institutions into the propaganda of Socialism, did certainly for a time greatly overaccentuate that conception and draw away attention from aspects that may be ultimately more essential.

Beginning with the proposition that the institutions and formulæ of the future must necessarily be developed from those of the present, that one cannot start *de novo* even after a revolution; one may easily end in an attitude of excessive conservatism toward existing machinery. In spite of the presence of such fine and original intelligences as Mr. Sydney Olivier and Mr. Graham Wallas in the Fabian counsels, there can be no denial that for the first twenty years of the society's career, Mr. Webb was the prevailing Fabian. Now his is a mind legal as well as creative, and at times his legal side quite overcomes his constructive element; he is extraordinarily fertile in expedients and skilful in adaptation, and with a real dread of open destruction. This statement by no means exhausts him, but it does to a large extent convey the qualities that were uppermost in the earlier years, at any rate, of his influence. His insistence upon continuity pervaded the society, was reëchoed and intensified by others, and developed into something like a mania for achieving Socialism without the overt change of any existing ruling body. His impetus carried this reaction against the crude democratic idea to its extremest opposite. There arose Webbites more Webbish than Webb. From saying that the unorganized people cannot achieve Socialism, they passed to the implication that organization alone, without popular support, might achieve Socialism. Socialism was to arrive, as it were, insidiously.

To some minds this new proposal has the charm of a schoolboy's first dark-lantern. Socialism ceased to be an open revolution, and became a plot. Functions were to be shifted, quietly, unostentatiously, from the representative to the official he appointed; a bureaucracy was to slip into power through the mechanical difficulties of an administration by debating representatives; and since these officials would by the nature of their positions constitute a scientific bureaucracy, and since Socialism is essentially scientific government as distinguished from haphazard government, they would necessarily run the country on the lines of a pretty distinctly undemocratic Socialism.

The process went even further than secretiveness in its reaction from the large rhetorical forms of revolutionary Socialism. There arose even a repudiation of "principles" of action, and a type of worker which proclaimed itself "Opportunist-Socialist." It was another instance of Socialism losing sight of itself; it was a process quite parallel at the other extreme with the self-contradiction of the Anarchist-Socialist. Socialism as distinguished from a mere Liberalism, for example, is an organized plan for social reconstruction, while Liberalism relies upon certain vague "principles"; it declares that good intentions and doing first-hand things and obvious things will not suffice. Now Opportunism is essentially benevolent adventure and the doing of first-hand things.

This conception of indifference to the forms of government, of accepting whatever governing bodies existed and using them to create officials and *get something done* was at once immediately fruitful in many directions, and presently productive of many very grave difficulties in the path of advancing Socialism. Mr. Webb, himself, devoted immense industry and capacity to the London County Council; it is impossible to measure the share he has had in securing such great public utilities as water-supply, traction, and electric supply, for example, from complete exploitation by private profit-seekers, but certainly it is a huge one, and throughout England and presently in America, there went on a collateral activity of Fabian Socialists. They worked like a ferment in municipal politics, encouraging and developing local pride and local enterprise in public works. In the case of large public bodies, working in suitable areas and commanding the services of men of high quality, striking advances in social organization were made, but in the case of smaller bodies in unsuitable districts and with no attractions for people of gifts and training, the influence of Fabianism did on the whole produce effects that have tended to discredit Socialism.   Aggressive, ignorant and untrained men and women, persons too often of wavering purpose and doubtful honesty, got themselves elected in a state of enthusiasm to undertake public functions and challenge private enterprise under conditions that doomed them to waste and failure.   This was the case in endless Parish Councils and Urban Districts; it was also the case in many London Boroughs. It has to be admitted by Socialists with infinite regret that the common borough council Socialist is too often a lamentable misrepresentative of the Socialist idea.

The creation of the London Borough Councils found English Socialism unprepared.   They were bodies doomed by their nature to incapacity and waste.   They represented neither natural communities nor any practicable administrative unit of area.   Their creation was the result of quite silly political considerations.   The slowness with which Socialists have realized that for the larger duties that they wish to have done collectively a new scheme of administration is necessary, that bodies created to sweep the streets, and admirably adapted to that duty, may be conspicuously not adapted to supply

electric power or administer education, is accountable
for much disheartening bungling. Instead of taking
a clear line from the outset, and denouncing these glori-
fied vestries as useless, impossible, and entirely unscien-
tific organs, the Socialists under the influence of the earlier
Fabianism tried to claim Bumble as their friend and use
him as their tool. And Bumble turned out to be a very
bad friend and a very poor tool. . . .

In all these matters the real question at issue is one
between the emergency and the implement. One may
illustrate by a simple comparison. Suppose there is a
need to dig a hole and that there is no spade available,
a Fabian with Mr. Webb's gifts becomes invaluable.
He seizes upon a broken old cricket bat, let us say, uses
it with admirable wit and skill, and presto! there is the
hole made and the moral taught that one need not
always wait for spades before digging holes. It is a
lesson that Socialism stood in need of, and which hence-
forth it will always bear in mind. But suppose we
want to dig a dozen holes, it may be worth while to spend
a little time in going to beg, borrow, or buy a spade. If
we have to dig holes indefinitely, day after day, it will
be sheer foolishness sticking to the bat. It will be
worth while then not simply to get a spade, but to get
just the right sort of spade in size and form that the soil
requires, to get the proper means of sharpening and

repairing the spade, to insure a proper supply. Or to point the comparison, the reconstruction of our legislative and local government machinery is a necessary preliminary to Socialization in many directions. Mr. Webb has very effectually admitted that, is in fact himself leading us away from that by taking up the study of local government as his principal occupation, but the typical "Webbite" of the Fabian Society, who is very much to Webb what the Marxist is to Marx, entranced by his leader's skill, still clings to the earlier Fabian ideal. He dreams of the most foxy and wonderful digging by means of box-lids, tablespoons, dish-covers — anything but spades designed and made for the job in hand — just as he dreams of an extensive expropriation of landlords by a legislature that includes the House of Lords. . . .

§ 3

It was only at the very end of the nineteenth century that the Fabian Socialist movement was at all quickened to the need of political reconstruction as extensive as the economic changes it advocated, and it is still far from a complete apprehension of the importance of the political problem. To begin with, Mr. and Mrs. Webb (receding a little from Fabian Society affairs and becoming more and more purely scientific in spirit) took up the study of local government and commenced that colossal task that still engages them, their book upon *English Local Government*, of which there has as yet appeared (1907) only one volume out of seven. (Immense as this service is, it is only one part of conjoint activities that will ultimately give constructive social conceptions an enormous armoury of scientifically arranged fact.)

As the outcome of certain private experiences, the moral of which was pointed by discussion with Mr. and Mrs. Webb, the present writer in 1902 put before the Fabian Society a paper on Administrative Areas[1] in which he showed clearly that the character and efficiency and possibilities of a governing body depend almost entirely upon the size and quality of the constituency it represents and the area it administers. This may be stated with something approaching scientific confidence. A local governing body for too small an area or elected upon an unsound franchise *cannot* be efficient. But obviously before you can transfer property from private to collective control you must have something in the way of a governing institution with a reasonably good chance of developing into an efficient controlling body. The leading conception of this Administrative Area

[1] See Appendix to *Mankind in the Making*. (Chapman and Hall, 1903.)

paper appeared subsequently running through a series of tracts, *The New Heptarchy Series,* in which one finds it applied first to this group of administrative problems and then to that.[1] These tracts are remarkable if only because they present the first systematic recognition on the part of any organized Socialist body of the fact that a scientific reconstruction of the methods of government constitute a necessary part of the complete Socialist scheme, the first recognition of the widening scope of the Socialist design that makes it again a deliberately constructive project.

It is only an initial recognition, a mere first raid into a great new unexplored province of study. This province is, in the broadest terms, social psychology. A huge amount of thought, discussion, experiment, is to be done in this field — needs imperatively to be done before the process of the socialization of economic life can go very far beyond its present attainments. Except for these first admissions, Socialism has concerned itself only with the material reorganization of society and its social consequences, with economic changes and the reaction of these changes on administrative work;

---

[1] 1. *Municipalization by Provinces.* 2. *On the Reform of Municipal Service.* 3. *Public Control of Electric Power and Transit.* 4. *The Revival of Agriculture; a National Policy for Great Britain.* 5. *The Abolition of Poor Law Guardians.* Others to follow. (Fabian Society, 1905–1906.)

s

it has either accepted existing intellectual conditions and
political institutions as beyond its control, or assumed
that they will obediently modify as economic and administrative necessity dictates. Declare the Social
revolution, we were told in a note of cheery optimism, by
the Marxist apostles, and political institutions will
come like flowers in May! Achieve your expropriation,
said the early Fabians, get your network of skilled
experts spread over the country, and your political forms,
your public opinion, your collective soul will not trouble
you. The student of history knows better. These
confident claims ignore the psychological factors in
government and human association; they disregard a
network of difficulties that lie directly in our way.
Socialists have to face the facts: firstly, that the political
and intellectual institutions of the present time belong
to the present condition of things, and that the intellectual methods, machinery, and political institutions of
the better future must almost inevitably be of a very
different type; secondly, that such institutions will not
come about of themselves — which indeed is the old
superstition of *laissez-faire* in a new form — but must be
thought out, planned, and organized just as completely
as economic socialization has had to be planned and organized; and thirdly, that so far Socialism has evolved
scarcely any generalizations even, that may be made the

basis of new intellectual and governmental — as distinguished from administrative — methods.   It has
preached collective ownership and collective control, and
it has only begun to recognize that this implies the necessity of a collective will and new means and methods
altogether for the collective mind.

The administrative Socialism which Mr. Webb and
the Fabian Society developed upon a modification of the
broad generalizations of the Marx phase is, as it were,
no more than the first courses above those foundations
of Socialism. It supplies us with a conception of
methods of transition and with a vision of a great and
disciplined organization of officials, a scientific bureaucracy appointed by representative bodies of diminishing activity and importance, and coming to be at
last the real working control of the Socialist state.   But
it says nothing of what is above the officials, what drives
the officials.   It is palace without living rooms, with
nothing but offices, — a machine, as yet unprovided with
a motor.   No doubt we must have that organization of
officials if we mean to bring about a Socialist state, but
the mind recoils with something like terror from the
conceptions of a state run and ruled by officials, terminating in officials, with an official as its highest expression.
One has a vision of a community with blue-books instead of a literature, and inspectors instead of a con-

science. The mystical democracy of the Marxist, though manifestly impossible, had in it something attractive, something humanly and desperately pugnacious, and generous, something indeed heroic; the bureaucracy of the Webbite, though far more attainable, is infinitely less inspiring. But that may be because the inspiring elements remain to be stated rather than that these practical constructive projects are in their nature, and incurably, hard and narrow. Instead of a gorgeous flare in the darkness, we have the first cold onset of daylight heralding the sun. If the letter of the teaching of Mr. and Mrs. Webb is bureaucracy, that is certainly not the spirit of their lives. The earlier Socialists gave Socialism substance, *rudis indigestaque moles*, but noble stuff; Administrative Socialism gave it a physical structure and nerves, defined its organs and determined its functions: it remains for the Socialist of to-day to realize in this shaping body of the civilized state of the future the breath of life already unconfessedly there, to state in clear terms the reality for which our plans are made, by which alone they can be realized; that is to say, the *collective mind of humanity, the soul and moral being of mankind.*

CHAPTER XIII

§ 1

SUCH an idea as Socialism, fundamentally true to the needs of life and arising as it does from the inevitable suggestion of very widely dispersed evils and insufficiencies, does not spring from any one source, nor develop along any single line. It breaks out like a smouldering fire, first taking on one form of expression and then another, now under this name and now under that.

The manifest new possibilities created by the progress of applied science, the inevitable change of scale and of the size and conception of a community that arises out of them, *necessitate* at least the material form of Socialism; that is to say, the replacement of individual action by public organization, first here, then there, in spite of a hundred vested interests. The age that regarded Herbert Spencer as its greatest philosopher, for example, was urged nevertheless, unwillingly and protestingly, but effectually, through phase after phase of more and more coördinated voluntary effort, until at last it had to undertake a complete system of or-

261

ganized free public primary education. There the moving finger of change halts not a moment; already it is going on to secondary education, to schemes for a complete public educational organization from reformatory school up to professorial chair. The practical logic of the case is invincible.

So, too, the public organization of scientific research goes on steadily against all prejudices and social theories, and, in a very different field, the plain inconveniences of a private control of traffic in America and England alike, force the affected property-owners whose businesses are hampered and damaged toward the realization that freedom of private property, in these services at least, is evil, and must end. Then again, the movement for public sanitation and hygiene spreads and broadens, and the natural alarm of even the most conservative at the falling birth-rate and the stationary infantile death-rate is evidently ripening for an advance toward public control and care even in the relation of child to parent, the most intimate of all personal affairs.

Inevitably all such movements must coalesce,— their spirit is one, the spirit of construction,— and inevitably their coalescence will take the form of a wide and generous restatement of Socialism. Nothing but a broader understanding of the broadening propositions of Socialism is needed for that recognition now.

Socialism, indeed, does not simply look, it appeals to the constructive professions at the present time, to the medical man, the engineer, the architect, the scientific agriculturist.

Each of these sorts of men, in just so far as he is concerned with the reality of his profession, in just so far as he is worthy of his profession, must resent the considerations of private profit, of base economies, that constantly limit and spoil his work and services in the interests of a dividend or of some financial manœuvre. So far they have been antagonized toward Socialism by the errors of its adherents, by the impression quite wantonly created, that Socialism meant either mob rule or the rule of pedantic, unsympathetic officials. They have heard too much of democracy, too much of bureaucracy, and not enough of construction. They have felt that on the whole the financial exploiter, detestable master as he often is, was better than the rule of either clamour on the one hand, or red tape on the other. But as I have been seeking to suggest, mob rule and official rule do not exhaust the possible alternatives. Neither ignorant democracy nor narrow bureaucracy can be the destined rulers of a Socialist state. The only conceivable rule in a Socialist civilization is through the operation of a collective mind that must be by its nature constructive and enterprising, because only through the creation of such a mind can Socialism be brought about. A Socialist state cannot exist without that mind existing also, and a collective mind can scarcely appear without some form of Socialism giving it a material body. Now it is only under an intelligent collective mind that any of the dreams of these constructive professions can attain an effective realization. Where will the private profit in a universal sanitation, for example, be found, in the abolition of diseases, in the planned control of the public health, in the abolition of children's deaths? What thought of private gain will ever scrap our obsolescent railroads and our stagnating industrial monopolies for new, clean methods? So long as they pay a dividend, they will keep on upon their present lines. The modern architect knows, the engineer knows, we might build ourselves perfectly clean, smokeless, magnificent cities to-day, as full of pure water as ancient Rome, as full of pure air as the Engadine, if private ownership did not block the way. Who can doubt it who understands what a doctor, or an electrical engineer, or a real architect, understands? Surely all the best men in these professions are eager to get to work on the immense possibilities of life, possibilities of things cleared up, of things made anew, that their training has enabled them to visualize! What stands in their way, stands in our way; social disorganization, individualist self-seeking, narrowness of outlook, self-conceit, ignorance.

With that conception they must surely turn in the end, as we Socialists turn, to the most creative profession of all, to that great calling which with each generation renews the world's "circle of ideas," — the Teachers!

The whole trend and purpose of this book from the outset has been to insist upon the *mental quality of Socialism*, to maintain that it is a business of conventions about property and plans of reorganization; that is to say, of changes and expansions of the ideas of men, changes and expansions of their spirit of action and their habitual circles of ideas. Unless you can change men's minds, you cannot effect Socialism, and when you have made clear and universal certain broad understandings, Socialism becomes a mere matter of science and devices and applied intelligence. That is the constructive Socialist's position. Logically, therefore, he declares the teacher master of the situation. Ultimately, the Socialist movement *is* teaching, and the most important people in the world from the Socialist's point of view are those who teach—I mean of course, not simply those who teach in schools, but those who teach in pulpits, in books, in the press, in universities, and lecture-theatres, in parliaments and councils, in discussions and associations, and experiments of every sort, and, last in my list but most important of all, those mothers and motherly women who teach little children in their earliest years.

Every one, too, who enunciates a new and valid idea, or works out a new contrivance, is a teacher in this sense.

And these teachers, collectively, perpetually renew the collective mind. In the measure that in each successive generation they apprehend Socialism and transmit its spirit, is Socialism nearer its goal.

§ 2

At the present time in America and all the western European countries, there is a collective mind, a Public Opinion made up of the most adventitious and interesting elements. It is not even a national or a racial thing, it is curiously international, curiously responsive to thought from every quarter, a something, vague here, clear there, here diffused, there concentrated. It demands the closest attention from Socialists, this something, this something which is so hard to define and so impossible to deny — civilized feeling, the thought of our age, the mind of the world. It has organs, it has media, yet it is as hard to locate as the soul of a man. We know that somewhere in the brain and body of a man lives his Self; that you must preserve that brain entire, aerate it, nourish it, lest it die and his whole being die, and yet you cannot say it is in this cell or in that. So with an equal mystery of diffusion the mind of mankind exists. No man, no organization, no authority, can be more than a part of it. Twice at least have there been attempts of parts to be the whole; the Catholic Church and the Chinese Academy have each in varying measure sought to play the part of a collective mind for all humanity, and failed. All individual achievement, fine books, splendid poems, great discoveries, new generalizations, lives of thought, are no more than flashes in this huge moral and intellectual being, which grows now self-conscious and purposeful, just as a child grows out of its early self-ignorance to an elusive, indefinable, indisputable sense of itself. This collective mind has to be filled and nourished with the Socialist purpose, to receive and assimilate our great idea. That is the true work of Socialism.

Consider the organs and media of the collective mind as one finds them in England or America now, how hazardous they are and accidental! At the basis of this strange thought-process is the intelligence of the common man, once illiterate and accessible only to the crude, inarticulate influences of talk and rumour, now rapidly becoming educated, or at any rate educated to the level of a reader and writer, and responding more and more to literary influences. The great mass of the population is indeed at the present time like clay, which has hitherto been a mere deadening influence underneath, but which this educational process, like some drying and heating influence upon that clay, is rendering resonant, capable of, in a dim answering way, *ringing* to the appeals made upon it. Reaching through this mass, appealing to it in various degrees at various levels and to various ends, there are a number of systems of organizations of unknown value and power. Its response, such as it is, robbed by multitudinousness of any personality or articulation, is a broad emotional impulse.

Above this fundamental mass is the growing moiety which has a conscious thought-process, of a sort. Its fundamental ideas, its preconceptions, are begotten of a mixture of social traditions learnt at home and in school and from the suggestions of contemporary customs and affairs. But it reads and listens more or less. And, scattered through this, here and there, are people really learning, really increasing, and accumulating knowledge, really thinking and conversing — the active mind-cells, as it were, of the world. Their ideas are conveyed into the mass much as impulses are conveyed into an imperfectly innervated tissue; they are conveyed by books and pamphlets, by lecturing, by magazine articles and newspaper articles, by the agency of the pulpit, by organized propaganda, by political display and campaigns. The gross effect is considerable, but it is just as well that the Socialist should look a little closely at the economic processes that underlie these intellectual activities at the present time. Except for the universities and much of the public educational organization, except for a few pulpits endowed for good under conditions that limit freedom of thought and expression, except for certain needy and impecunious propagandas, the whole of this apparatus of public thought and discussion to-day has been created and is sustained by commercial necessity.

For example, consider what is I suppose by far the most important vehicle of ideas at the present time, which for a huge majority of adults is the sole vehicle of ideas, the newspaper. It is universal because it is cheap, and it is cheap because the cost of production is paid for by the advertisements of private enterprise. The newspaper is to a very large extent parasitic upon competition; its criticism, its discussion, its correspondence, are, from the business point of view, written on the backs of puffs of competing tobaccos, soaps, medicines, and the like. No newspaper could pay upon its sales alone, and the same thing is true of most popular magazines and weekly publications. It is highly probable that whatever checks public advertisement in other directions, the prohibition of bill-posting upon hoardings, for example, the protection of scenery, railway carriages, and architecture from the advertiser, stimulates the production of attractive literature. Necessarily what is published in newspapers and magazines must be acceptable to advertising businesses and not too openly contrary to their interests. With that limitation the newspapers provide a singularly free and various arena for discussion at the present time. It must, however, be obvious that to advance toward Socialism is, if not to undermine the newspaper altogether, at least to change very profoundly this material vehicle of popular thought. . . .

The newspaper disseminates ideas. So, too, does the book and the pamphlet, and so far as these latter are concerned, their distribution does not at present rest in the same degree upon their value as vehicles of advertisement. They are salable things unaided. The average book of to-day, at its nominal price of six shillings, pays in itself and supports its producers. So in a lesser degree does the sixpenny pamphlet, but neither book nor pamphlet reach so wide a public as the halfpenny and penny press. The methods and media of the book trade have grown up, no man designing them; they change, and no one is able to foretell the effect of the changes. At present there is a great movement to cheapen new books, and it would seem the cheapening is partly to be made up for in enhanced sales and partly by an increased use of books for advertisement. Many people consider this cheapening of new books as being detrimental to the interests of all but the most vulgarly popular authors. They believe it will increase the difficulty of new writers, and hopelessly impoverish just the finest element in our literary life,—those original and exceptional minds who demand educated appreciation and do not appeal to the man in the street. This may or may not be true; the aspect of interest to Socialists is that here is a process going on which is likely to produce the most far-reaching results upon the collective mind, upon that thought-process of the whole community which is necessary for the progressive organization of Society. It is a process which is likely to spread one type of writer far and wide, which may silence or demoralize another, which may vulgarize and debase discussion. Yet, as Socialists, they have no ideas whatever in this matter, their project of activities ignores it altogether.

Books and newspapers constitute two among the chief mental organs of a modern community, but almost if not equally important is that great apparatus for the dissemination of ideas made up of the pulpits and lecture halls of a thousand sects and societies. Toward all these things Socialism has hitherto maintained an absurd attitude of *laissez-faire*. . . .

So far I have looked at the collective mind as a thought-process only, but it has much graver and more im-

mediate functions in a democratic state. It has, one
must remember, to *will* social order and development.
In every country the machinery for determining and
expressing this will is complex. The common method
in the modern Western state is through the voting of a
numerous electorate, which tends, it would seem, to become more and more the entire manhood, if not the
entire adult population of the country. It is a curious
but perhaps inevitable method. Practically thought
has to percolate down to the common man through all
these strange and accidental channels, — newspapers
which are advertisement sheets, books which may be
boycotted in a "Book War," pulpits pledged to doctrine, and lecture halls kept open by rich people's sub-
scriptions; it has to reach him, to mingle itself with
generalized emotional forces in the heat of mysteriously
subsidized election campaigns, and then return as a collective determination. For the Statesman and the Socialist there could hardly be any study more important,
one might think, than the science of these processes and
methods. Yet the world has still to produce even the
rudimentary generalizations of this needed science of
collective psychology.

§ 3

Now I ask the reader to consider very carefully how
the Socialist movement, using that expression now in its

wider sense, stands to this very vague and very real outcome of social evolution, the collective mind; what it is really aspiring to do in that collective mind.

One has to recognize that this mind is at present a mind in a state of confusion, full of warring suggestions and warring impulses. It is like a very disturbed human mind: it is without a clear aim; it does not know except in the vaguest terms what it wants to do; it has impulses; it has fancies; it begins and forgets. In addition it is afflicted with a division within itself that is strictly analogous to that strange mental disorder, which is known to psychologists as multiple personality. It has no clear conception of the whole of itself, it goes about forgetting its proper name and address. Part of it thinks of itself as one great being, as, let us say, Germany; another thinks of itself as Catholicism, another as the White Race, or Judea. At times one might deem the whole confusion not so much a mind as incurable dementia, — a chaos of mental elements, haunted by invincible and mutually incoherent fixed ideas. This, you will remember, is the gist of that melancholy giant torso of irony, Flaubert's *Bouvard et Pécuchet*.

In its essence the Socialist movement amounts to this: it is an attempt in this warring chaos of a collective mind to pull itself together, to develop and establish a governing idea of itself. It is like a man saying to himself

T

resolutely, "What am I? What am I doing with myself? Where am I drifting?" and making an answer,
hesitating at first, crude at first, and presently clear
and lucid.

The Socialist movement is from this point of view, no
less than the development of the collective self-consciousness of humanity. Necessarily therefore it must be
international as well as outspoken, making no truce with
prejudices against race and colour. These national and
racial collective consciousnesses of to-day are things as
vague, as fluctuating as mists or clouds; they melt,
dissolve into one another; they coalesce; they split. No
clear isolated national mind can ever maintain itself under
modern conditions; even the mind of Japan now comes
into the common melting-pot of thought. We Socialists
take up to-day the assertion the early Christians were
the first to make, that mankind is of one household and
one substance; the Samaritan who stoops to the wounded
stranger by the wayside our brother rather than that
Levite. . . .

In a very different sense, indeed, the Socialist propaganda must be *the germ of the collective self-consciousness of mankind in the coming time.* If the purpose of
Socialism is to prevail, its scattered writings, its dispersed, indistinct, and confused utterances, must increase in height and breadth and range, increase in power

and service, gather to themselves every means of expression, grow into an ordered system of thought, art, literature, and will. The Socialist Propaganda of to-day must beget the whole Public Opinion of to-morrow, or fail. The Socialists must play the part of a little leaven to leaven the whole world. If they do not leaven it, then they are altogether defeated. . . .

§ 4

Now this conception of Socialism, as being ultimately an intellectual synthesis of mankind, sets a fresh test of value upon all the activities of the Socialist, and opens up altogether new departments for research. We propose to destroy the competitive capitalistic system that owns and sustains our present newspapers, gives and leaves money to universities, endows fresh pulpits, publishes, advertises, and buys books; we have to ask, as reasonable creatures, what new media we propose to give in the place of these accidental and unsatisfactory methods of distributing and exchanging thought. It would almost seem as though current Socialism breathes public opinion as the Middle Ages breathed air, without realizing that it existed, that it might be vitiated or withheld. And so we are beyond the range of prepared and digested Socialist proposals here altogether. It is

still open to the anti-Socialist to allege that Socialism
may incidentally destroy itself by choking the channels
of its own thinking, and the Socialist has still to reply
in vague general terms.

We must insure the continuity of the collective mind.
The attempt to realize the Marxist idea of a democratic Socialism without that might easily fail into the
abortive birth of an acephalous monster; the secular
development of administrative Socialism give the world
over to a bureaucratic mandarinate, self-satisfied, interfering, and unteachable, with whom wisdom would
die.   Here I can now suggest methods only in the most
general terms, and even before methods are suggested,
certain principles need to be laid down as vitally necessary to Socialism.   They are essentially principles of
that Liberalism out of whose generous aspirations Socialism sprang, but they are principles that even to-day, un-
happily, do not figure in the fundamental creed of any
Socialist body.

The first of these is the principle of *freedom of speech;*
the second, *freedom of writing;* and the third, *universality
of information.*   In the civilized state every one must be
free to know, knowledge must be patent and at hand, and
any one must be free to discuss, write, suggest, and per-
suade.   These freedoms must be guarded as sacred
things.   It is not in the untutored nature of man to

respect any of these freedoms; it is not in the bureaucratic habit of mind. Indeed, the desire to suppress
opinions adverse to our own is almost instinctive in
human nature. It is an instinct we have to conquer.
Fair play in discussion is sustained by a cultivated respect, by a correction of natural instinct; men need to
be *trained* to be jealous of obscurantism, of unfair argument, of authoritative interference with opinion when
that opinion is against them. In England such a
jealousy does already largely exist; it has been cultivated with us since the seventeenth century at least.
America, it seemed to me during my short visit to the
States, has somewhat retrograded from its former British
standard in this respect; there is a crude majority tyranny in the matter of publication, an un-English disposition to boycott libraries, books, authors, and publications upon petty issues, a growing disposition to
discriminate in the mails against unpopular views.
These interferences with open statement and discussion
are decivilizing forces.

Given a clear public understanding of these necessities as primary, then one may point out that the next
necessity for the mental existence of a Socialist state is
an extension and cheapening of the impartial universal
distributing activity of the public post so that it becomes
not only the means of correspondence, but also of dis-

tributing books and newspapers, pamphlets, and every form of printed matter. The post-office must become bookseller and news-agent. In France this is already the case with the press, and newspapers are handed in, not by the newsboy, but by the public mail. In England, Messrs. Smith and Mudie and so forth may censor what they like among periodicals or books. The remedy is more toilsome and vexatious than the injury. Neither England nor America has any security against finding its public supply of magazines or literature suddenly choked by the manœuvres of some black-mailing book or news trust "fighting" author or publisher for some squalid increase in its proportion of profits, or interested in financial exploitations liable to exposure. Neither country is secure against the complete control of its channels of thought by some successful monopolistic adventurer. . . .

The Socialist state will not for a moment permit such risks as these; it must certainly be the universal news-vender and bookseller; every news-vender and book-seller must become an impartial state official, working for a sure and comfortable salary instead of for precarious profits. And this amplification of the book and news post and the book and news trades will need to be not simply a municipal but a state service of the widest range.

Distribution, however, is only the beginning of the

problem. There is the more difficult issue of getting books and papers printed and published. And here we come to an intricate puzzle in reconciling the indisputable need for untrammelled individual expression on the one hand with public ownership on the other, and also with the difficult riddle, how authors may be supported under Socialist conditions. It is not within the design of this book to do more than indicate a possible solution. At present authors with business shrewdness and the ability to be interesting get an income from the sale of their books, and it seems possible that they might continue to be paid in that way under Socialism. It is difficult outside the field of specialist work (which under any Socialist system has to be endowed in relation to colleges and universities) to find any other just way of discriminating between the author who ought to get a living from writing, and the author who has no reasonable claim to do so. But under Socialism, in addition to the private publisher or altogether replacing him, there will have to be some sort of public publisher.

Here again difficulties arise. It is difficult to see how, if there is only one general state publishing department, a sort of censorship can be altogether avoided, and even if, for example, one insists upon the right of every one who cares to pay for it to have matter printed, bound, and issued by the public presses and binders, it still leaves a disagreeable possibility of uniformity haunting the mind. But the whole trend of administrative Socialism is toward a conception of great local governments, of land, elementary education, omnibus-transit, power-distribution, and the like, vesting in the hands of municipalities as great as mediæval principalities, and it seems possible to look to these great bodies and to the municipal patriotism and intermunicipal rivalries that will develop about them, for just that spirited and competitive publishing that is desirable, just as one looks now to their rivalries as a stimulus for art and architecture and public dignity and display.[1] Already, as I have pointed out in a previous chapter (Chapter VIII, § 5), the decorative arts had to be rescued from the degrading influence of private enterprise; no one wants to go back now to the early Victorian state of affairs, and so it is reasonable to hope that out of the municipal art and technical schools which teach printing, binding, and the like, public presses, public binderies, and all the machinery of book production may be developed in a natural and convenient manner. So, too, the municipalities might publish, seek out, maintain, and honour writers and sell the books they produced, against each

[1] I visited Liverpool and Manchester the other day for the first time in my life, and was delighted to find how the inferiority of the local art galleries to those of Glasgow rankled in people's minds.

other all over the world.   It would be a matter of pride for authors still unrecognized to go forth to the world with the arms of some great city on their covers, and it would be a matter of pride for any city to have its arms upon work become classic and immortal.   So at least one method of competition is possible in this matter. . . .

This, however, is but one passing suggestion out of many possibilities.   But in all these issues of the intellectual life, it is manifest that public ownership must be so contrived and can be so contrived as to avoid centralization and a control without alternatives.   Moreover, whatever public publishing is done, it must be left open to any one to set up as an independent publisher or printer, and to sell and advertise through the impartial public book and news-distributing organization. . . .

I lay some stress upon this matter of book issuing because it is a remarkable thing about contemporary Socialist discussion that it does not seem to be in the least alive to the great public disadvantage of leaving this vitally important service to private gain-getting. Municipal coal, municipal milk, municipal house-owning, the Socialists seem prepared for, and even municipal theatres, but municipal publication they still do not take into consideration. . . .

The problem of the press is perhaps to be solved by some parallel combination of individual enterprise and public resources. All sorts of things may happen to the newspaper of to-day even in the near future; it cannot but be felt that in its present form it is an extremely transitory phenomenon, that it no longer embodies and rules public thought as it did in the middle and later Victorian period, and that a separation of public discussion from the news-sheet is already in progress. Both in England and America the popular magazine seems taking over an increasing share of the public thinking. . . .

But I will not go into the future of the newspaper here. All these suggestions are merely thrown out in the most tentative way to indicate the nature of the field for study that lies open for any intelligent worker to cultivate. . . .

The same truth that controls must be divided, and a competition, at least for honour and repute, kept alive under Socialism, needs also to be applied to schools and colleges and all the vast machinery of research. It is imperative that there should be overlapping and competing organizations. An educated and prosperous community, such as we hypotheticate for the Socialist state, will necessarily be more alert for interest and intellectual quality than our present "driven" multitude; its ampler leisure, its wider horizons, will keep it critical and exacting of what claims its attention. The rivalries of institutions and municipalities will be part

of the drama of life. Under Socialism, with the extension of the educational process it contemplates, universities and colleges must become the most prominent of
facts; nearly every one will have that feeling for some
such place which now one finds in a Trinity man for
Trinity; the sort of feeling that sent the last thoughts
of Cecil Rhodes back to Oriel. Everywhere balanced
against the town hall or the Parliament house will be
the great university buildings and art museums; the
lecture halls open to all comers, the great noiseless libraries, the book exhibitions, and book and pamphlet
stores, keenly criticised, keenly used, will teem with un-
hurrying, incessant, creative activities.

And all this immense publicly sustained organization
will be doing greatly and finely what now our scattered
line of Socialist propagandists is doing under every disadvantage; that is to say, it will be developing and sustaining the social self-consciousness, the collective sense
of the state.

§ 5

I am naturally preoccupied with the Mind of that Civilized State we seek to make because my work lies in this
department. But while the writer, the publisher and
printer, the bookseller and librarian and teacher and
preacher, must chiefly direct himself to developing this

great organized mind and intention in the world, other sorts of men will be concerned with parallel aspects of the Socialist synthesis. The medical worker and the medical investigator will be building up the body of a new generation, the body of the civilized state, and he will be doing all he can, not simply as an individual, but as a citizen, to *organize* his services of cure and prevention, of hygiene and selection. And the specialized man of science will be concerned with his own special synthesis, the knowledge of the civilized state, whether he measure crystals or stain microtome sections or count stars. A great and growing multitude of men will be working out the Apparatus of the Civilized State; the student of transit and housing, the engineers in their incessantly increasing variety, the miners and geologists, estimating the world's resources in metals and minerals, the mechanical inventors perpetually economizing force. The scientific agriculturist again will be studying the food-supply of the world as a whole, and how it may be increased and distributed and economized. And to the student of law comes the task of rephrasing his intricate and often quite beautiful science in relation to the new social assumptions we have laid down. All these and a hundred other aspects are integral to the wide project of constructive Socialism as it shapes itself now.

And to the man or woman who looks at these issues,

not as one specialized in relation to some constructive calling, but as a common citizen, a mere human being eager to make and do from the standpoint of personal liberty and personal affections, the appeal of this great constructive project is equally strong. You want security and liberty. Here it is, safe from the greed of trust and landlord. Here is investment with absolute assurance and trading with absolute justice; this is the only safe way to build your own house in perfect security, to make your own garden safe for yourself and for your children's children, the only way in which you can link a hundred million kindred wills in loyal coöperation with your own, and that is to do it not for yourself alone and for your children alone, but for all the world, — all the world doing it also for you, — to join yourself to this great Making of a permanent well-being for mankind.

And here finally let me set out a sort of programme of constructive Socialism, as it seems to be shaping itself in the minds of contemporary Socialists, in order that the reader may be able to measure this fuller and completer proposition against the earlier Fabian Socialism whose propositions are set out in Chapter XI, § 1. All these are incorporated in this that follows: there is no contradiction whatever between them, but there is amplification; new elements are taken into consideration,

once disregarded difficulties have been faced and partially resolved.

First, then, the constructive Socialist has to do
whatever lies in his power toward *the enrichment of the
Socialist idea.* He has to give whatever gifts he has
as artist, as writer, as maker of any sort to increasing and
refining the conception of civilized life. He has to em-
body and make real the state and the city. And the
Socialist idea, constantly restated, refreshed, and elaborated, has to be made a part of the common circle of ideas;
has to be grasped and felt and assimilated by the whole
mass of mankind, has to be made the basis of each
individual's private morality. That mental work is
the primary, most essential function of constructive
Socialism.

And next, constructive Socialism has in every country
to direct its energies and attention to *political reform,*
to the scientific reconstruction of our representative and
administrative machinery, so as to give power and real
expression to the developing collective mind of the community and to remove the obstructions to Socialization
that are inevitable where institutions stand for "interests" or have fallen under the sway of aggressive private
property or of narrowly organized classes. Governing
and representative bodies, advisory and investigatory
organizations of a liberal and responsive type, have to be

built up, — bodies that shall be really capable of the immense administrative duties the secular abolition of the great bulk of private ownership will devolve upon them.

Thirdly, the constructive Socialist sets himself to forward the *resumption of the land by the community*, by increased control, by taxation, by death duties, by purchase, and by partially compensated confiscation as circumstances may render advisable, and so to make the municipality the sole landlord in the reorganized world.

And meanwhile the constructive Socialist goes on also with the work of *socializing the main public services*, by transferring them steadily from private enterprise to municipal and state control, by working steadily for such transfers, and by opposing every party and every organization that does not set its face resolutely against the private exploitation of new needs and services.

There are four distinct systems of public service which could very conveniently be organized under collective ownership and control now, and each can be attacked independently of the others. There is first the need of public educational machinery, and by education I mean not simply elementary education, but the equally vital need for great colleges, not only to teach and study technical arts and useful sciences, but also to enlarge learning and sustain philosophical and literary work. A civilized community is impossible without great public libraries, public museums, public art schools, without public honour and support for contemporary thought and literature, and all these things the constructive Socialist may forward at a hundred points.

Then next there is the need and opportunity of organizing the whole community in relation to health, the collective development of hospitals, medical aid, public sanitation, child welfare, into one great loyal and efficient public service. This too may be pushed forward either as the part of the general Socialist movement or independently as a thing in itself by those who may find the whole Socialist proposition unacceptable or inconvenient.

A third system of interests upon which practical work may be done at the present time lies in the complex interdependent developments of transit and housing, questions that lock up inextricably with the problem of replanning our local government areas. Here, too, the whole world is beginning to realize more and more clearly that private enterprise is wasteful and socially disastrous, that collective control, collective management, and so on to collective enterprise and ownership of building land, houses, railways, tramways, and omnibuses give the only way of escape from an endless drifting entanglement and congestion of our mobile modern population.

The fourth department of economic activity in which collectivism is developing, and in which the constructive Socialist will find enormous scope for work, is in connection with the more generalized forms of public trading, and especially with the production, handling, and supply of food and minerals. When the lagging enterprise of agriculture needs to be supplemented by endowed educational machinery, agriculturist colleges, and the like, when the feeble intellectual initiative of the private adventure miner and manufacturer demands a London "Charlottenburg," it must be manifest that state initiative has altogether outdistanced the possibilities of private effort, and that the next step to the public authority instructing men how to farm, prepare food, run dairies, manage mines, and distribute minerals, is to cut out the pedagogic middleman and undertake the work itself. The state education of the expert for private consumption (such as we see at the Royal School of Mines) is surely too ridiculous a sacrifice of the community to private property to continue at that. The further inevitable line of advance is the transfer from private to public hands by purchase, by competing organizations, or what not, of all those great services, just as rapidly as the increasing capacity and experience of the public authority permits.

This briefly is the work and method of constructive

U

Socialism to-day.   Under one or other head it can utilize almost every sort of capacity and every type of opportunity.   It refuses no one who will serve it.   It is no narrow doctrinaire cult.   It does not seek the best of an argument, but the best of a world.   Its worst enemies are those foolish and litigious advocates who antagonize and estrange every development of human Good Will that does not pay tribute to their vanity in open acquiescence.   Its most loyal servants, it may be its most effectual helpers on the side of art, invention, and public organization and political reconstruction, may be men who will never adopt the Socialist name.

CHAPTER XIV

SOME ARGUMENTS *AD HOMINEM*

§ 1

BEFORE I conclude this compact exposition of modern Socialism, it is reasonable that the reader should ask for some little help in figuring to himself this new world at which we Socialists aim.

"I see the justice of much of the Socialist position," he will say, "and the soundness of many of your generalizations. But it still seems to remain — generalizations; and I feel the need of getting it into my mind as something concrete and real. What will the world be *like* when its state is really a Socialist one? That's my difficulty."

The full answer to that would be another book. I myself have tried to render my own personal dream in a book called *A Modern Utopia*,[1] but that has not been so widely read as I could have wished; it does not appeal strongly enough perhaps to the practical everyday side of life, and here I may do my best to give very briefly

---

[1] (Chapman and Hall, 3/6.)

some intimation of a few of the differences that would strike a contemporary if he or she could be transferred to the new order we are trying to evolve.

It would be a world and a life in no fundamental respect different from the world of to-day, made up of the same creatures as ourselves, as limited in capacity if not in outlook, as hasty, as quick to take offence, as egotistical essentially, as hungry for attention, as easily discouraged — they would indeed be better educated and better trained, less goaded and less exasperated, with ampler opportunities for their finer impulses and smaller scope for rage and secrecy, but they would still be human. At bottom it would still be a struggle for individual ends, albeit ennobled individual ends; for self-gratification and self-realization against external difficulty and internal weakness. Self-gratification would be sought more keenly in self-development and self-realization in service, but that is a change of tone and not of nature. You might, indeed, were you suddenly flung into it, fail to note altogether for a long time the widest of the differences between the Socialist state and our present one, the absence of that worrying urgency to earn, that sense of constant economic insecurity, which afflicts all but the very careless or the very prosperous to-day. Painful things being absent are forgotten. On the same principle certain common objects of our daily life you might not miss at all.   There would be no slums, no hundreds of miles of insanitary, ignoble homes, no ugly, health-destroying cheap factories.   If you were not in the habit of walking among slums and factories, you would scarcely notice that.   Din and stress would be enormously gone.   But you would remark simply a change in the atmosphere about you and in your own contentment that would be as difficult to analyze as the calm of a Sunday morning in sunshine in a pleasant country.

Let me put my conception of the Socialist world to a number of typical readers, as it were, so that they may see clearly just what difference in circumstances there would be for them if we Socialists could have our way now.   Let me suppose them as far as possible exactly what they are now, save for these differences.

Then first let us take a sample case and suppose yourself to be an elementary teacher.   So far as your work went you would be very much as you are to-day; you would have a finer and more beautiful schoolroom, perhaps, better supplied with apparatus and diagrams; you would have cleaner and healthier, that is to say, brighter and more responsive children, and you would have smaller and more manageable classes.   Schools will be very important things in the Socialist state, and you will find outside your classroom a much ampler building with open corridors, a library, a bath, refectory for the children's midday meal, and gymnasium, and beyond the playground, a garden. You will be an enlisted member of a public service, free under reasonable conditions to resign, liable under extreme circumstances to dismissal for misconduct, but entitled until you do so to a minimum salary, a maintenance allowance, that is, and to employment. You will have had a general education from the state up to the age of sixteen or seventeen and then three or four years of sound technical training so that you will know your work from top to bottom. You will have applied for your present position in the service, whatever it is, and have been accepted, much as you apply and are accepted for positions now, by the school managers, and you will have done so because it attracted you, and they will have accepted you because your qualifications seemed adequate to them. You will draw a salary attached to the position, over and above that minimum maintenance salary to which I have already alluded. You will be working just as keenly as you are now and better because of the better training you have had, and because of shorter hours and more invigorating conditions, and you will be working for much the same ends, that is to say, for promotion to a larger salary and wider opportunities and for the interest and sake of the work. In your leisure you may be studying, writing, or doing some work of supererogation for the school or the state — because *under Socialist conditions it cannot be too clearly understood that all the reasons the contemporary Trade Unionist finds against extra work and unpaid work will have disappeared.* You will not, in a Socialist state, make life harder for others by working keenly and doing much if you are so disposed. You will be free to give yourself generously to your work. You will have no anxiety about sickness or old age; the State, the universal Friendly Society, will hold you secure against that; but if you like to provide extra luxury and dignity for your declining years, if you think you will be amused to collect prints or books, or travel then, or run a rose garden, or grow chrysanthemums, the State will be quite ready for you to pay it an insurance premium in order that you may receive in due course an extra annuity to serve that end you contemplate.

You will probably live as a tenant in a house which may either stand alone or be part of a terrace or collegiate building, but instead of having a private landlord, exacting of rent and reluctant of repairs, your house landlord will very probably be, and your ground landlord will certainly be, the municipality, the great Birmingham or London or Hampshire or Glasgow or such-like municipality, and your house will be built solidly and prettily, instead of being jerry-built and mean-looking, and it will have bathroom, electric light, electrically equipped kitchen, and so forth, as every modern civilized house might have and should have now.   If your taste runs to a little close garden of your own, you will probably find plenty of houses with one; if that is not so and you want it badly, you will get other people of like tastes to petition the municipality to provide some, and, if that will not do, you will put yourself up as a candidate for the parish or municipal council to bring this about.   You will pay very much the sort of rent you pay now, but you will not pay it to a private landlord to spend as he likes, at Monte Carlo or upon foreign missions or in financing "Moderate" bill-posting, or what not, but to the municipality, and you will pay no rates at all.   The rent will do under Socialism what the rates do now.   You cannot grasp too clearly that *Socialism will abolish rates* absolutely. Rates for public purposes are necessary to-day because the landowners of the world evade the public obligations that should, in common sense, go with the rent.

Light, heating, water, and so on will either be covered by the rent or charged for separately, and they will be supplied just as near cost price as possible. I don't think you will buy coals because I think that in a few years' time it will be possible to heat every house adequately by electricity; but if I am wrong in that, then

you will buy your coals just as you do now, except that
you will have an honest coal merchant, the Public Coal
Service, — a merchant not greedy for profit nor short
in the weight, calculating and foreseeing your needs, —
not that it may profit by them, but in order to serve
them, — storing coal against a demand and so never
raising the price in winter.

I am assuming you are going to be a house occupier;
but if you are a single man, you will probably live in
pleasant apartments in an hotel or college and dine in a
club, and perhaps keep no more than a couple of rooms,
one for sleep and one for study and privacy of your own.
But if you are a married man, then I must enlarge a
little further upon your domestic details because you will
probably want a "home of your own." . . .

§ 2

Now just how a married couple lives in the Socialist
state will depend very much, as indeed it does now, on
the individual relations and individual tastes and pro-
clivities of the two people most concerned. Many
couples are childless now and indisposed for home and
children, and such people will also be found in the Socialist state, and in their case the wife will probably have an
occupation and be a teacher, a medical practitioner, a

government clerk or official, an artist, a milliner, and earn her own living. In which case they will share apartments perhaps, and dine in a club and go about together, very much as a childless couple of journalists or artists or theatrical people do in London to-day. But, of course, if either of them chooses to idle more or less and live on the earnings of the other, that will be a matter quite between themselves. No one will ask who pays their rent and their bills; that will be for their own private arrangement.

But if they are not childless people but have children, things will be on a rather different footing. Then they will probably have a home all to themselves, and that will be the wife's chief affair; only incidentally will she attend to any other occupation. You will remember that the state is to be a sort of universal Friendly Society, supplying good medical advice and so forth, and so soon as a woman is likely to become a mother, her medical adviser, man or woman as the case may be, will report this to the proper officials and her special income as a prospective mother in the state will begin. Then when her child is born, there will begin an allowance for its support, and these payments will continue monthly or quarterly, and will be larger or smaller according first to the well-being of the child, and secondly, to the need the state may have for children — so long as the children are in their mother's care. All this money for maternity will be the wife's independent income, and normally she will be the house-ruler, just as she is now in most well-contrived households. Her personality will make the home atmosphere; that is the woman's gift and privilege, and she will be able to do it with a free hand. I suppose that for the husband's cost in the household the present custom of cultivated people of independent means will continue, and he will pay over to his wife his share of the household expenses.

After the revenue in the domestic budget under Socialism one must consider the expenditure. I have already given an idea how the rent and rates, lighting and water, are to be dealt with under Socialist conditions. For the rest, the housewife will be dealing on very similar lines to those she goes upon at present. She will buy what she wants and pay cash for it. The milkman will come in the morning and leave his "book" at the end of the week, but instead of coming from Mr. Watertap Jones' or the Twenty-per-cent Dairy Company, he will come from the Municipal Dairy; he will have no interest in giving short measure, and all the science in the state will be behind him in keeping the milk clean and pure. If he is unpunctual or trying in any way, the lady will complain just as she does now, but to his official superiors instead of his employer, and if that does not do, she and her aggrieved neighbours (all voters you will understand) will put the thing to their representative in the parish or municipal council. Then she will buy her meat and groceries and so on, not in one of a number of inefficient little shops with badly assorted goods under unknown brands, as she does now if she lives in a minor neighbourhood, but in a branch of a big well-organized business like Lipton's or Whiteley's or Harrod's. She may have to go to it on a municipal electric car, for which she will probably pay a fare just as she does now, unless perhaps her house rent includes a season ticket. The store will not belong to Mr. Lipton or Mr. Whiteley, or Mr. Harrod, but to the public — that will be the chief difference; and if she does not like her service, she will be able to criticise and remedy it, just as one can now criticise and remedy any inefficiency in one's local post-office. If she does not like the brands of goods supplied, she will be able to insist upon others. There will be brands, too, different from the household names of to-day in the goods she will buy. The county arms of Devon will be on the butter paper, Hereford and Kent will guarantee her cider, Hampshire and Wiltshire answer for her bacon, just as now already Australia brands her wines and New Zealand protects her from deception (and insures clean, decent slaughtering) in the matter of Canterbury lamb. I rather like to think of the red dagger of London

on the wholesome bottled ales of her great (municipalized)
breweries, and Maidstone or Rochester, let us say, boast-
ing a special reputation for jam or pickles. Good
honest food, all of it will be, made by honest, unsweated
women and men, with the pride of broad vales and up-
lands, counties, principalities, and great cities behind it.
Each county and municipality, will be competing freely
against its fellows, not in price but quality : the cheeses
of Cheshire against the cheeses of France and Switzerland, the beer of Munich against the Kentish brew,
bread from the bakeries of London and Paris, biscuits
from Reading town, chocolate from Switzerland and
Bourneville, side by side with butter from the meadows
of Denmark and Russia.

Then when the provisions have been bought, she will
go perhaps to the other departments of the great store
and buy or order the fine linen and cotton of the Manchester men, the delicate woollens of the Bradford city
looms, the silks of London or Mercia, Northampton
or American boots and so forth, just as she does now in
any of the great stores. But, as I say, all these goods
will be honest goods, made to wear as well as look well,
and the shopman will have no "premiums" to tempt
him to force rubbish upon her instead of worthy makes
by specious "introduction."

But suppose she wants a hat or a dress made. Then

probably, for all that the world is under Socialism, she will have to go to private enterprise; a matter of taste and individuality, such as dress, cannot be managed in a wholesale way. She will probably find in the same building as the big department store, a number of little establishments, of Madame This, of Mrs. That, some perhaps with windows displaying a costume or so, or a hat or so, and here she will choose her particular artist and contrive the thing with her. I am inclined to think the dressmaker or milliner will charge a fee according to her skill and reputation for designing and cutting and so on, and that the customer will pay the store separately for material and the municipal workshop for the making under the artist's direction. I don't think, that is, that the milliner or dressmaker will make a trading profit, but only an artist's fee.

And if the lady wants to buy books, music, artistic brac-a-brac, or what not, she will find the big store, displaying and selling all these things on commission for the municipal or private producers all over the world. . . .

So much for the financial and economic position of an ordinary woman in a Socialist state. But management and economies are but the basal substance of a woman's life. She will be free not merely financially; the systematic development of the social organization and of the mechanism of life will be constantly releasing her more and more from the irksome duties and drudgeries that have consumed so much of the energies of her sex in the past. She will be a citizen and free as a man to read for herself, think for herself, and seek expression. Under the law, in politics and all the affairs of life she will be the equal of a man. No one will control her movements or limit her actions or stand over her to make decisions for her. All these things are implicit in the fundamental generalization of Socialism which denies property in human beings.

§ 3

Perhaps now the reader will be able to figure a little better the common texture of the life of a teacher or a housewife under Socialism. And incidentally I have glanced at the position a clever milliner or dressmaker would probably have under the altered conditions. The great mass of the employees in the distributing trade would obviously be living a sort of clarified, dignified version of their present existence, freed from their worst anxieties, the terror of the "swap," the hopeless approach of old age, and from the sweated food and accommodation of the living-in system. Under Socialism the "living-in" system would be incredible. Their conditions of life would approximate to those of the

teacher. Like him they would be enrolled a part of a
great public service, and like him entitled to a minimum
wage, and over and above that they would draw salaries
commensurate with the positions their energy and [1]
ability had won. The prosperous merchant of to-day
would find himself somewhere high in the hierarchy
of the distributing service. If, for example, you are a
tea merchant or a provision-broker, then probably if
you like that calling, you would be handling the same
kind of goods, not for profit but efficiency, "shipping into
the Midlands" from Liverpool, let us say, much as you
do now. You would be keener on quality and less keen
on deals; that is all. You would not be trying to
"skin" a business rival, but very probably you would be
just as keen to beat the London distributors and dis-
tinguish yourself in that way. And you would get a
pretty good salary; modern Socialism does not propose
to maintain any dead level to the detriment of able men.
Modern Socialism has cleared itself of that jealous hatred
of prosperity that was once a part of class-war Socialism.
You would be, you see, far more than you are now, one
of the pillars of your town's prosperity — and the Town
Hall would be a place worth sitting in. . . .

So far as the rank and file of the distributing service is
concerned, the chief differences would be a better education, security for a minimum living, an assured old

age, shorter hours, more private freedom, and more opportunity. Since the whole business would be public and the customer would be one's indirect master through the polling booth, promotion would be far more by merit than it is now in private businesses, where irrelevant personal considerations are often overpowering, and it would be open to any one to apply for a transfer to some fresh position if he or she found insufficient scope in the old one. The staff of the stores will certainly "live out," and their homes and way of living will be closely parallel to that of the two people I have sketched in §§ 1 and 2.

In the various municipal and state transit services the state of affairs would be even closer to a broadened and liberalized version of things as they are. The conductors and drivers will no doubt wear uniforms, for convenience of recognition ; but a uniform will carry with it no association with the idea of a livery as it does at the present time. Mostly this service will be run by young men, and each one, like the private of the democratic French army, will feel that he has a marshal's *baton* in his knapsack. He will have had a good education; he will have short hours of duty and leisure for self-improvement or other pursuits, and if he remains a conductor or driver all his life, he will have only his own unpretending qualities to thank for that. He will probably remain a conductor if he likes to remain a conductor, and

x

get out if he does not. He is not obliged to take that *baton* out and bother with it if he has quiet tastes.

The great organized industries, mining, cotton, iron, building, and the like, would differ chiefly in the permanence of employment and the systematic evasion of the social hardship caused nowadays by new inventions and economies in method. There will exist throughout the world an organized economic survey, which will continually prepare and revise estimates of the need of iron, coal, cloth, and so forth in the coming months; the blind speculative production of our own times is due merely to the dark ignorance in which we work in these matters, and with such a survey, employment will lose much of the cruel intermittence it now displays. The men in these great productive services, quite equally with teachers and railway men, will be permanently employed. They will be no more taken on and turned off by the day or week than we should take on or turn off an extra policeman or depend for our defences upon soldiers casually engaged upon the battlefield at sixpence an hour. And if by adopting some ingenious device we dispense suddenly with the labour of hundreds of men, the Socialist state will send them, not into the casual wards and colonies as our state does, to become a social burthen there, but into the technical schools to train for some fresh use of their energies. Taken all round, of course, these men, even the least enterprising or able, will be better off than they are now, with a fuller share of the product of their industry. Many will no doubt remain as they are, rather through want of ambition than want of push, because under Socialism life will be tolerable for a poor man. A man who chooses to do commonplace work and spend his leisure upon chess or billiards, or gossip, or eccentric studies, or amusing but ineffectual art, will remain a poor man, indeed, but not be made a wretched one. Sheer toil of a mechanical sort there is little need of in the world now; it could be speedily dispensed with at a thousand points were human patience not cheaper than good machinery, but there will still remain ten thousand undistinguished sorts of work for unambitious men. . . .

If you are a farmer or any sort of horticulturist, a fruit or flower grower, let us say, or a seedsman, you will probably find yourself still farming under Socialism; that is to say, renting land and getting what you can out of it. Your rent will be fixed, just as it is to-day, by what people will give. But your landlord will be the municipality or the county, and the rent you pay will largely come back to you in repairs, in the guiding reports and advice of the Agricultural Department, in improved roads, in subventions to a good electric car service to take your produce to market, in aids and education for your children. You will probably have a greater fixity of tenure and a clearer ownership in improvements than you have to-day. I am inclined to think that your dairying and milling and so forth will be done wholesale in big public dairies and mills because of the economy of that; you will send up the crude produce and sell it perhaps to the county association to brand and distribute. It is probable you will sell your crops standing and the public authority will organize the harvesting and bring out an army of workers from the towns to gather your fruit, hops, and corn. You will need therefore only a small permanent staff of labourers, and these are much more likely to be partners with you in the enterprise than wage-workers needing to be watched and driven.

In your leisure you will shoot, perhaps, or hunt if your tastes incline that way; it is quite likely that scattered among the farms of the future countryside will be the cottages and homes of all sorts of people with open-air tastes who will share their sports with you. One need not dread the disappearance of sport with the disappearance of the great house. In the dead winter time you will probably like to run into the nearest big town with your wife and family, stay in a hotel for a few weeks, talk to people in your clubs, see what plays there are in the municipal theatres, and so forth. And you will no doubt travel also in your holidays. All the world will know something of the pleasures and freedom of travel, of wandering and the enjoyment of unfamiliar atmospheres, of mountains and deserts and remote cities and deep forests and the customs of alien peoples.

§ 4

A medical man or woman or a dentist or any such skilled professional, like the secondary schoolmaster, will cease to be a private adventurer under Socialism, concerned chiefly with the taking of a showy house and the use of a showy conveyance; he (or she) will become part of one of the greatest of all the public services in the coming time, — the service of public health. Either he — I use this pronoun and imply its feminine — will be on the staff of some of the main hospitals (which will not be charities but amply endowed public institutions) or he will be a part of a district staff, working in conjunction with a nursing organization, a cottage hospital, an isolation hospital and so forth, or he will be an advising specialist or mainly engaged in research or teaching and training a new generation in the profession.

He must not judge his life and position quite by the lives and position of publicly endowed investigators and medical officers of health to-day. At present, because of the jealousy of the private owner who has, as he says, to "find the funds," almost all public employment is badly paid relatively to privately earned incomes. The same thing is true of all scientific investigators and of most public officials. The state of things to which Socialism points is a world that will necessarily be harmonious with these constructive conceptions and free from those jealousies. Whitehall and South Kensington have much to fear from the wanton columns of a vulgarized capitalistic press and from the greedy intrigues of syndicated capital, but nothing from a sane constructive Socialism. To the public official therefore of the present time the Socialist has merely to say that he will probably be better paid, relatively, than he is now, and in the matter of his house rents and domestic marketing, *vide supra*. . . .

But now suppose you are an artist — and I use the word to cover all sorts of art, literary, dramatic, and musical, as well as painting, sculpture, design, and architecture — you want before all things freedom for personal expression, and you probably have an idea that this is the last thing you will get in the Socialist state. But, indeed, you will get far more than you do now. You will begin as a student, no doubt, in your local municipal art schools, and there you will win prizes and scholarships and get some glorious years of youth and work in Italy or Paris or Germany or London or Boston or New York or wherever the great teachers and workers of your art gather thickest, and then you will compete, perhaps, for some public work, and have something printed or published or reproduced and sold for you by your school or city; or get a loan from your home municipality for material — if your material costs money — and set to work making that into some salable, beautiful thing. If you are at all distinguished in quality, you will have a competition among public authorities from the beginning, to act as sponsors and dealers for your work; benevolent dealers they will be and content with a commission. And if you make things that make many people interested and happy, you may by that fortunate gift of yours, grow to be as rich and magnificent a person as any one in the Socialist state. But if you do not please people at all, either the connoisseurs of the municipal art collection or private associations of art patrons or the popular buyer, well, then your lot will be no harder than the lot of any unsuccessful artist now; you will have to do something else for a time and win leisure to try again.

Theatrical productions will be run on a sort of improvement upon contemporary methods, but there will be no cornering of talent possible, no wild advertisement of favoured stars upon strictly commercial lines, no theatrical trust. The theatres will be municipal buildings, every theatre-going voter will be keen to see them

comfortable and fine; they will perhaps be run in some
cases by a public repertoire company and in another by
a lessee, and this latter may be financed by his own
private savings or by subscribers or partners, or even
by a loan from the public bank, as the case may be. This
latter method of exploitation by a lessee will probably
also work best in the public Music-Halls, but it is quite
equally possible that these may be controlled by managers under partly elected and partly appointed public
committees. In some cases the theatrical lessee might
be a kind of stage society organized for the production
of particular types of play. The spectators will pay for
admission, of course, as they do now, but to the Municipal
Box-Offices, and, I suppose, the lessee or the author and
artists will divide up the surplus after the rent of the
theatre has been deducted for the Municipal Treasury.
In every town of any importance there will be many
theatres, music-halls, and the like, perhaps under competing committees. In all these matters, as every intelligent person understands, one has to maintain variety
of method, a choice of avenues, freedom from autocracies,
and since the Socialist community will contain a great
number of intelligent persons with leisure and opportunity for artistic appreciation, there is little chance of
this important principle being forgotten, much less
than there is in this world where a group of dealers can

often make an absolute corner in this artistic market or
that. You will not, under Socialism, see Sarah Bern-
hardt playing in a tent as she had to do in America, because all the theatres have been closed against her
through some mean dispute with a trust about the
sharing of profits.

And if it is not too sudden a transition, it seems most
convenient in a Socialist state to leave religious wor-
ship entirely to the care of private people; to let them
subscribe among themselves, subject, of course, to a
reasonable statute of Mortmain, to lease land and build
and endow and maintain churches and chapels, altars and
holy places and meeting-houses, priests and devout
ceremonies. This will be the more easily done since the
heavy social burthens that oppress religious bodies at the
present time will be altogether lifted from them; they
will have no poor to support, no schools, no hospitals,
no nursing sisters, the advance of civilization will have
taken over these duties of education and humanity that
Christianity first taught us to realize. So, too, there
seems no objection and no obstacle in Socialism to religious houses, to nunneries, monasteries, and the like,
so far as these institutions are compatible with personal
freedom and the public health, but of course factory laws
and building laws will run through all these places, and
the common laws and limitations of contract override

their vows, if their devotees repent. So that you see Socialism will touch nothing living of religion, and if you are a religious minister, you will be very much as you are at the present time, but with lightened parochial duties. If you are an earnest woman and want to nurse the sick and comfort the afflicted, you will need only, in addition to your religious profession, to qualify as a nurse or medical practitioner. There will still be ample need of you. Socialism will not make an end of human trouble, either of the body or of the soul, albeit it will put these things into such comfort and safety as it may.

§ 5

And now let me address a section to those particular social types whose method of living seems most threatened by the development of an organized civilization, who find it impossible to imagine lives at all like their own in the Socialist state.

But first it may be well to remind them again of something I have already done my best to make clear, that the modern Socialist contemplates no swift change of conditions from those under which we live, to Socialism. There will be no wonderful Monday morning when the old order will give place to the new. Year by year the great change has to be brought about, now by this socialization of a service, now by an alteration in the incidence of taxation, now by a new device of public trading, now by an extension of education. This problem at the utmost is a problem of adaptation, and for most of those who would have no standing under the revised conceptions of social intercourse, it is no more than to ask whether it is wise they should prepare their sons or daughters to follow in their footsteps or consent to regard their callings as a terminating function.

So far as many professions and callings go, this matter may be dismissed in a few words. Under Socialism, while the particular trade or profession might not exist, there would probably be ample scope in the public machine for the socially more profitable employment of the same energies. A family solicitor, such as we know him now, would have a poor time in a Socialist state, but the same qualities of watchful discretion would be needed at a hundred new angles and friction surfaces of the state organization. In the same way the private shopkeeper, as I have already explained, would be replaced by the department managers and buyers of the public stores; the rent collector, the estate bailiff — one might make long lists of social types who would undergo a parallel transformation.

But suppose now you are a servant, I mean a well-trained, expert, prosperous servant; would the world

have no equivalent of you under the new order? I
think probably it would. With a difference, there will
be room for a vast body of servants in the Socialist state.
But I think there will be very few servants to private
people, and that the "menial" conception of a servant
will have vanished in an entirely educated community.
The domestic work of the ordinary home, one may
prophesy confidently, will be very much reduced in
the near future, whether we move toward Socialism or
no. All the dirt of coal, all the disagreeables attendant
upon lamps and candles, most of the heavy work of
cooking, will be obviated by electric lighting and heating,
and much of the bedroom service dispensed with through
the construction of properly equipped bath-dressing-
rooms. In addition, it is highly probable that there will
be a considerable extension of the club idea; ordinary
people will dine more freely in public places, and con-
veniences for their doing so will increase. The single-
handed servant will have disappeared, and if you are
one of that class, you must console yourself by thinking
that under Socialism you would have been educated up
to seventeen or eighteen and then equipped for some
more interesting occupation. But there will remain
much need of occasional help of a more skilled sort, in
cleaning out the house thoroughly every now and then,
probably with the help of mechanisms, in recovering and

repairing furniture; and in all this sort of "helping" which will be done as between one social equal and another, many people who are now, through lack of opportunity and education, servants, will no doubt be employed. But where the better type of service will be found will probably be in the clubs and associated homes, where pleasant-mannered, highly paid, skilful people will see to the ease and comfort of a considerable *clientele* without either offence or servility. There still remains, no doubt, a number of valets, footmen, maids, and so on, who under Socialism would not be servants at all, but something far better, more interesting and more productive socially.

But this writing of servants brings me now to another possibility, and that is that perhaps you are, dear reader, one of that small number of fortunate people, rich and well placed in the world, who even under existing conditions seem to possess all that life can offer a human being. You live beautifully in a great London house, waited upon by companies of servants; you have country seats with parks about them and fine gardens; you can travel luxuriously to any part of the civilized world and live sumptuously there. All things are done for you, all ways are made smooth for you. A skilled maid or valet saves you even the petty care of your person, skilled physicians, wonderful specialists, intervene at any threat of illness or discomfort; you keep ten years younger in appearance than your poorer contemporaries and twice as splendid. And above all you have an immense sense of downward perspectives, of being special and apart and above the common herd of mankind.

Now, frankly, Socialism will be incompatible with this patrician style. You must contemplate the end of all that. You may still be healthy, refined, free, beautifully clothed and housed, but you will not have either the space or the service or the sense of superiority you enjoy now, under Socialism. You will have to take your place among the multitude again. Only a moiety of your property will remain to you. The rents upon which you live, the investments that yield the income that makes the employment of that army of butlers and footmen, estate workers and underlings, possible, that buys your dresses, your jewels, your motor cars, your splendid furnishings and equipments, will be public property yielding revenue to some national or municipal treasury. You will have to give up much of that. There is no way out of it, your way to Socialism is through "the needle's eye." From your rare class and from your class alone does Socialism require a real material sacrifice. You must come down to a simpler, and in many material aspects a less distinguished, way of living.

This is so clearly evident that to any one who believes

self-seeking is the ruling motive, the only possible motive in mankind, it seems incredible that your class will do anything than oppose to the last the advancement of Socialism. You will fight for what you have, and the Have-nots will fight to take it away. They preach a class war, to my mind a lurid, violent, and distasteful prospect. We shall have to get out of the miseries and disorder of to-day, if not by way of château-burning and tumbrils, at least by a mitigated equivalent of that. But I am not altogether of that opinion. I have a lurking belief that you are not altogether eaten up by the claims of your own magnificence. While there are, no doubt, a number of people in your class who would fight like rats in a corner against, let us say, the feeding of poor people's starving children, or the recovery of the land by the state to which it once belonged, I believe there is enough of nobility in your class as a whole to considerably damp their resistance. Because you have silver mirrors and silver hair-brushes, it does not follow that you have not a conscience. I am no believer in the theory that to be a *sans-culotte* is to be morally impeccable, or that a man loses his soul because he possesses thirty pairs of trousers beautifully folded by a valet. I cherish the belief that your very refinement will turn — I have seen it in one or two fine minds visibly turning — against the social conditions that made it possible. All this space, all this splendour, has its traceable connection with the insufficiencies and miseries from which you are remote.   Once that realization comes to you, the world changes.   In certain lights, correlated with that, your magnificence can look, you will discover — forgive the word! — a little *vulgar*. . . .   Once you have seen that, you will continue to see it.   The *nouveau riche* comes thrusting among you, demonstrating that sometimes quite obtrusively.   You begin by feeling sorry for his servants and then apologetic to your own.   You cannot "go it" as the rich Americans and the rich South Africans, or prosperous bookmakers or music-hall proprietors "go it," their silver and ivory and diamonds throw light on your own.   And among other things you discover you are not nearly so dependent on the numerous men in livery, the spaces and enrichments, for your pride and comfort as these upstart people.

I trust also to the appeal of the intervening spaces. You cannot so entirely close your world in from the greater world without, that, in transit at least, the other aspects do not intrude.   Every time you leave Charing Cross for the Continent, for example, there are all those horrible slums on either side of the line.   These things *are*, you know, a part of your system, part of you; they are the reverse of that splendid fabric and no separate thing : the wide rich tapestry of your lives comes through on the other side, stitch for stitch, in stunted bodies, in children's deaths, in privation and anger. Your grandmothers did not realize that. You do. You *know*. In that recognition and a certain nobility I find in you, I put my hope, much more than in any dreadful memories of 1789 and those vindictive pikes. Your class is a strangely mixed assembly of new and old, of base and fine. But through it all, in Great Britain and western Europe, generally, soaks a tradition truly aristocratic, a tradition that transcends property; you are aware and at times uneasily aware of duty and a sort of honour. You cannot bilk cabmen nor cheat at cards; there is something in your making forbids that as strongly as an instinct. But what if it is made clear to you, and it is being made clear to you, that the wealth you have is, all unwittingly on your part, the outcome of a colossal, if unpremeditated, social bilking?

Moreover, though Socialism does ask you to abandon much space and service, it offers you certain austere, yet not altogether inadequate, compensations. If you will cease to have that admirable house in Mayfair and the park in Kent and the moorlands and the Welsh castle, yet you will have another ownership of a finer kind to replace those things. For all London will be yours, a city to serve indeed, and a sense of fellowship that is, if

Y

you could but realize it, better than respect. The common people will not be common under Socialism. That is a very important thing for you to remember. But better than those thoughts is this, that you will own yourself, too, more than you do now. All that state, all that prominence of yours — do you never feel how it stands between you and life?

So I appeal from your wealth to your nobility, to help us to impoverish your class a little and make all the world infinitely richer by that impoverishment. And I am sure that to some I shall not appeal in vain. . . .

§ 6

And lastly, perhaps you are chiefly a patriot and you are concerned for the flag and country with which your emotions have interwoven. You find that the Socialist talks constantly of internationalism and the world state, and that presents itself to your imagination as a very vague and colourless substitute for a warm and living reality of England or "these states" or the Empire. Well, your patriotism will have suffered a change, but I do not think it need starve under Socialist conditions. It may be that war will have ceased, but the comparison and competition and pride of communities will not have ceased. Philadelphia and Chicago, Boston and New York, are at peace, in all probability forever at peace so

far as guns and slaughter go, but each perpetually criticises, goads, and tries to outshine the other. And the
civic pride and rivalry of to day will be nothing to that
pride and rivalry when every man's business is the city,
and the city's honour and well-being is his own. You
will have, therefore, first, this civic patriotism, your
pride in your city, a city which will be like the city of the
ancient Athenian's or the mediæval Italian's, the centre
of a system of territories, the property and chief interest
of its citizens. I, for instance, should love and serve,
even as I love to-day, these home counties about London,
the great lap of the Thames Valley and the Weald and
Downlands, my own country in which all my life has been
spent; for you the city may be Ulster, or Northumbria, or
Wales, or East or West Belgium, or Finland, or Burgundy,
or Berne, or Berlin, or Venetia, Pekin, Queensland, or
San Francisco. And keeping the immediate peace
between these vigorous giant municipal states and holding them together, there will still be in many cases the
old national or imperial government and kindred municipalities with a common language and a common history and a common temper and race. The nation and
the national government will be the custodian of the
national literature and the common law, the controller
and perhaps the vehicle of intermunicipal and international trade and an intermediary between its municipal

governments and that great Congress to which all things are making, that permanent international Congress which will be necessary to insure the peace of the world.

That, at least, is my own dream of the order that may emerge from the confusion of distrusts and tentatives and dangerous absurdities, those reactions of fear and old traditional attitudes and racial misconceptions which one speaks of as international relations to-day.

CHAPTER XV

§ 1

AND here my brief exposition of the ideals of modern Socialism may fitly end.

I have done my best to set out soberly and plainly this great idea of deliberately making a real civilization by the control and subordination of the instinct of property and the systematic development of a state consciousness out of the achievements and squalor, out of the fine forces and wasted opportunities of to-day. I may have an unconscious bias, perhaps, but so far as I have been able, I have been just and frank, concealing nothing of the doubts and difficulties of Socialism, nothing of the divergencies of opinion among its supporters, nothing of the generous demands it makes upon the social conscience, the Good Will in man. Its supporters are divergent upon a hundred points, but upon its fundamental generalizations they are all absolutely agreed, and some day the whole world will be agreed. Their common purport is the resumption by the community

325

of all property that is not justly and obviously personal, and the substitution of the spirit of service for the spirit of gain in all human affairs.

It must be clear to the reader who has followed my explanations continuously, that the present advancement of Socialism must lie now along three several lines: —

FIRST, and most important, is the primary intellectual process, the elaboration, criticism, discussion, enrichment, and enlargement of the project of Socialism. This includes all sorts of sociological and economic research, the critical literature of Socialism, and every possible way — the drama, poetry, painting, music — of expressing and refining its spirit, its attitudes, and conceptions. It includes, too, all sorts of experiments in living and association. In its widest sense it includes all science, literature, and invention.

SECONDLY comes the propaganda; the publication, distribution, repetition, discussion, and explanation of this growing body of ideas, until this conception of a real civilized state as being in the making becomes the common intellectual property of all intelligent people in the world; until the laws and social injustices that now seem, to the ordinary man, as much parts of life as the east wind and influenza, will seem irrational, unnatural, and absurd. This educational task is at the present time the main work that

Socialists have before them. Most other possibilities wait upon that enlargement of the general circle of ideas. It is a work that every one can help forward in some measure, by talk and discussion, by the distribution of literature, by writing and speaking in public, by subscribing its propagandist organization.

And THIRDLY, there is the actual changing of practical things in the direction of the coming Socialist State, the actual socialization, bit by bit and more and more completely, of the land, of the means of production, of education and child welfare, of insurance and the food-supply, — the secular realization, in fact, of that great design the intellectual process of Socialism is continually making more beautiful, attractive, and worthy. Now this third group of activities is necessarily various and divergent, and at every point the conscious and confessed Socialist will find himself coöperating with partial or unintentional Socialists, with statesmen and officials, with opportunist philanthropists, with Trades Unionists, with religious bodies and religious teachers, with educationists, with scientific and medical specialists, with every sort of public-spirited person. He should never lose an opportunity of explaining to such people how necessarily they are Socialists, but never should he hesitate to work with them because they refuse the label. For, in the house of Socialism, as in the house of God, there are many mansions.

These are the three main channels for Socialist effort, thought, propaganda, and practical, social, and political effort, and between them they afford opportunity for almost every type of intelligent human being. One may bring leisure, labour, gifts, money, reputation, influence, to the service of Socialism; there is ample use for them all. There is work to be done for this idea, from taking tickets at a doorway and lending a drawing-room for a meeting, to facing death, impoverishment and sorrow for its sake.

§ 2

Socialism is a moral and intellectual process, let me in conclusion reiterate that. Only secondarily and incidentally does it sway the world of politics. It is not a political movement; it may engender political movements, but it can never become a political movement; any political body, any organization whatever, that professes to stand for Socialism, makes an altogether too presumptuous claim. The whole is greater than the part, the will than the instrument. There can be no official nor pontifical Socialism; the theory lives and grows. It springs out of the common sanity of mankind. Construc-

tive Socialism shapes into a great system of developments
to be forwarded, points to a great number of systems of
activity amidst which its adherents may choose their
field for work.   Parties and societies may come or go, parties and organizations and names may be used and aban-
doned; constructive Socialism lives and remains.

There is a constantly recurring necessity to insist on
the difference between two things, the larger and the
lesser, the greater being the Socialist movement, the
lesser the various organizations that come and go.   There
is this necessity because there is a sort of natural antagonism between the thinker and writer, who stand by the
scheme and seek to develop and expound it, and the
politician who attempts to realize it.   They are allies,
but allies who often pull against each other, whom a
little heat and thoughtlessness may precipitate into a
wasteful conflict.   The former is perhaps too apt to
resent the expenditure of force in those conflicts of
cliques and personal ambition that inevitably arise among
men comparatively untrained for politics, those squabbles
and intrigues, reservations and insincerities that precede
the birth of a tradition of discipline; the latter is equally
prone to think literature too broad-minded for daily life
and to associate all those aspects of the Socialist project
which do not immediately win votes, with fads, kid
gloves, "gentlemanliness," rosewater, and such like

contemptible things. These squabbles of the engineer and the navigating officer must not be allowed to confuse the mind of the student of Socialism. They are quarrels of the mess-room, quarrels on board the ship and within limits; they have nothing to do with the general direction of Socialism. Like all indisciplines they hinder but they do not contradict the movement. Socialism, the politicians declare, can only be realized through politics. Socialism, I would answer, can never be narrowed down to politics. Your parties and groups may serve Socialism, but they can never be Socialism. Scientific progress, medical organization, the advancement of educational method, artistic production and literature are all aspects of Socialism; they are all interests and developments that lie apart from anything one may call — except by sheer violence to language — politics.

And since Socialism is an intellectual as well as a moral thing, it will never tolerate in its adherents the abnegation of individual thought and intention. It demands devotion to an idea, not devotion to a leader. No addicted follower of so-and-so or of so-and-so can be a good Socialist any more than he can be a good scientific investigator. So far Socialism has produced no great leaders at all. Lassalle alone of all its prominent names was of that type of personality which men follow with enthusiasm. The others, Owen, Saint Simon, Proudhon,

Fourier, Marx, Bebel, Webb, contributed to a process they never seized hold upon, never made their own, they gave enrichment and enlargement and the movement passed on; passes on gathering as it goes.   Kingsley, Morris, Ruskin — none are too great to serve this idea, and none so great they may control it or stand alone for it. So it will continue. Socialism under a great leader, or as a powerfully organized party, would be the end of Socialism. No doubt it might also be its partial triumph, but the reality of the movement would need to take to itself another name, to call itself " constructive civilization" or some such synonym in order to continue its undying work. Socialism no doubt will inspire great leaders in the future, and supply great parties with ideas; in itself it will still be greater than all such things.

§ 3

So this general account of Socialism concludes. I have tried to put it as what it is, as the imperfect and still growing development of the social idea, of the collective Good Will in man. I have tried to indicate its relation to politics, to religion, to art and literature, to the widest problems of life. Its broad generalizations are simple and I believe acceptable to all right-thinking minds. And in a sense they simplify life. Once they have been understood they clear away and render impossible a thousand confusions and errors of thought and practice. They are, in the completest sense of the word, illumination.

But Socialism is no panacea, no magic "Open Sesame" to the millennium. Socialism lights up certain once hopeless evils in human affairs and shows the path by which escape is possible, but it leaves that path rugged and difficult. Socialism is hope, but it is not assurance. Throughout this book I have tried to keep that before the reader. Directly one accepts those great generalizations, one passes on to a jungle of incurably intricate problems through which man has to make his way or fail, the riddles and inconsistencies of human character, the puzzles of collective action, the power and decay of traditions, the perpetually recurring tasks and problems of education. To have become a Socialist is to have learnt something, to have made an intellectual and a moral step, to have discovered a general purpose in life and a new meaning in duty and brotherhood. But to have become a Socialist is not, as many suppose, to have become generally wise. Rather in realizing the nature of the task that could be done, one realizes also one's insufficiencies, one's want of knowledge, one's need of force and training. Here and in this manner, says Socialism, a palace and safety and great happiness may be made for mankind. But it seems to me the Socialist, as he turns his hand and way of living towards that common end, knows little of the nature of his task if he does so with any but a lively sense of his individual weakness and the need of charity for all that he achieves.

In that spirit and with no presumption of finality this book of explanations is given to the world.

www.ingramcontent.com/pod-product-compliance
Lightning Source LLC
Chambersburg PA
CBHW022208010726
47493CB00002B/463